G. M. Malliet attended Oxford University and holds a graduate degree from the University of Cambridge. She is the author of the bestselling St Just Mysteries and Max Tudor novels. She lives in the US.

Visit her online at gmmalliet.com.

In Prior's Wood

A MAX TUDOR MYSTERY

G. M. MALLIET

CONSTABLE · LONDON

CONSTABLE

First published in the USA in 2018 by St. Martin's Publishing Group

This edition published in Great Britain in 2018 by Constable

1 3 5 7 9 10 8 6 4 2

A CIP catalogue record for this book
is available from the British Library.

ISBN 978-1-47212-518-7

Printed and bound in Great Britain by CPI Group (UK), Croydon CR0 4YY

Papers used by Constable are from well-managed forests
and other sustainable sources

Constable
An imprint of
Little, Brown Book Group
Carmelite House
50 Victoria Embankment
London EC4Y 0DZ

An Hachette UK Company
www.hachette.co.uk

www.littlebrown.co.uk

To the people of the city of Manchester, England,
especially Stephen Jones and Chris Parker

May 2017

CONTENTS

PART III: AS IT LAYS

PART IV: THE WORLD AND THE FLESH

ACKNOWLEDGMENTS

Once again, I would like to express my gratitude for the assistance and support of agent Vicky Bijur and series acquiring editor Karyn Marcus, as well as Sarah Melnyk, Martin Quinn (led by Paul Hochman), Andy Martin, Kelley Ragland, Pete Wolverton, and Jennifer Donovan of Minotaur Books. I am further indebted to jacket designer David Rotstein, production editor Kevin Sweeney, production manager Yolanda Pluguez, interior designer Omar Chapa, and copy editor Debbie Friedman.

It takes a village to usher a book through to the end, and these villagers make it all possible.

AUTHOR'S NOTE

Sometimes I am asked why I write crime novels. People often find it vaguely disturbing that anyone—a woman, in particular—would willingly choose such a pastime. Some will ask me if I'm "still writing," as if writing were a temporary affliction, like a bad head cold. I can only reply, with apologies for taking words from Stephen King, "What makes you think I have a choice?" Authors don't write so much as write down what is in their heads, demanding release on that particular day. This process of writing—or painting, or building bridges, or programming computers—is part of the gift of being human. There is nothing voluntary about it.

I should mention that Nether Monkslip, Chipping Monkslip, and all the villages of Monkslip County exist only in my imagination. They are anchored somewhere in a parallel universe where I go to escape boredom and fear and every condition in between. I am privileged to be allowed to visit these villages every day, and I am grateful to those who tell me the villages offer them the same sort of respite.

I should add that like the villages, the characters in any story I write are imaginary. There is no fun whatsoever in writing about real people. I write to escape real people.

Also, all mistakes as to Great British idiom and custom are my own.

The typos, however, belong to everyone.

CAST OF CHARACTERS

THE REV. MAXEN "MAX" TUDOR—A dashing MI5 agent turned clergyman with a talent for solving crime.

AWENA OWEN—Max's wife, the mother of his son, Owen, and the owner of the New Age shop Goddessspell in Nether Monkslip.

MRS. HOOSER—Max's housekeeper at the vicarage and the mother of Tildy Ann and Tom.

THE REV. DESTINY CHATSWORTH—Max's curate at St. Edwold's.

DAVID, LORD DUXTER OF MONKSLIP—A publisher knighted for services to the arts and charity, he opens up Wooton Priory as a writers' retreat, with calamitous result.

MARINA, LADY DUXTER OF MONKSLIP—She is discovered in scandalous circumstances, sending shockwaves through the area.

COLIN FROST—A cybersecurity expert based in Saudi Arabia.

JANE FROST—Colin's wife, the Wooton Priory librarian and archivist.

POPPY FROST—Colin's precocious sixteen-year-old daughter by his first wife.

STANLEY ZITHER—Poppy's loyal boyfriend.

NETTA HENSLOWE—The widow of Leo Henslowe, Netta dies in her sleep following her husband's hunting accident.

ELKA GARTH—Owner of the Cavalier Tea Room and Garden in Nether Monkslip, also known as Gossip Central.

SUZANNA WINSHIP—Sister of the local doctor, ambitious Suzanna often finds herself at sixes and sevens in a small village.

DETECTIVE CHIEF INSPECTOR COTTON—The dapper DCI is once again dispatched from Monkslip-super-Mare to investigate a most suspicious death.

ADAM BIRCH—Owner of The Onlie Begetter bookshop.

CARVILLE RASMUSSEN—A famous crime writer staying at Wooton Priory. He claims to be working on his magnum opus but he seems to spend most of his time "thinking."

THE RIGHT REVEREND BISHOP NIGEL ST. STEPHEN—The bishop wants to know why Max Tudor has once again become involved in murder, and when it's all going to stop.

LUCAS COOMBEBRIDGE—A famous seascape artist living in Monkslip Curry, Lucas may once again hold a clue to a baffling murder.

Shine on the poor girl's grave.

– The Cross Roads, Robert Southey

In Prior's Wood

PART I

Absent in the Spring

Chapter 1

NOW YOU SEE IT

Lord Duxter had always disliked card tricks. He detested everything to do with magic, actually: rabbits pulled from hats, women sawn in half, the whole sleight-of-hand nonsense. But in particular and mostly, he disliked card tricks.

To him, tricks and magic and all that sort of thing were the hobbies of a twelve-year-old boy—one of stunted emotional development, at that. A grown man should have outgrown such childish pastimes.

But Colin Frost had not. Oh, no, not he. It summed him up, this idiotic interest, which Colin insisted on regarding as some sort of skill set, the specialty of a highly trained artist emerged from his magician's cave after years of study and practice to bore the world with his "pick-a-card" trickeries. It didn't matter to Lord Duxter that he could never figure out the trick—he did not regard that as a commentary on his intelligence. It was more that he didn't care how it was done. One had to *care*, somehow. He saw it as a sort of social mask Colin hid behind, something to hide the fact that he had no conversation—at least none that would interest any sane person. Colin dealt in software and computers and God knew what-all forms of geekery. Apps, for God's sake. He was always on about the latest apps. He was a cybersecurity expert, with skills ostensibly much in demand. The magic tricks were simply an extension of his preference for dealing with numbers and things rather than engaging with people.

Lord Duxter blamed the mother—she had been much the same way as Colin, and the whole village knew it. Cold as ice, she'd been. And Netta, the grandmother. No doubt she was the prototype for the mother. A cold fish if ever one swam in the small social pond of the Monkslip villages.

It was odd, Lord Duxter reflected. On the surface, Colin had everything going for him: still only in his thirties, he had a high IQ (or at least mathematical ability, if not what one might call actual intelligence); a good, slender physique; and a handsome if rather blank countenance, rather like an Easter Island statue. You could read him as profound or stupid, take your pick. None of these qualities, however, added up to having a personality—that spark of life that lit a man from within. Colin was, in fact, a good-looking dolt, rather naïve and pliable. A man of modest accomplishments married to a woman of stunning ordinariness.

Look at her now, in a frock at least two sizes too big and thick-soled shoes a decade out of style—if they'd ever been in style. They were the kind of shoes one wore if one were worried about a stack of bricks landing on one's toes at any moment. Jane could have been twenty-five or forty but Lord Duxter knew she had just celebrated her thirtieth birthday. Her eyes behind the oversized, rose-tinted lenses conveyed intelligent awareness, so much so that compared with her husband, at least, she was a dynamo.

She was doing a good and meticulous job sorting the books

and albums and other materials that had been discovered by a maid clearing out the attic not long before. Lord Duxter knew he was underpaying Jane Frost and resolved to do something about that, soon. Quite soon. No one had ever accused Lord Duxter of being a tightwad, not even his wife, who had accused him of many things. He hired the best and was willing to pay for the best, a lesson he'd learned watching his father penny-pinch over the years with disastrous result. He was also known for his philanthropic impulses, which had earned him an OBE for services to charity and publishing. His little joke was that given the slim profit margins in publishing these days, the whole publishing scene was tantamount to running a charity. But in fact the writers' retreats he sponsored, in which he threw open the doors of his home to struggling authors for up to a month, were what had brought him to the notice of the Queen. He was an incubator for talent, of which he was enormously proud. He wished being an incubator paid better, but one couldn't have everything, he supposed.

Now Colin was actually waving his hands over the pack of cards as he said "Abracadabra" in his deep, booming voice. What an asshole. It's a wonder he wasn't wearing a pointy hat and a cape with moons and stars painted on. Lord Duxter supposed he should feel pity for a man raised in such a stifling environment as that of Hawthorne Cottage but Lord Duxter was not a man much given to fellow feeling, and he certainly did not care about this oaf. He preferred to assist mankind at a vast, safe distance whenever possible. As Charles Schultz had said, "I love mankind; it's people I can't stand." Yes, at arm's length was quite the best way. Otherwise, people tried to embroil one in all their little problems.

Now he tried desperately to catch his wife's eye but she was too enthralled by this idiot display. The writers' retreats had in fact been her idea, and much of the work that went into establishing and funding the program had been hers as well, facts he chose to forget when the subject of his OBE came up. For that OBE was without question the crowning achievement of his entire life. Wooton Press was his brainchild and in a tough business he had prevailed, so it was only right the powers that be had finally acknowledged it. And not, in his estimation, before time.

Then there was the house itself to be proud of. He had bought Wooton Priory from King's College, Cambridge, which had owned the building and grounds since the time of the Dissolution of the Monasteries. A small, deconsecrated church, formerly the Priory Church of St. George, still stood on the grounds. It had been converted into a private en suite writers' studio, which Lord Duxter reserved for his bestselling authors. The midlisters were penned up in the main house where they shared the bathing facilities, not without a great deal of grumbling. Lord Duxter had found it beneficial thus to promote competition and friction and if possible ill-will among his authors, always dangling before them the carrot of being invited to stay at the St. George Studio provided they sold enough books for him. It kept them from bitching about their publicity, or lack thereof, if not for long.

King's College had sold the place to him with certain conditions attached, among them that it be used in part for educational purposes, and of course he'd had to fulfill conditions set by the Anglican Church before they released the building into his care. Like it was any of their business anymore, really, but he pretended to be delighted to cooperate with everyone in order to gain his heart's desire. The main buildings of the priory, huddled against the ancient forest and pond and next to the churchyard where for centuries monks had been laid to rest, had been shambolic wrecks when he first saw and fell in love with the place: saw the sunlight streaming through stark, empty windows and splaying patterns against stone floors tufted with weeds. With the success of Wooton Press he began to refurbish the buildings in earnest. Establishing Wooton Priory as a writers' retreat was the next natural step—it required no genius for Marina to have thought of it. And besides, there was that stipulation from King's to think of.

As to further thoughts: his only idea at the moment was that he might leap out of his chair, fling himself across the room, and strangle Colin in front of both their wives if he did not bring this *stupid* magician's act to an end soon. Lord Duxter drummed his fingers impatiently against the velvet-covered arms of his eighteenth-century chair. He sat before the fireplace in his vast drawing room, where a fire laid by his manservant crackled gleefully. Spring was on the way, and Lord Duxter liked putting the fireplace to use as much as possible. Normally he found it relaxing. Not tonight.

Now he pulled his lips into somewhat of a rictus smile as Colin guessed, correctly, the card he had chosen from the deck. Ace of spades. What a surprise. Colin's own face wore a smile of childlike happiness—a misplaced smile of achievement. Lady Duxter looked genuinely thrilled and overflowing with admiration; she enjoyed this sort of spectacle, while Colin's wife, Jane, much more a sensible sort, could barely be troubled to conceal her boredom. Lord Duxter clapped weakly, politely, in such a way as to discourage Colin from starting in on another trick. In fact, Lord Duxter rose from his chair, still clapping, and said, loudly, "Excellent! That calls for another drink." And before Colin or anyone else could stop him, he headed for the door. He didn't give a tinker's damn if he was being rude. He didn't see a reason why people should be subjected to such torment in their own homes without a little something to dull their senses.

This whole evening had been his wife's idea—she'd invited these people to dinner for reasons of her own. She wanted, she said, to discuss the priory's history with Jane, who was fast becoming an expert on the subject. What fascinated Marina most of all was some stupid legend about a girl's grave in Prior's Wood. Fine. That didn't mean *he* had to suffer. The women had all day to talk about such things together if they wanted. But Marina felt, she said, that they didn't entertain enough, and she blamed her depression on her isolation. Again, fine. If inviting the village idiot and his harvest-mousy little wife to dine was not a recipe for depression he didn't know what was, but Marina seemed to enjoy planning the meal and arranging the flowers on the table and so on. It gave her an interest. Which was good; she was getting thin as a reed again—always a sign she was agitated by something. But being forced to endure magic tricks had not been part of his concession to getting through the evening. What sort of nitwit, apart from Colin, kept a deck of cards in his pocket at all times—presumably on the off chance someone would beg him to perform? Could he not see that Marina's request had only been made out of politeness? She couldn't be so far gone she saw this nursery-room folly as fun.

Although she did look as though she were enjoying herself. Incredible. An educated, cultivated woman like Marina. Perhaps not having had a child of her own had finally made her lose all her senses. Look at the way she'd taken Colin's teenager under her wing—swapping decorating tips or whatever it was females talked about when they were alone. Marina seemed to be getting rather desperate on the subject of children, longing for what might have been. None of it was healthy, in his opinion.

Lord Duxter's internal monologue continued mining the same vein until he had knocked back a large glass of bourbon, which helped restore his equanimity. Meanwhile, from the sounds emerging from the drawing room, he gathered that yet another performance was underway. Oh, sweet merciful heaven. Colin had moved on from card tricks to tarot cards. He was prattling on, telling someone's fortune: "Now, there's the Emperor. He's always a symbol of monogamy. That would be Lord Duxter, of course." Lord Duxter's ears pricked up. He had been faithful to his lady wife, that much was true. Thick and thin. Mostly. "Oh, and there's the Magician! I suppose tonight that's me. Ha ha! In this position it means an event is coming that will open up new worlds and perspectives."

Lord Duxter, topping up his drink, thought sending Colin to another world might be a splendid idea, if he took that deck of cards with him.

"And next, we have the Pope in the position of career. This means a change of situation." From where Lord Duxter stood he couldn't tell for whom Colin was reading the cards. It could have been Marina or Jane. But if Colin was telling his own fortune, certainly a change could be arranged for him.

It went against all his years of acquired breeding but Lord Duxter decided he could not stand any more. They probably wouldn't notice he was gone anyway, he told himself, with more than a tinge of self-pity. He had reached an age where he felt he had tended to the needs of others long enough. (This was patently untrue, but this sort of thing was the sort of thing he told himself.) His wife with her chronic illnesses and complaints and air of melancholy was the last straw. He was still paying off the bill for that expensive clinic she'd stayed at in Switzerland. He didn't deserve this. It was now *his* turn to enjoy *his* life.

Carrying his again-refilled glass, he took himself up the wide carpeted stairs to his bedroom. The trouble with sending Colin away was that he would come back, but at least there would be a respite from the card tricks. He would call his friend Sir Braithminster in the morning—he had been saying just the other day that his oil company in Saudi Arabia was desperate for geeks like Colin. And Colin was desperate for a job. And by the looks of things, his wife Jane was desperate for a little "me" time, as well as a new frock and hairdo.

Overall, the sooner the man was out of everyone's hair, the happier everyone would be. Lord Duxter wondered what the Saudis would make of him.

That was their problem. Perhaps he'd have a little accident. Maybe a camel would sit on him. Now *that* would be a change of situation.

As Lord Duxter reached the top of the stairs, he could faintly hear Colin exclaim, "Oh! The Death card. No, no . . . not to worry, Marina, it doesn't always mean . . . you know. It can just mean the end of an era. A new beginning."

Lord Duxter, amazed that Colin had the cheek to call his wife so familiarly by her first name, heard her exclaim nervously, "Are you sure, Colin? How can you be sure?" She had always been a gullible ninny when it came to rubbish like this.

"No, no," Colin assured her. "It doesn't necessarily mean death. Almost never. Just that a change is in the works, that's all. Now, enough of this. It seems Lord Duxter isn't coming back. Anyone up for a game of Widow Whist?"

Chapter 2

MAY DAY

"I can't believe it's almost the first of May," said Awena, looking at the calendar hanging on the kitchen wall. "It's nearly time for Beltane—how did that happen? I'll need to find the dried meadowsweet to make the May wine—but I wonder where I put it?" She reached into a kitchen drawer, pulling out a pair of scissors. The gilt-edged embroidery of her dress reflected morning sunlight into the room. Awena, it was said, might have invented boho chic. On her feet she wore jeweled sandals. "It's probably too early to hope to find fresh meadowsweet growing."

"Beltane?" asked her husband, the Reverend Max Tudor, over the top of that day's *Monkslip-super-Mare Globe and Bugle*.

"Do you know," Awena continued, "I suppose I really should add the recipe for May wine to my newest cookbook, but the recipe is so easy it hardly seems worth it. You simply add the meadowsweet to white wine and let it steep for twenty-four hours. It does give me an idea, though. I wonder if it would be a good idea to organize the book by the four seasons. What do you think, Max?"

The cookbook was only one of the plates Awena kept in the air, in a manner of speaking. She also now had a meditation app. Free to download, of course, and developed for her by a rather intense, bespectacled young man in London with an astonishing collection of video and voice recording equipment. Meditation was a free gift, she maintained, and no one should charge for it.

"It's always good to be organized," said Max vaguely, folding back the newspaper to the crossword puzzle. "But what happens if you write a follow-up book? You'll have used up all the seasons. Did you say, Beltane?"

Not offended that her husband was listening with only half his attention, Awena nodded. She stood back from the kitchen counter, where she had been arranging spring flowers, and cast a critical eye over the bluebells. The cottage she shared with Max and their still-sleeping child, Owen, always smelled of fresh blossoms that were never allowed to stand in yesterday's water. By some seemingly miraculous process, flowers arranged by Awena lasted twice as long as anyone else's. This made her presence less, not more, desired by the women of the St. Edwold's Church Flower Guild. Beloved as Awena was, there was always a certain amount of jockeying for position on the flower rota, for decorating the altar often meant coveted face time with Max, their handsome vicar. Parishioners were known to borrow or even invent problems to bring to Max when they had no real problems of their own. There was something so soothing in his manner they felt the lightening of a burden shared, before they remembered there had been no real problem in the first place.

"Beltane, yes," said Awena. "'Bright Fires.' It's halfway between the spring equinox and the summer solstice. Beltane will start at sundown April thirtieth and last all day May first. You must remember this from last year, Max?"

"I think I'm meant officially to look the other way," said Max. "But yes, I remember."

"Beltane was huge around these parts, until Christianity drove it out—or underground," she said. "The Church tried to turn it into May Day—a much tamer event. It is one of the few pagan festivals they failed to repurpose into a Christian one. The people liked it as it was. But officials did try."

"It probably looked as though the villagers were having too much fun," said Max. "We can't have that. For us it's either sackcloth and ashes or nothing." Max thought the Protestant reformers had been by and large a humorless bunch, a trait shared by extremists down to the present day. Too often it had been their way or the highway. Or prison, or the stake. May Day in Calvinist Scotland had been erased from the calendar, as best they could manage, and the Puritans later banned Maypoles around the time they were setting sail for the Americas to spread their peculiar brand of joy in the New World.

"You're joking, but that's exactly what was going on. Since Beltane celebrates the return of the sun, it's a time of new life and growth, a flowering, fertile time. It is also a period when it is easiest to pierce the veil between this world and the next. Just like at Samhain—these are days of 'no time.'"

"I see," said Max. "This isn't the one where they did the human sacrifice, is it?" He had put down the paper to listen to his wife; he often learned something new from these rare chats about Awena's beliefs. And he often came away seeing the many places where her theories and practices intersected with his own. He also carried off many an idea for his next sermon.

"Max, really. Dancing and bonfires and music, yes. Human sacrifice, no. Well, maybe just the once or twice. All that was probably just jealous Romans carrying tales. There was no Wicker Man. Probably not. It's more that the usual order of things was suspended and a few people got carried away, as people will."

He wondered why the Romans would be jealous of a lot of hovel-dwelling peasants who probably stank of animal dung and ate gruel laced with gristle, but he thought it politic not to ask. He and Awena—Anglican vicar and Wiccan—got along so well by making every allowance for the other's religion.

"Beltane was—and still is—a fertility rite. There was all manner of carry-on around here, especially in those woods over by Wooton Priory. Not just the young ones but people of all ages. A bit of an orgy in some cases, it is supposed, but also there were greenwood marriages—a sort of tryout to see if the union of a betrothed couple was going to be fertile."

"An audition for the main event. I see."

"The birthrate soared nine months later—there would be a sort of Beltane baby boom; this is all well documented—and finally it was felt a line had to be drawn. The Victorians finally succeeded in stamping out the festivities for a very long while."

"To replace them with tea parties and ghastly good-works projects for fallen women."

Awena paused in snipping off the bottoms of some yellow daffodil stems. "Do you remember me telling you about Viola, that local girl? From Chipping Monkslip? It was during the Beltane festivities one year that she went missing in Prior's Wood—this was back in Victorian times. It was her disappearance that put a stop to the celebrations, in keeping with the surge of Victorian disapproval. The timing of her departure confused things for a good while—the fact that she disappeared when there was a lot of organized chaos and debauchery going on anyway. People really did assume she'd run off, possibly because after spending all night in the woods with her lover, a lowly gardener, no 'decent' family would take her back in."

"Not even her own family?"

"Especially not her own family. Her people had a place in the community—the father was one of the local squires—and the girl was now damaged goods, whether or not anything much actually happened in the woods. Remember these were Victorians and this is how they thought. There wasn't a dowry big enough to erase from people's minds the image of Viola skipping off with the local gardener, flowers in her hair and wearing, at best, a sort of skimpy toga."

"Really, it sounds delightful. I shall have to make a note to buy you a toga."

"*Max*."

"All right. It was a different era but yes, I can see how the girl must have been distressed. Terrified, actually. She could guess how her family would react and I would imagine she didn't feel she could face the consequences. But where would she go? London? Then as now, you need money to run off to London with your boyfriend. A gardener would need references and, call me mad, but taking off with the local squire's daughter in tow would probably ruin your chances of a good reference."

"It would seem the young couple thought of that. The boy gave notice to the head gardener just before Beltane that he was off to join the army or something, but later he surfaced somewhere in Yorkshire. No one at his new employer's realized his connection to the young girl of the house—he had one of those names like James Smith—and I guess no one verified his references."

"The gardener showed up in Yorkshire, then. But where was she?"

"Her family assumed she was with him and no one could be bothered to go and find out. There had been a bit of a family row, you see, and they just wrote her off. There's a family Bible Lord Duxter got hold of somehow that he keeps in the archives at the old priory—he can show you it with her name and date of birth cut out of the page by someone using a sharp knife. The rub is that her young man—the gardener—thought she'd changed her mind about joining him. I suppose he couldn't just take a week off from work to come down here and ask. He was too low on the totem pole to expect any serious time off. It wasn't until later he learned she was missing. A villager he ran into quite by accident in his local recognized him. He thought right then and there he was in trouble but he could prove, you see, that he was nowhere around when she went missing. He had witnesses—his new employer, for one. Then a theory took hold that she must have gone out into Prior's Wood with someone else entirely and that is where the mystery lies. Who was she with? And did he do away with her?"

"Undoubtedly, the chances are good he did. But the gardener didn't get in touch with the family? Once he realized she was missing? I mean, really missing?"

"Not directly. I imagine he didn't dare. He told this villager—it was one of your predecessors in office, by the way—he told him the whole story, or what he knew of it. The vicar knew the young man and could vouch for his character. It was the vicar who got in touch with the authorities on his return from his travels. So a desultory search of the woods began, a sort of thrashing around the bushes and branches, knowing it was all much too late. Then songs and poems began to be written about her, and her legend was passed down. 'The Girl's Grave' is still sung around these parts every May Day."

"If she was anywhere," said Max, catching the spirit of the tale, "it's a good guess she ended up in the lake in those woods."

"Hmm," said Awena. "What makes you think she was put in the lake? It's more a pond these days, by the way."

"I don't know. If you had a body to hide, isn't that where you'd put it?"

"I've never given any thought to where I'd hide a body."

"Well, no, of course not," Max said. "But do consider it now. Let's say she was killed accidentally in some sort of struggle or she was murdered outright. Something happened, in any event, that would cause trouble for someone if her body were found. The killer only had to tip the body into the lake to conceal the crime—he'd weigh her down with stones knotted in the hem of her dress or something. The most likely scenario is that he took her out to the center of the water in a rowboat. Either he rowed out with the body or he strangled her in the boat and then tipped her in. I would think the latter was the simpler way, assuming she was willing to go with him. If she didn't suspect she was being lured to her death by some sort of maniac."

"That's too awful to think about," said Awena. "I prefer to think killing her was a spur-of-the-moment thing. They quarreled; perhaps he hit her with an oar."

"No serious attempt at a search was made at the time?"

Awena shook her head. "Not given that family row; she told them she was leaving and sort of flounced off the way girls her age tend to do, then as now. So no, no real search, because they thought she was alive. Very angry and defiant, and very alive. They also didn't drain the lake, even when they finally realized she may not simply have run off. In any event it would have been pointless. It had been years before they realized what the true situation may have been and if she were down there in those waters she was gone for sure. Even today, the best they could hope for would be to find a ring or necklace or something at the bottom. Her bones . . . well, you know."

Max shook his head. "Not necessarily. It depends. There's water and then there's water. That's why bog people have been found well preserved after hundreds of years."

"But that's dreadful, to think she could have been recovered and no one could be bothered. Even after it was apparent she had not after all disgraced the family by running off."

"Oh, but in their minds she had, remember—disgraced the family. By being in those woods at all that Beltane night."

"I'll ask Jane about this," said Awena. "She might know something, or she may have come across more information in the archives she's been sorting through."

"Jane? Oh, right, of course. Jane Frost."

Awena paused to coax a recalcitrant stem into the dead center of a tall vase packed with flowers. "She's been organizing the archives over at Wooton Priory, where I'll be working during the day in the autumn. For the writers' retreat, you know. I figure by then I'll have enough of the book roughed out it will be the perfect time to get the manuscript trimmed into final shape for the publishers."

"For Lord Duxter." Whose Wooton Press owed a great deal of its success to the unforeseen explosion in popularity of Awena's all-things-natural recipes, her television show having added to the surge of interest in her written recipes as well as her general approach to a simpler life uncluttered by possessions. Awena felt a debt of gratitude in return, that Lord Duxter had early on seen the potential in what others had dismissed as a faddish harking back to earlier times.

"You're sure you'll be all right while I'm in London for the next few days?" she asked.

"No worries. Owen will be fine with me. We have reached an understanding. If he does not throw his cereal on the floor he gets to watch telly cartoons. And Tara of course fills in as needed."

"Owen likes being at Goddessspell with her. It's too bad

goat yoga was such a failure. He loved watching the classes but the goats got to be too big a distraction. And then there was the cleanup . . ."

"I think anyone but Tara could have foreseen what would happen."

Awena smiled. "Worth a try, anyway. But my mind rests easy, knowing I'm free to go. I really need to see the original recipes and try to intuit what it is they meant to say. So much gets lost in translation. Jane's been helpful in pointing me toward sources in the British Library."

"Her husband is headed for Saudi Arabia right about now, isn't he?" Max asked.

Awena stepped back to admire the artistry of her arrangement, saying, "Colin left last week. I've been thinking of inviting Jane over. She might like a break from Mrs. Henslowe—her grandmother-in-law, I suppose you'd call her. And I imagine Jane will be feeling a bit lonely without Colin around."

Awena was always inviting people over "to make sure they didn't feel alone."

"Whatever induced Colin to take a job so far away from his family?" Max asked. "I heard there was some discussion beforehand. It seemed a bit up in the air whether he would accept the offer."

"The financial rewards, purely, according to Jane. Colin had been unemployed almost a year and I don't think they had a lot of options left. He can be a bit of a square peg, you know. I don't think job offers were thick on the ground."

"I see. Of course, that makes sense."

"But now Jane has her hands so full she never gets to see her own family, she told me. Not that she cares about that greatly—they don't appear to be close-knit—but what seemed to bother her was the idea that Colin's family and needs came first in his mind, with his never having a thought that, for one thing, taking care of an ang-sty teenager like Poppy was hardly a laugh a minute for Jane."

"That's right, there's the stepdaughter," Max said. "Should we also invite her over?"

"Probably she'd be needed to stay with Netta Henslowe if Jane came over." After a moment Awena added, "Living with Mrs. Henslowe must be a lot like living alone. Or perhaps it's more like being an unpaid companion."

"Netta Henslowe can be difficult, I know. Since her husband was killed in that hunting accident—"

"Since well before that."

"You are quite right," said Max. "She was always difficult, prob-ably from birth. So Jane's not only been left to cope with Mrs. Henslowe, she's been put in charge of a stepdaughter, who tolerates her at best. I see the problem too often. Poppy didn't ask for this situation, it was created for her by adults, and she can only think of getting away from the evil stepmother."

"I don't think it's quite as bad as that, actually. I think she and Poppy get along, but that is mainly because Jane can't really be both-ered to keep close tabs on the girl. It's a good thing that at sixteen Poppy is old enough to fend for herself, for the most part. And she's always hanging about the abbey, so her stepmother isn't too far out of reach if needed."

"They say the teen years are the worst. I hope we avoid all that with Owen." Max turned a page in his newspaper and saw there were no obituaries. Good.

"They all came here from London, am I right?" Awena asked. "Colin, Jane, and Poppy?"

Max folded the paper and took a final sip of coffee. "I believe so. Yes, I think that's where Jane and Colin met originally. He was a widower, but I don't know when his first wife died. It's only certain Poppy lost her natural mother at far too young an age. I would be willing to bet she never bargained on finding herself in a small village."

"And that's all the more reason to get Jane out of the house, don't you think?" Awena asked. "Give the situation a chance to air out a bit? Besides, Jane's found a sort of treasure trove of stuff at the priory. Letters and books, and an old history of the village. She thinks some of it may be valuable or at least of interest to someone like me. I'd like to hear more about it."

"By all means, let's give her a ring. Maybe we could plan a small dinner party. Make sure she feels part of village life."

"I'll ring her today."

But regrettably, in light of future events, Jane never made it to dinner.

PART II

In the Cards

Chapter 3

THE FOOL

It was the sort of apple-crisp September day that tempted the villagers of Nether Monkslip out of doors on any pretext that could be manufactured. A trip to the shops to buy ground pepper and a knitting pattern might be drawn out into an all-afternoon event, rounded off with a stop for tea and biscuits at Elka Garth's Cavalier Tea Room and Garden.

But the Reverend Max Tudor stood indoors in the amber glow of St. Edwold's Church, the knuckles of one hand pressed hard against his mouth as he stared aghast at a just-delivered stained glass window. The small delivery lorry had driven away minutes before with cheery waves of farewell from Sam, the driver, and his young mate Robbie. Sam and Robbie had removed the window from its custom-made wooden encasement but had left the packaging untouched to await the glass installers, who were scheduled to mount the window into its wooden frame in a few days' time.

Having seen the delivery team off, Max had torn the seal on the padded wrappings. After leaning the stained glass gently against the plywood currently boarding up the window, he'd stood back with great anticipation to assess the work. There was just enough light for him to see by from the flickering candles on the altar and from sunlight filtering in through the stained glass windows adjacent to the one being replaced. He stared for a long while, still and motionless, taking it all in, the church cat Luther mewling for attention at his feet until Max scooped him up and began idly ruffling the fur at his neck. But Max's was not the enthralled, rapt gaze of the art enthusiast viewing a long-awaited treasure. Rather, a frown altered the handsome features of the vicar of St. Edwold's into an expression conveying distress atop astonished disbelief. All he could think was that it would have to be redone. And at what cost?

The funds to re-create the old stained glass depiction of the Good Shepherd, which had been destroyed during a vicious storm by an uprooted tree driven through the window, had been donated by old Mr. Henslowe, now deceased. For the timeliness and generosity of his gift, Max was profoundly grateful, although it had to be said, for Leo Henslowe, the timing had been quite unexpected and rather awful. He had been the victim of a shooting accident while out with a hunting party on his eightieth birthday.

If not for the bequest he'd recently had attached as a codicil to his will, the sheet of plywood might have covered the window indefinitely while the village's fundraising efforts dragged on and on. The villagers, after all, could only buy so many jars of preserves to help replace the stained glass, and there was a limit to the income generated from the sale of hand-knitted hats and booties and the like. The surplus fund for emergency repairs had been drawn down too many times in fixing the church's old plumbing to allow for acts of God, which, ironically, were not covered by the church's insurance policy.

But what was it, that creature surrounded by colorful shards of leaded glass in the iron frame? Surely . . . surely it was not a goat? The rather demented-looking crystal-blue eyes with their horizontal, rectangular pupils said that it was. It was either a goat or it was a lamb as designed by someone who had not been raised anywhere near a farm and had only the weakest grasp on animal husbandry. The eyes were goat's eyes, with that blank, rather sinister stare of the goat. And surely the ears, too, were the wrong shape for a lamb.

And weren't those horns? And a beard? A goatee, in fact.

Max, settling the cat on a nearby pew, supposed he should have been more suspicious of the artist, who was famously eccentric, unconventional, and contrary as it suited him, which was often. Lucas Coombebridge had been plumping for a great unveiling of the new stained glass artwork, a ceremony to be held in front of all the village worthies, and he had often stated his wish that Max should be as surprised as anyone else in the audience. But Max had prevailed, insisting on seeing the work before it was revealed in a ceremonial presentation to the villagers. He knew Lucas's character well enough to doubt him and his motives.

The trouble was that Henslowe had donated the money for the window conditionally, with strict instructions as to who the artist must be. He had also been specific as to the colors, the materials, and of course the theme. It must be a Good Shepherd to replace the one that was lost to the storm. When Henslowe had passed to his reward not long afterward—or rather, been blown sky high—his wishes had taken on added weight and authority. In fact, old Leo's codicil dictated that extra funds be directed to the routine cleaning and upkeep of "his" window. After his death, his widow, Netta, had seized the fallen banner and run with it. Max thought the choice of Lucas as artist may in fact have been her idea, for Lucas famously had a way with the ladies, even ladies in their eighties.

Max took a judicious step back, and concluded that he was not being hasty in his judgment. The window was a fright. It was not just the goat, it was the whole thing. It was hideous. Incorrect by any biblical standard, and bordering on the blasphemous. Surely a goat draped about the neck of the Good Shepherd—the traditional image of a benevolent Jesus retrieving a lost lamb—was just plain wrong.

Jesus, too, when it came right down to it, had a rather crazed look about him: the wide-eyed stare of the fanatic, the whites of his eyes showing all the way round. It was frightening was what it was. And the Good Shepherd was most people's favorite depiction of the gentle and compassionate man sent by God to save mankind. This man looked, in a word, insane. What had Lucas been thinking? Very likely he'd been thinking of all the commotion he could cause. Lucas was like that.

But the window, in addition to being a horror, was done and paid for and had been executed and delivered in accordance with the terms of the benefactor's will. Max could refuse it and probably he would have to, but how awkward. Much better to see if the artist was amenable to making a few alterations.

Hah. The chances were slim but he had to try.

Max was rehearsing the request in his mind ("It looks as if it would be a matter of painting out the goat's beard, you see, and doing something about the shape of the eyes . . . Of course, I'm no artist but I rather feel we've gone off in the wrong direction here . . .") when the Rev. Destiny Chatsworth hauled open the heavy doors of the church and stepped briskly inside. She wore the large Birkenstock sandals she favored, making a splat-splat sound against the flagstones. Max knew it was Destiny without having to turn to look.

"Ah, there you are, Max," she said. "I've been looking all o—what in God's name is that?" The window actually stopped her in her tracks, her mouth falling open in a gratifying little "o" of astonishment. The untamable spirals of her hair seemed to spring even further out from her head in surprise. Max did not feel so alone in his assessment of the art, like some philistine unable to appreciate greatness when it was set before him. It was as shocking as he had thought. Nether Monkslip would be a laughingstock.

"Lucas. He was commissioned to replace the old window, you know. Leo Henslowe gave rather explicit instructions in his bequest. And this is what Lucas turned up with."

Echoing Max's earlier reaction, she stepped back to attempt a more judicious gaze. Finally she said, "Did he not submit a design for approval?"

"He did, actually," Max replied with a touch of asperity. "Of course he did. In the design he submitted, the lamb looked like a cute fuzzy toy, and the Christ did not look like, like . . ."

"Like a serial killer?"

"If that's not going too far to say so, yes. He looked like, well, normal. Gentle and kind. Like you'd expect the Good Shepherd to look."

"At least Lucas gave his shepherd dark hair," she offered cautiously. "Jesus looks Swedish in so many renderings."

"Hmm."

"What a shame," she said. "It was wonderful to think of that window being repaired at last. Perhaps you could pass it off as a modern interpretation of the scriptures?" The glass on an earlier occasion had nearly been blown out of its frame by an explosion detonated by a lunatic set on the destruction of Max's happiness, but some act of Providence had largely preserved it then. While the criminal was safely in prison now, it looked like his mission was continuing, with Mother Nature and Lucas now in charge.

Max aimed lifted eyebrows in Destiny's direction.

"No, I suppose not," she said. "We'd have to come up with an entire new theology to explain this. 'The Lord is my goatherd' doesn't have the same ring somehow."

"No."

"I don't know whether to laugh or cry."

"Me either. You said you had been looking for me. Was there something in particular you wanted to tell me?"

"Yes, and it is rather an odd coincidence," said Destiny. "There's been another death in the village. It happens to be Mrs. Henslowe this time."

"Oh, I'm so sorry to hear that," said Max, thinking it was a relief she hadn't lived to see how her husband's bequest had been spent. "Her heart, was it? She was a nice woman." This was patently untrue but Max felt when someone died it is hardly the moment to start listing their shortcomings. "It's not surprising—she was eighty last spring, as I recall—but even so."

"Lots to go wrong at eighty. Her eyesight and hearing had been fading for years. Still, up until about a year ago she could get around fairly well—she rode her bicycle everywhere, nearly knocked me down a few times. Never could be bothered to apologize or ring the bicycle bell in the first place: one was supposed to just *know* one was in her way. Sometimes I'd see her walking to the shops, all dressed up and her hair done just so. It seemed to take her an hour to buy a loaf of bread, but she'd get there in the end. Her gooseberry jam was still a fixture at the Harvest Fayre, however. Fought over, it was. It was thought she made limited quantities so she could drive up the price, but that's a story Miss Pitchford likes to put about."

"A bit of jealousy there, between those two." Max nodded sagely. "Going back decades. It's understandable, really. Miss Pitchford could never match Netta for her gooseberry jam. And Netta was said to be a famous beauty in her prime. I believe—now don't quote me—but I believe Miss Pitchford may have fancied old Leo for herself, when they were all young together. But he only ever had eyes for Netta."

"That may be. Well, as I say, Netta Henslowe seemed to be doing all right, if only all right for her age. Perhaps getting a bit paranoid; she was always rather suspicious by nature and it does seem to me as we get older basic traits get more ingrained. But her heart was giving her trouble, especially after Leo passed. People do die of broken hearts."

"There are no surviving children, but there's a grandson. I suppose he's been notified?"

"Colin Frost. Right. Both his parents have passed already. He's been working over in Saudi Arabia. Something to do with oil. Or some sort of computer thing they use in the oil fields. Cybersecurity, is it? Don't ask—I'm sure I couldn't explain it even though Colin tried to tell me, several times. Everything over there is something to do with oil or banking. Anyway, yes, he's on his way home. Netta was actually living with Colin's wife and daughter, you know. To be precise, they were living with her—she has that good-sized cottage with the thatched roof on the outskirts of the village. Beautiful little place it is."

"Hawthorne Cottage, yes. I go past it all the time on my way to take the services at Chipping Monkslip."

"Mrs. Henslowe refused ever to go into a nursing home and the two women and the girl all seemed to shove along well enough, so it was a good arrangement."

"Dr. Winship has been in attendance on Netta?"

"Oh, yes—he's been her doctor for ages. She went suddenly, though, and that's a shame—she had specifically asked for unction if and when she started to fail. There just wasn't time for me to get there—I live closest to her cottage. She went peacefully in her sleep."

"It's a blessing of sorts. I considered getting her to intervene over this once I saw it—" And here he waved his hand in the direction of the offending artwork, averting his eyes. "But perhaps it's just as well. I am rather glad she didn't live to see her husband's last wishes carried out in such a . . . well, such a strange way."

"What are you going to do?"

"Cover it up, for now. I'll get on to the artist and see what can be done."

"It's funny," said Destiny. "Everything in the depiction looks quite, quite mad. Including the goat. The flowers are rather nice, though."

"I should have known from the moment I heard Coombebridge was involved. It is probably his idea of a joke."

"He's famous in these parts, isn't he? Well, he's famous, period, if I've heard of him. I'm not much of a connoisseur of art."

"Oh, yes, as an oil painter he's quite famous. As a person he's notorious. His personal life has always been a ramshackle scandal. I suppose he took this window on as a challenge. It's not his usual medium at all."

"There's that—that might explain it. I suppose if you're not used to working in stained glass, it might be tricky to get the exact effect you want."

"Knowing Lucas, this was probably exactly the effect he wanted."

"Ah," said Destiny. "Probably you're right."

"I should have double-checked what he was up to. Gone out there to see him, on any pretext. I knew his character. Rather, his reputation. I feel such a fool. No one in his senses would have left Lucas to his own devices. It's like handing matches and dry hay to a toddler."

"So we got a billy goat instead of a little lamb."

"It looks like it. At least he got the prescribed colors right, although I doubt very much that Leo was hoping to see purples and greens of such virulent shades."

"But it is a *small* billy goat," said Destiny, doubtfully. "A young one. So maybe Lucas's intention was . . . not what we think."

"When it comes to Lucas Coombebridge you can be sure the symbolism is exactly what we imagine it to be and what he intended it to be. The goat has long been a pagan symbol for fertility. Or for the devil himself. Perhaps it was all meant to be a joke, a sort of dig at Awena and her beliefs."

"My. That is convoluted."

"He's a complicated man. If anyone could take the goat as his symbol or mascot, it would be Lucas Coombebridge." Max paused and added, under his breath, "The old goat."

Chapter 4

STRENGTH

"I was sorry to hear about Netta today," said Awena, settling Owen into his high chair in preparation for his dinner. She liked to feed him before she and Max had their meal so they had a better chance to talk. "When was Leo's accident . . . over a year ago, wasn't it?"

"It may have been closer to a year and a half. I remember holding the service for him." Max handed her Owen's bib. A small tussle ensued because Owen wanted to tie it on without anyone's help. He vigorously shook his small head with its thatch of dark hair until his father relented. The bib had a small pink lamb embroidered on it. *I don't*, thought Max, *seem able to escape the animal kingdom today*.

An expert in handling firearms, Max had been horrified at the manner of Leo Henslowe's death—shot in the head by a fellow hunter, the old man had died instantly, which was a mercy. It was another accident that need not have happened, and none of Max's usual bromides had had any effect: Netta, who had railed against the unfairness of it all, had seen no point in going on without Leo by her side.

"Too many people without proper firearms training or even common sense blow themselves and other people to kingdom come each year," Max said now. "There is really no excuse for it."

Awena, who abhorred anything to do with guns and hunting, could only nod in grim agreement.

"So she leaves behind Colin and his daughter, Poppy," Max said. "And Colin's wife, of course—Poppy's stepmother, Jane. What exactly happened to her own children—Netta's, I mean?" Awena had been in the village far longer than Max, and knew all the relationships, legends, feuds, and entanglements going way back.

"Netta and Leo had a son, named Lawrence, and a daughter," said Awena. "The daughter's name was—let me see; it's been years . . . Yes, her name was Lenore. Both are deceased. Lenore was Colin's mother."

"Yes, all well before my time here," said Max, setting the table. "Tell me a bit about the dynamics. Every family has its own ways. I need to start thinking what to say at the service for Netta."

"'*De mortuis nil nisi bonum,*'" quoted Awena. "'Say only good of the dead.' That may be a struggle in this case. I wouldn't want your job some days, Max." She handed Owen his bottle to keep him occupied until his food arrived. "Netta was very nice and proper but she was also a bit of a grande dame. Always perfectly turned out, makeup and hair and so on. Thin as a runway model. Exquisite, really. Well, you've seen her; she'd only become more grand with age. Her children—well, Lawrence and Lenore were merely props in her personal pageant, or so it seemed to most people. They were never the main event. And when they became a bit of a problem for her in their teens she sort of—oh, I don't know. Sort of shut them down. She didn't turn them out into the street or anything, but she was so clearly disappointed they wouldn't just go away and leave her to her perfect marriage. Their usefulness as props, particularly as they grew, was gone."

"You mean when they were no longer small and cuddly?"

She shook her head and thought a moment before saying, "No. Difficult to explain . . . It was more than that. They were in her way at *any* age. My sense was that she tired of them, or grew *more* tired of them—not that they became more or less attractive to her. It's more that the maternal instinct just wasn't there to begin with. It was her husband she loved. Him and him alone, in a way that may not have been entirely healthy. She was heard to say that the only time she and Leo had difficulty in their marriage was when the children were teenagers, and her intense dislike, particularly of Lenore, seemed to start around that time. Apparently she and Lenore quarreled over Lenore's hairdo, of all things. People generally felt that the children were born out of Netta's desire to please Leo, not because she wanted children herself. Does that make sense?"

"Well, no, although I understand what you mean. He wanted children to carry on the family name and she saw having children somehow as her duty—part and parcel of making her husband happy."

"Yes, I think so. Lenore was born first, you see, and I gather the disappointment was great that she was 'only' a girl." Awena sketched little quotation marks in the air at "only." "So then Lawrence came along. General rejoicing, a son and heir to carry on the name, praise heaven."

"What an outdated point of view. Positively archaic. I'd have been delighted if Owen had been a girl. I truly did not care either way about primogeniture or any of the other rot." Headed for the kitchen, he asked, "Will we need soup spoons?"

"Yes," she said, "to the spoons."

On his return, she continued, "And yes, dear Max, but that is you. For someone like Leo—and by extension, Netta—the birth of Lenore was a disappointment. Think of Henry the Eighth's displeasure at his daughter Elizabeth's birth and you won't miss the mark by much. But with Lawrence's birth, I suppose Leo felt he had ticked that box and now he could move on."

"I don't suppose Lenore fared too well, especially if her parents couldn't hide their disappointment at her existence."

Again Awena shook her head. "Do you know, the rumor went round that she killed herself, although officially she died in a skiing accident in the Alps. Fell off a ski lift, of all things, and plunged to her death. She wasn't yet in her forties."

"That's hard to do these days—fall off, I mean. With all the safety features built into those lifts."

"That was the general thinking around the village, too, but it seemed kinder to those left behind—to Colin—to call it an accident. There was never a thought it was foul play—Lenore was alone in the lift."

"But that's appalling," said Max. "The poor soul."

"We'll never know what was in her mind. She didn't leave a suicide note, if the fall was intentional. Nothing—no hint. Anyway, by that point Netta had long since sort of written her off, her and her brother both. From the moment Netta finished giving birth to the two children, she regarded her job as done, and she could focus her energies back where they belonged: on her husband's happiness. The children were sent off to boarding school at the first opportunity. But worse followed worse: Lenore fell off that ski lift, and Lawrence died a year later—definitely a suicide. Drugs. So there were two people of the same generation of the family gone too soon, and then their father Leo taken in such a horrific and sudden way. If Netta seemed a bit sharp-tempered at times, it was no wonder."

Sharp-tempered was an understatement, from all Max had heard and knew of the woman firsthand. But like Awena, he had made allowances. Everyone carried a secret burden, and it was impossible to gauge how he himself might react to such a cascade of losses. He'd nearly lost Awena once and he still didn't know how he'd managed to hang on to his sanity.

"There is no question," Awena continued, "that losing Leo was a last straw. Every time I ran into Netta she seemed to have shrunk an inch, and withdrawn further into herself. I saw her less and less often around the village, in fact. She'd gotten rather doddery—you know what I mean. But if you offered her your arm to help her cross the High she'd refuse. Once Jane came along, most of the shopping and running errands fell to her. And to the great-granddaughter: Poppy helped out as she could."

"Another teenager in the house," said Max. "I wonder how she and Netta got on."

"Interesting you should say that. I did hear Poppy's experiments with her hair and nails were a renewed source of friction. Sometimes you need to pick your fights with greater care. Anyway, Netta never shed a tear during any of this, not even at losing Leo. That was when her reputation as a cold fish began to solidify. Some people were scandalized, but I thought that rather unfair. Netta was stoical by nature."

"We all grieve in different ways." This was always Destiny's stance, and Max knew it to be true. "People assume roles to get themselves through it. They do their crying in private."

"Yes, I'm sure you're right," said Awena. "We have to make allowances for shock. But the son's drug use—well, Netta had hardened against him a long time before because of it. The disgrace, you know. I don't suppose she ever acknowledged that addictions like that run in families, as does depression. And that his difficult relationship with her may have exacerbated things. But it's going to be hard for you to carve a fitting homily out of any of this. You'll have to sand down the bumpy parts. 'Funerals are for the living,' Netta would always say. But who else, I wonder, would they be for?"

"That expression is a coping mechanism," said Max. "Used by people who tend to distance themselves emotionally. It's a form of self-defense against pain and loss. I've seen it often in people with difficult childhoods—they build these walls, you know. No one can hurt you if you refuse to feel any pain. It's a form of strength, but God knows the damage it causes—to oneself, and to others."

"And if you pride yourself on your stiff upper lip and common sense, it makes matters worse. I do see. Yes, that was how she operated. Nothing must mar the perfection of her life as she presented it to her public. I admired her for years and I still do. But one day I realized such perfectionism comes at a price. At too high a price for those closest to you."

"But when Leo died, Netta couldn't entirely hide her grief behind platitudes."

"Yes," agreed Awena. "It became more of a struggle. I suppose her death can be put down to a sort of wasting away to grief. Outwardly she was strong, for her age, and tough as a nut. Inwardly—that can be a different story."

"Destiny said she died of a broken heart. It does happen all the time. One of my biggest fears is that, God forbid, anything should happen to you. I doubt I'd survive. At least, I know I wouldn't want to." He and Awena having had one close call in that regard, Max felt he knew what he was speaking of.

"I'm going to live to a very ripe old age and so are you," said Awena briskly. "But not if we don't have our dinner soon. I'm famished, aren't you? However, tonight's meal is a bit of a failed experiment, I'm afraid—the main course is from one of the recipes I'm trying to adapt for my book. I think I'm starting to dream in Middle English—I'm so steeped in this 'Ye Olde' project—but the onion and mushroom tart just isn't right. Some of the spices for it either hadn't been discovered or weren't common in England in the Middle Ages. It will taste all right, I think, but I do need it to be more authentic than that."

"I'm sure it will be grand," said Max absently. Awena had never offered him a bad meal since he'd known her. And "authentic" should have been Awena's middle name.

She disappeared momentarily into the kitchen and reemerged carrying Owen's little dish. "But the fennel soup with ginger turned out well," she continued. "And there's braised spinach with roasted courgettes as a side dish, and the last of the runner beans."

"Wonderful," said Max, taking Owen's meal from her and placing it before him.

"I've spent untold hours in the London archives reading up on all this. And as it turns out, Lord Duxter has quite a good collection of books on the history of food and agriculture and cooking and so on in his library. Jane Frost has been good in helping me find what I need. She's taken up cooking as a hobby, too, I gather. The problem I'm finding is that vegetables were often frowned upon back in those days. Anything that grew out of the ground was considered to be peasant food, suitable only for those who had to grub about for a living."

"I'm glad Jane has been of help," said Max. "She appears to be rather a good-natured sort and she may welcome the distraction. Not everyone could put up with Netta Henslowe with such patience."

Awena looked at him. "Do you think so? I suppose Jane is good-natured around you. Most women are, Max. They want you to like them."

"How extraordinary," said Max.

Awena smiled. "Personally, I've always found Jane to have a bit of an edge, but it's understandable, given her situation there at Hawthorne Cottage. Rather trapped, yes? She's nice, but sometimes it seems rather forced—a bit of an effort. As if she had to remind herself how to behave around other people."

"Ah." Max had found this to be not uncommon. Despite Awena's warm and accepting nature, which won most people to her side, there were women in the village who were, well, envious. That reaction never lasted long after meeting her but it was painful to see while it did last.

"I don't suppose she's having an easy life with Colin gone so much," Awena added. "I don't know what I'd do if you were gone for months at a time. It was bad enough when you were crime solving in Monkslip-super-Mare, and you were only away a few days."

"I can never wait to get back home, even after just a long day at the vicarage."

"At least the book is coming along nicely with Jane's help, although with Colin's return I may have less to do with her than before. I'm really having to scrounge to create a casserole for the modern palate using only what would have been available to the medieval cook. I rather regret agreeing to the whole project, but Lord Duxter was persuasive. And he offered a generous advance."

"Well, whatever you create will be delightful, as always," said Max, whose knowledge of casseroles had been limited to the frozen Sainsbury's varieties before he had met Awena. "If there are leftovers, could I take them over to Destiny's? I know she's working late tonight. I'm afraid that despite my best intentions, much of the drudge work of the parish is falling on her shoulders."

"Better yet, why don't you invite her over to join us? I'll just put Owen down and we'll have a proper grown-up meal for a change."

"What a good plan. I'm sure she'll welcome the break. I'll ring her now."

Chapter 5

THE HIGH PRIESTESS

Was there a sound more inviting than the cracking of firewood in the first fire of the season? Max breathed in deeply of the aroma as he stood from his chair to add a few small logs to the flames. Thea, his Gordon setter, lolled as near the hearth as she dared without having her black-and-tan fur burst into flames.

Max, Awena, and Destiny were having a late dinner at a small table Max had set before the fireplace, Destiny having gratefully accepted the last-minute invitation. Owen had gone down without a fuss and was fast asleep upstairs in his room. Awena had had to wait until he'd drifted off to remove the lamb bib. She'd rinse it out tonight and have it dry for him to wear tomorrow; the child suddenly could not be parted from it.

Destiny had quickly become a mainstay of village life, someone on whom Max increasingly relied to help run the parish churches in his care—two in addition to St. Edwold's. In recent years, more duties within the Anglican Church fell on fewer shoulders, and every priest of his acquaintance was stretched thin, trying to balance pastoral care with many other practicalities of day-to-day life in a parish. Destiny's arrival as his assistant felt like a literal godsend.

"You don't drive the car to Wooton Priory?" Destiny asked Awena, accepting a glass of red wine. "When you go to use their library? It must be a walk of what—three miles?"

"Unless I'm carrying a lot of heavy books for my research, I walk. I'm used to it. I generally put a thermos in my knapsack and have my tea at the Girl's Grave."

"Well, that sounds rather grim. The what?"

"It's the local name for a spot near the pond in Prior's Wood," Max informed her. "It's been called the Girl's Grave since I've lived here, certainly. But you'll not find it on any map. An exception being a map in Frank Cuthbert's *Wherefore Nether Monkslip*—the original unreliable source."

Destiny was an even more recent arrival to the village than Max. Max had noticed that only Nether Monkslippers who could claim ancestors going back several generations were not considered newcomers. Like Destiny, Max would always be a bit of an outsider. Even Awena had been born in Wales, not in the village, and while she was greatly loved and admired, she, too, was tarred with the outsider brush. The "real" villagers closed ranks when and as it suited them.

"The woods are vast and dense, with trees that come right up to Wooton Priory," Max continued. "Those woods used to be rather a hangout for local teens."

"They still are," said Awena. "And that's a tradition that goes back many centuries."

"Where does the girl of the name come from?" asked Destiny. "Who's in the grave, I mean?"

"It's a bit of a misnomer," said Awena, leveling honeyed slices of the fragrant onion and mushroom tart onto their plates. "There was a young girl who went missing in Prior's Wood. If she's buried there, no one ever found her. It's just assumed she's there—somewhere."

"All of this happening at some time in the last century?" Max reached for the bread, which was still warm from the oven.

"Yes," said Awena. "Meaning of course the eighteen hundreds, not the nineteen hundreds. That's so confusing, isn't it, when we are so newly into this century."

Max, using small wooden tongs to lift runner beans onto his plate, paused. "There seems to have been a great deal of that sort of thing going on in these parts. Missing women, I mean. The young nun who was murdered in Nunswood up on Hawk Crest, for example."

Awena nodded solemnly. "The Crest has its own tales, its own secrets." She knew her husband was thinking also of the suicide committed up there, not that long ago. He counted it as one of his failures, although there was nothing he could have done to prevent its happening. "And there was another nun found dead in the Wooton Priory church, her body covered with an altar cloth," she continued. "This one was also some time in the Middle Ages, when the priory was still a religious house. She'd been stabbed."

"I remember hearing something about this," said Destiny, nodding her acceptance of a serving of vegetables from Max. "A priest did it, right?"

"Yes," said Awena. "It turned out she'd been killed by a rogue priest in a failed attempt to cover up their affair. Her ghost still walks the night."

"Awena, listen to yourself," said Max, but he was smiling. "'Walks the night.' It's just an old folk tale that the nun's been seen in those woods. Lucky thing she was a novice wearing a white habit. A ghostly nun in a black habit would melt into the trees."

Awena smiled, the gentle, forbearing smile she used when dealing with skeptics. The "none so blind as those who will not see" smile.

Max went on, heedless, spearing a small nib of carrot from the mushroom tart with his fork. "Sadly, that sort of carry-on in religious houses wasn't rare. Not nearly so rare as it should have been. It was common in those days for a girl to be handed over as a postulant, sometimes as a sort of tribute or offering by a pious family, and sometimes as a punishment for a teenager who was difficult to control. The hope, then as now, was that the nuns might be able to straighten her out. It was along the same lines as sending a troubled boy into the army, hoping to make a man of him. It was often a recipe for disaster, of course. The girls would rebel against all the rules and strictures, as teenagers will do, and often they became the source of scandals that plagued the monasteries for decades. Centuries."

"You mean sex scandals," said Destiny, reaching for the cruet of olive oil.

"Is there any other kind? Well, all right, there were financial scandals as well, although nothing electrifies the populace so much as a nun who turns up pregnant after a visit from an itinerant monk or priest. And it goes without saying, young boys also were sent into monasteries at a too-tender age and fell into trouble there or invented trouble where none was before. By our standards, and even by theirs, these were children thrown into an adult world, unprepared for it. There is no question the system too often became corrupt— corroded by weak leadership, and by recruiting and promoting the wrong sorts of people in the first place."

"So what happened in Prior's Wood?" asked Destiny. "The Girl's Grave?"

"It's funny but Max and I were talking about this not long ago," said Awena. "A local girl went missing during the Beltane festivities. Not a nun but the daughter of a prosperous Victorian landowner with holdings near Chipping Monkslip. She was sixteen years old and she vanished off the face of the earth. The story that was put about was that she had run off with the gardener. But the boy turned up later and swore he knew nothing about her disappearance. No one else was missing from around Chipping Monkslip—no likely young man, I mean—and the authorities at the time grilled everyone who might have known something, in an ever-widening circle of suspects. The son of the lord of the manor was questioned—handled with kid gloves, of course. Villagers always thought he may have been involved—jealous or simply drunk, you know the sort of thing. She never was found. Her name was Viola. It's such a beautiful, old-fashioned name, I've always remembered it."

"I think I've heard that story, or some version of it," said Destiny. "And a song—some boy was singing it and strumming his guitar at the last Harvest Fayre. Is it true?"

Awena shrugged. "Most of these stories that get handed down have at least a kernel of truth, like the legend of King Arthur. Viola is one of the stories told to frighten children into staying out of those woods at night and never going there alone, because it's dark and dense and easy to get lost. The murdered novice also does a good job of frightening them into steering clear."

"They never figured out what happened to Viola?"

Awena shook her head. "No. She may have been abducted by a passing stranger but they never found any evidence for or against that theory. The family believed she had run away and wanted to low-key the whole affair."

"*What* a sad story," said Destiny. "You always think children will be safer in the country, don't you? When I think of the worry I put my parents through, staying out all hours at that age, I want to write them a letter of apology. Can you pass me more of the bread, please?"

"There is nothing bucolic about country life," said Awena. "Once you scratch the surface it's a struggle for survival straight down the line—at least, among the farmers and those trying to make a living off the land."

"I wonder," said Destiny, continuing her train of thought, "how Poppy is faring over there at Hawthorne Cottage. With Netta gone, it's just her and Jane. I should stop by."

"That's a good idea," said Max. "I'll be seeing Jane soon, I would imagine. With Colin. About the arrangements for Netta, you know. It seems an age since I've seen Jane; we did invite her for dinner one night but she couldn't make it."

"I saw her this afternoon coming out of the Cut and Dried Salon," said Awena. "It's sweet, her wanting to look nice for Colin's return."

"I imagine Poppy has missed her father while he's been gone," said Max.

"Enormously," said Awena. "There's a bit of hero worship going on there, if you ask me."

"It does seem a lot of people go missing hereabouts," Destiny remarked, absently slathering butter on a slice of the homemade wholegrain bread.

"It's true," admitted Max. "It's a low-density population, then as now, to have so many people unaccounted for." He might have added that a lot of murders had been committed in and around Nether Monkslip in recent years—that there'd been quite an alarming spike in the numbers of those cases. That the murders seem to have started when Max came on the scene as vicar was something he chose not to dwell on. His bishop seemed to think there was a connection, that Max had been sent by Providence to deal with an outbreak of evil. As if crime solving were some new form of pastoral care.

Max wasn't himself sure if Providence might see him as the cure or the cause. Or if it weren't all pure coincidence.

"Which is why," Awena said, "when farmer Johnson's wife

disappeared about the same time as Kevin, the man from the local gardening center, everyone began rehashing the tale of the missing Viola. But remote as we are, you can't keep a secret in this village for long: the couple was spotted in London years later, living together quite happily."

"When did this happen?"

Awena paused to sip her water as she totted up the years. "It's been ten years or so, I think. Miss Pitchford would know. She keeps a diary of such things. Let's hope she never decides to publish it."

It was unspoken, but it never needed to be said: Miss Pitchford knew where all the bodies were buried.

Awena put down her fork to stare at Max. "I never put it together before now. It *is* an awful lot of women gone missing from one area, not counting Judith Johnson and Kevin. The Victorian girl, and Lord Duxter's nun, and the other nun up on Hawk Crest."

"And those are just the ones we know of," said Max. "I doubt Lord Duxter would like the nun thought of as 'his,' but perhaps I'm wrong about that. It makes a good story to lure writers to his retreats."

"I hear he turned the little priory church into a sort of writers' chalet after it was deconsecrated," said Destiny. "Nice and spooky. Perhaps someone will write another *Frankenstein* there."

Max nodded. "Perhaps. Now, who would like cream with their coffee?"

The talk drifted over to Lord and Lady Duxter and their renovation of the priory. The clock on the mantelpiece struck the hour.

"That can't be right!" said Awena. "Max, what's the time?"

He looked at his watch.

"It's nine o'clock. The night is still young."

"I'll stay just a while if I'm not intruding," said Destiny. "I've got nothing on the schedule until nine tomorrow morning."

"You're more than welcome," said Awena. "We don't get nearly enough chances."

As Max poured brandy, Destiny offered to help serve the individual blackberry tarts. Awena sat staring into the fire, recalling a conversation she'd had not long before with another of Lord Duxter's authors. They had met signing books at a library conference and had shared a coffee afterward. Dominique le Grande, not her real name, was a writer of what used to be called potboiler romances—stories that kept food on the table for the author because of the sheer volume of books she was able to produce in a year. Dominique was in fact one of Wooton Press's success stories. She was a comfortable woman of fifty or so years, smartly dressed, never married, pretty in a faded-pink way.

"Didn't he start a charitable foundation?" Dominique had asked Awena.

"Yes, it's called the Wooton Wishing Well. It provides books to schools. It's one of the reasons he was made an OBE, for services to publishing and charity."

"Ah, yes. An Officer of the Most Excellent Order of the British Empire." She'd put a mocking emphasis on the word "excellent." "It's funny, but Lord Duxter never struck me as being a man often in the grip of charitable impulses."

"Well, no," said Awena. "He doesn't strike me that way, either. Of course it is a tax haven of sorts but I do think a well-intended one. At least, it does no real harm and it may do some good."

"And of course, it provides some good publicity for him and his publishing interests, too."

"Yes, there's that." She peered closely at her new friend. "You don't like him, do you?"

Dominique, blushing, busied herself with the little sugar packets, rearranging them in their holder by color and type. Awena, abundantly gifted with sixth sense, intuited what the matter was. Dominique had had an affair with Lord Duxter—an affair that probably had ended badly, as had several of his affairs before. Awena acknowledged that this intuition was more along the lines of a lucky if logical guess: Lord Duxter was known to have a roving eye.

"It's neither here nor there if I do," said Dominique. "He's a businessman. Businessmen have to be, well, ruthless to succeed. Don't they?"

"I'm a businesswoman and I haven't found that to be the case, no. Quite the opposite. I wouldn't last in business very long if no one trusted me to be honest and to deal fairly with them."

"Well, Awena, there's you, and then there is the rest of the world. People like our David keep an eye on the main chance."

"I'm sorry," said Awena. "Was he quite rotten to you?"

"He let me down," she had said with a shrug. But it was a dismissal of feeling that seemed to cost her dearly. "Led me on, and let me down. And of course, the irony is that now I have to produce gushing romances for his sodding publishing company, so he can get rich. Richer. Oh, I'm not explaining this well!" A tear had sprung to her eye and she paused to dab a paper serviette at her running makeup. "I hate him, that's all. And there's nothing to be done. I knew he was married, so what did I think would happen? My bad choices do me in every time. Such selfish foolishness is a curse. Let's talk of something else."

Awena never repeated this conversation to Max or to anyone. It would be, she decided, carrying tales. Even in days to come, when Lord Duxter's character would be held under a microscope, Awena saw nothing to be gained by bringing up past indiscretions.

Chapter 6

THE EMPEROR AND EMPRESS

The object of the after-dinner conversation among Max, Awena, and Destiny was at that moment at the large oak desk in his study at Wooton Priory, choosing the list of titles he would publish for next year.

The whole business of book publishing was a matter of luck, it had always seemed to Lord Duxter. Pure, blind, stupid luck. Who could have predicted the Hilary Mantel phenomenon? Those *Shades of Grey* books? Stieg Larsson? Assuredly not Lord Duxter, who to his everlasting chagrin had declined to publish all those books and authors. The Lord Duxter whose personal tastes in reading inclined toward nonfiction titles on business and finance and fly fishing was not a man often found to have his finger on the pulse. He regarded the whole enterprise of publishing as a gamble, almost an addiction, and a dangerous one at that. He tended to put everything to win on either black or red and to close his eyes tightly as the croupier spun the wheel of fortune. It sometimes worked, and he'd got lucky in the case of Awena, and that Dominique romance person, and Carville Rasmussen the Insufferable, his best-selling crime writer.

He picked up a piece of paper outlining a proposed fiction series and tried to concentrate, adjusting his glasses higher on his nose. Some author wanted to write about a vicar who was formerly an agent for MI5. Well, that sounded boring as hell. He started wadding up the proposal to aim it at the trash bin beside his desk when he stopped midgesture. Wasn't there a sort of rock-star vicar in nearby Nether Monkslip who was rumored to be MI5? In fact—yes, of course. He was married to Awena. How could he have forgotten? Well, he wasn't sure he wanted to publish a book about a vicar. That sort of religious twaddle never sold well. Readers today wanted—what was it readers today wanted? Damned if he knew. Action, flashing lights, car chases, dismembered corpses. Quaint Canadian villages seemed to be popular, though. He wondered if he could persuade the author to switch locales and have the vicar be a former Mountie. It was a thought.

He struggled to recall something that John le Carré had written in *The Pigeon Tunnel*. Pushing himself away from the desk, he trundled across the room of linen-fold paneled walls to take the book down from the shelves, wishing he had been able to woo le Carré to his stable—another missed opportunity, but Lord Duxter knew he'd made a lowball bid there. Yes, there it was: "Spying and novel writing are made for each other. Both call for a ready eye for human transgression and the many routes to betrayal." Aloud he muttered the phrase, "many routes to betrayal," never imagining it had anything to do with him. He wondered if he could persuade this vicar fellow to try his hand at writing a spy novel. Or perhaps a crime story, to give Rasmussen some competition to worry about. The vicar would probably jump at the chance. Those sorts of people were always as poor as church mice and probably bored with little to do, as well.

He smoothed out the wrinkles he'd created in the proposal and put it atop a small stack on the left side of the desk.

And so we find Lord Duxter. Aged fifty-two years and six months. Balding and with a cherubic face and twinkly blue eyes. The face and eyes are deceptive, however. When he is angry the eyes turn to splinters of glassy blue ice refracting sunlight. And his face turns red, like a balloon about to burst, the veins around those eyes looking set to explode. He is on the thin side and rangy so that in approach he might appear quite fit and trim but that, too, is deceptive, for he carries before him a pot belly, largely hidden from world view by expert tailoring.

He wears glasses in trendy frames, for he is near-sighted from decades of reading small print. Tonight's glasses have red frames but when he is photographed, which is often, he wears dark frames that make him look, he hopes, like Arthur Miller. Now if only Lady Duxter looked like Arthur's Marilyn Monroe—now, that would be something.

He attended Eton and Cambridge but he had dropped out after two years to travel the world. No one in his bewildered and exasperated family could stop him and really it was just as well. He was taking up space that perhaps a more deserving and diligent student could put to good use. Eventually he returned to England and his travels brought him to the county of Monkslip on a hiking trip, and thus to Wooton Priory. His mind then began to play with various schemes for turning a profit on the falling-down, empty buildings. Using his connections in the Church of England, in academia, and in his gentlemen's club, he pulled things and people together and made the place a going concern.

Now, Lord Duxter was rather bored and looking for new worlds to conquer. Not in a literary sense but in a personal one. His marriage to Marina, now Lady Duxter, was one of convenience, although he often had to wonder who was being convenienced by their union. She cost him a packet, she did, for her wardrobe alone. She might sometimes remind him that it was her own money she was spending but after so many years together it was *their* money, surely, and he was doing her a favor by helping her keep tabs on it. The medical bills were what he had not bargained for, not at all. Nor the long, sulky silences shot through with moments of hysteria. Nor the nights spent alone. Incredibly, it was his own father who had talked him into the match. He'd thought Marina was classy, as well as rich.

On being awarded the OBE Lord Duxter had felt he'd reached the pinnacle of everything he'd ever striven toward. He was a man who liked honors, being unable to gauge his own worth without such outward signs and reassurances. Long before he had been named Lord Duxter of Monkslip he had picked out the name, writing it on the flyleaf of the first book he'd acquired for his fledgling publishing company. That one author of his who believed in manifesting good luck would have said he had manifested his OBE. Actually, if he were manifesting anything it would be a hereditary peerage— one of his fantasies was of rescuing the Queen when she'd fallen off her horse or a madman had barged into her bedroom or something; in gratitude she would create a new peerage just for him. It could happen. "Ask, Believe, Receive," right? But he declared himself satisfied with having risen so far above a rather dodgy upbringing, emotionally speaking. It was no good getting greedy. His father, Monty Bottom, had worked in trade, as had his father before him. The publishing trade, to be sure—the family owned several large printing presses. But Lord Duxter liked to tell people his father had worked in publishing and few were interested enough to parse the actual truth behind that statement. Marina had only found out after their marriage, for example. If she felt she had bought a pig in a poke, well. Everyone knew the buyer must beware.

Besides. Marina should consider herself damned lucky to have him.

Several doors down, Marina, Lady Duxter, sat at the vanity table in her dressing room applying face powder to her forehead, her nose, her chin, her décolletage, and much of the tabletop. She applied it rather too liberally, and ended up ghostly pale with powder settled into the wrinkles around her eyes because her mind was not on her task. She was thinking of *him*. It was as if he blotted out the sun, and had become all she could see before her. The laughter in his eyes, the way he loved to make *her* laugh. When was the last time a man had made her laugh—intentionally, that is?

It was like that whenever he came near—a sort of electricity shot through her being until only he was left in her world. He brought her out of herself, and in her experience, few people could be bothered to take the time. Certainly her husband could not be bothered. As to making her laugh—well. She supposed there was humor in David's pompous self-absorption, but it was not humor of the laugh-out-loud variety.

She sat back in the little pink satin chair, closing her eyes, almost liquid with longing. She remembered, she could sense again, the warmth of his skin against hers, the feel of his strong, muscular arms as he held her close. How good it felt to be in his embrace, how safe; how comforting was his deep voice in her ear as he said "It won't be long now, darling." She said the words aloud for what must have been the hundredth time, as if she could make it all come true, as if she could conjure him up. "It won't be long." Like *she* could be a magician and make him appear before her now! But he was so far away, so very far away in spirit, not just in physical distance, and she reminded herself she must be careful. No one must know. Not yet. There would be scenes, recriminations, probably a messy and costly divorce, no matter how she struggled to rise above her opponent—her husband—and not to stoop to his level, to what were sure to be his dirty tactics. But how she longed for this distance to dissolve and for him—*him*, the dearest darling of her heart!—to be in this room, right now, standing beside her, his hands caressing her shoulders until she would stand and turn and fling herself into his waiting arms, surrendering again and again to his kiss. She'd be seeing him soon; David would be in London meanwhile, and they'd be free—free!

She sighed, a deep and melancholy sigh. She hadn't felt like this since she was a girl in school, just setting out in the world and full of dreams of what was possible, thinking everything was possible, and all at once. Not knowing anything about the world, alas. Life wasn't like one of the romances in the books she read. No. Life was, well it was like one of the day's headlines, full of despair, and people making awful, foolish choices. People dying, dying because they could stand no more . . .

She opened a drawer in the vanity table and rooted around among the several plastic containers inside. Choosing one, she took out of it one of her antidepressant pills and washed the little capsule down with wine. She hesitated but a brief moment and shook another capsule out of the container.

This was not good. She'd told herself—how many times?—she would stop this, she would start taking better care of herself. That she could get through a day without a pill or a drink to bolster her. Some days she lasted as long as noontime before she caved in to the mind-numbing anxiety that ruled her days.

She wanted to weep—not an unusual feeling for Marina, Lady Duxter. The only time she didn't want to weep was when *he* was around, holding her close. Then she would soar.

She wondered if there weren't time left for her, for her to start her life again. Was having a child even possible? Movie stars older than she were doing it, probably with a surrogate or some hormone therapy or other. But it was possible.

She and David were a childless couple. That had long since ceased to bother him but it bothered her. She knew this was why she had taken Poppy Frost under her wing, especially now that Poppy was in mourning for her great-grandmother. Netta may have been a battle-axe but her passing was bound to affect the girl, who was such a sensitive sort. She wanted so desperately to be a writer, to make a mark on the world, and they spent hours together discussing authors, particularly women authors like the Brontës and Woolf and Austen and du Maurier and Colette, Marina's particular favorite.

She was of an age, Poppy, that she could have been her own child, if the fates had been kinder.

Chapter 7

THE LOVERS

The next day Poppy Frost and Stanley Zither sat under a tree in Prior's Wood with a breakfast picnic of coffee and home-baked bread and butter and jam. Poppy had made the bread and preserves herself, as well as the coffee. She knew her way very well around the kitchen at home.

Their topics were the usual ones for people their age: the state of the world, the latest music, and the tiresome adults that surrounded them, Poppy's stepmother in particular. Of course with Poppy's great-grandmother dying, there was one less adult to complain about. Stanley was already noticing a softening in Poppy's attitude to the old lady, which was only natural. He could barely remember the quarrels with his own mother anymore. He just missed her terribly.

"How are things at home?" he asked. He was lying stretched out on a blanket under an enormous old tree in Prior's Wood. He liked to gaze up through the branches, his eyes half-closed against the sun's feeble autumn warmth. The air around them was filled with dust motes that swirled and danced. His mother used to say they were fairies too small for humans to see. Stanley knew that was daft but she really had seemed to believe it so he tried to, as well.

"Much the same as always," replied Poppy, stretched beside him with her hands behind her head. "Except that now we have all these people ringing and leaving food and writing and dropping by. Wanting to know about the funeral, you know. Wanting to talk about her 'last hours.'"

"That must be rough."

Poppy shrugged.

"I'm not home much—I make a point of it; I'd rather hang about the priory, talk with Lady Duxter and stuff. Marina. It's quiet and no one bothers me there. There's always a nook or a cranny where I can scribble in my notebook, undisturbed."

"But you will miss her, I know."

Poppy screwed up her face in the expression of confusion and worry that always made him want to kiss her. "I always thought she was all right," she admitted grudgingly, at last. "Others had their problems with her. She could be a bit of an autocrat." Seeing his puzzled look, she explained: "That means tyrant." "Autocrat" was a word Poppy had just come across in her reading. She had made a New Year's vow to use a new word in a sentence three times a day to be sure she'd learnt it off by heart. She wanted to be a writer one day—actually, if the dozens of notebooks she'd filled since childhood were any indication, she was already a writer. What she wanted to be was a *published* writer, a very different thing.

First she would go to Oxford and study the greats and later take the publishing world by storm. All before the age of twenty-five, her target goal. She wanted to be one of the wunderkinds the university was famous for producing, the sort reviewed fawningly in the newspaper book columns, and photographed looking dark and quirky and quite interesting, oftentimes with weird clothing and haircuts and lots of eye makeup behind retro eyeglasses. Sometimes they were photographed standing in the sea, as if they were contemplating suicide by drowning or perhaps just thinking of swimming to France. Whatever. She had already decided she would be photographed standing in the sea for her first jacket cover. She thought being photographed in the nude would make for a particularly arresting cover that would sell lots of books but she had the idea publishers might resist the (very good) idea.

She hadn't decided yet if the best way to achieve all this instant acclaim requiring photographers would be to read the classics or to go straight for the moderns. But for now she collected words the way other girls collected shoes and dresses. Or boys.

Luckily, Stanley supported this vast, sprawling dream, even though he had no interest in writing and only barely understood the allure of scribbling in a notebook or staring at a computer screen all day. He wanted to read theoretical cosmology, and for that he would be going to the University of Cambridge. His own dream was to take lectures from Stephen Hawking, and his only prayer was that Hawking, having already beaten the odds many times, would live long enough to oblige him. In the meantime, Stanley played guitar in a band called the Godsforsakens, and was wise enough to realize that while the band was popular at local dances, it was unlikely this success would translate onto a larger stage, and would at best amount to a garage hobby in midlife.

Poppy, perhaps fortunately for her and for their relationship, was tone deaf. But this difference as to tastes and the physical distance between the two renowned centers of learning troubled Poppy at times. The universities were not light-years away but her interests and Stanley's certainly were. Sometimes she wondered if they would survive the three to five years during which they would be separated, apart from the holidays. No train ran directly between the universities—one had to take the train to London and switch over, a journey that involved Paddington and King's Cross, and which was so convoluted an excursion as to seem a deliberate ploy by both the railroads and the universities to keep their students separate, to not encourage cross-pollination of ideas or of any other sort.

"When is the funeral again?" Stanley asked.

"That hasn't been decided. My dad is headed home to handle the details. *She* called him last night and I could hear them talking about it."

Who "she" was required no explanation. "She" in a tone that dripped acid, and that was said with a particular curl of the lip, was always Poppy's stepmother, Jane. Poppy seldom used her actual name. Personally, Stanley thought Jane was all right, but he understood that relations with a stepmother, even a good stepmother, could be fraught with opportunities for misunderstanding. Poppy's mother had been killed by a drunk driver when she was only ten. Three years later, her father, Colin, had married Jane. Not too much later Poppy had ended up living in Hawthorne Cottage with her grandmother, Netta. That was a lot of change packed into a few short years.

Nearly everyone in the village thought she and Jane got along swimmingly, a fiction Poppy said Jane liked to encourage. Stanley thought the truth was that all stepchildren disliked their stepparents, especially when their biological parent had been taken so violently from them.

Poppy had had an extra large burden, losing her mother in that way. And her father had remarried within minutes, from Poppy's perspective. And then he became unemployed. And then he was shipped off to a place Poppy didn't even want to visit, let alone live. All her views of Saudi Arabia had been formed by her reading in school, and there was no question she agreed with her stepmother on this score: it was no place for a British woman used to the normal freedoms.

"Once she stopped trying to be my friend we got along all right," Poppy once had explained to Stanley. "Better, anyway. What I couldn't abide was her wanting to swap makeup and hairstyling tips with me like we were at some never-ending sleepover and completely ignoring the fact that her idea of makeup, what little she wears, is about a thousand years out of date. And besides, I'm not a girlie girl at all. I'm more like Jo March, if I'm like anyone. Jane keeps trying to turn me into, oh, I don't know. Her idea of a 'young lady.' I am seriously tempted to cut all my hair off and sell it, like Jo did. At least then Jane would shut the fuck up about the color."

Stanley had no idea who Jo March was, but he nodded, looking up through the tree branches at the sky with its scudding clouds, trying to imagine them into the shapes of galloping animals. It was a perfect autumn day, warm and close and blue, and he had eaten more of the bread and butter and preserves than was good for him. It was all making him groggy. Sometimes of an afternoon Poppy would bring wine she had managed to smuggle out of the house, and then he really did have trouble staying awake. What he wanted even now was to doze off into a half sleep. Poppy had other ideas. Seeing his eyes close, she shook him awake. This conversation was important and she wanted Stanley's input.

"I am hoping," she said, "that once my father comes home, he'll figure out a way he can stay. I think Jane wants that, too. You should hear her on the phone with him, all lovey dovey about how much she misses him. She's even been learning how to cook all his favorite meals. Really, it would make a cat sick to hear her. It makes me wonder what she's really up to."

"Maybe she's going to deliver an ultimatum. Tell him he must get a job in the UK. Or else."

Poppy said, "Who, her? My stepmother? Won't ever happen. But she has her ways. If she wants him back he'll stay."

Chapter 8

THE STAR

That same morning, as Poppy and Stanley were having their breakfast in Prior's Wood, Awena was setting out for Wooton Priory, packing her knapsack with everything she would need for the day. Owen was already in the care of Tara at Goddessspell, where he would play quite happily until Max came to collect him around noontime. The shop was filled with sparkly trinkets to capture the infant eye.

"This week," Awena was saying, wrapping a sandwich in a cloth napkin, "the only writers at the priory are me and Carville Rasmussen. He's a crime writer. You may have heard of him? No? Oh, but he'd be crushed to hear that. He seems to thrive on publicity. It's the very air he breathes."

"A bit like our Frank, then," said Max. Frank Cuthbert was a local historian who had risen to prominence with his largely fictionalized depiction of Nether Monkslip and surrounding areas, *Wherefore Nether Monkslip*. The book had grown from a self-published, photocopied-and-stapled pamphlet to reach the heights of the bestseller lists in London and the U.S., despite being hailed by critics as "pointless." It continued to be available on shop bookshelves, a perennial favorite. That Frank was a relentless self-promoter had cost him more than a few friendships, a fact of which he remained blithely unaware, or perhaps, uncaring. Every villager owned a copy of the book, purchased in the desperate, futile belief that they were only required to buy the one copy and were never required actually to read it. It was rather, some said, like owning a copy of the Bible or *War and Peace*. But this proved a fruitless hope when Christmas rolled round and Frank besieged the villagers with suggestions that the book would make a great gift for even their most distant relatives.

"Exactly like Frank, now you come to mention it," said Awena. "I was wondering the other day who he reminded me of. One can't go near Carville without being offered a glossy bookmark advertising his latest book, which is always hailed as a bestselling masterpiece. I can't imagine it, personally, but the books do seem to be everywhere you look. He writes these very modern, present tense stories: 'She stabs him; he bleeds; she cries.' You know the kind of thing. I think he fancies himself a sort of Hemingway figure and I'm sorry to say there is a resemblance. He's sort of barrel-chested and has masses of wavy white hair and a beard. He likes to wear rollneck jumpers, too, like in that famous "Papa" photo, and he always carries a pipe he doesn't seem actually to smoke, thank heaven. I don't think he drinks a lot, either, which rather ends the comparisons."

Max was taking an inventory of the contents of the kitchen cupboards with an eye to doing a shop that afternoon at the village general store. "We can't be out of courgettes already; no one ever runs out of courgettes—wait, there one is. So, it's just him at the manor house this week?"

"That's right. Of the writers who will come up to stay at Wooton Priory for an extended period, he's the first to arrive. It's strange, though."

"What?"

"Well, he's there to write, but I've yet to see him writing anything. He does carry a notebook in his pocket, and what looks like a very expensive pen, but he's always just . . . I don't know. Sort of *lurk*ing about." Awena hunched her shoulders and did a rather amusing Count Dracula imitation. Max laughed. "If he notices anyone noticing him, he goes into this sort of rapture—a thinker's pose, as if he's been struck dumb by some profound idea. That sounds unkind of me to say, doesn't it? I suppose it's just that I don't really much care for him. But I do try."

"Ah," said Max. Awena was the least unkind of people, so Carville must be a real pain. "Well, you must avoid him as much as possible. I suppose with its being just him at the priory, that's a bit tricky. He's always around."

She nodded. "Unlike me—I'm a day-tripper, just there for a bit of focus and to potter among the library shelves with no distractions, and relieved to come home to you and Owen in the evenings. I'll light a candle for Carville tonight when I pray, and wish him well. It's quite the best way to deal with people who are . . . well, tiresome." She snapped shut the fastenings of the knapsack and hefted it, testing its weight. "Umph," she said. "You'd think I'd be used to the extra weight by now, after hauling Owen about."

"Ah," said Max again, his mind on picking up a bottle of white wine from Mme Cuthbert's shop. "Quite right you are, about praying for Carville. So, the following week . . . ?"

"The following week will be a full house—I find I've met most of them at conferences and whatnot: A poet or two, looking rather ghastly and lost, you know. A husband-and-wife team writing about personal finance, the Blannings—handsome couple, polished, immediately forgettable, I'm afraid. A children's book author—this one I've always thought was a bit of a scary person, but children seem to love his tales of vampire bats and so on. Then there will be another crime writer but, I gather, a cozier, past-tense sort of crime writer: 'She stabbed him, but gently and with great precision, like a woman doing needlepoint. No blood was spilt on the carpet, for which the servants would be grateful.' There will also be a former nun writing a memoir about life in the cloister. The priory will no doubt provide inspiration. Who else? There was one more. Oh, yes, how could I forget? The Major will be staying there to work on that interminable military history book of his, or whatever it is he's been writing for yonks. I'll be glad if I miss that, actually, because he does so like to read aloud from his work in progress during the Writers' Square meetings, so no one else gets a lot of work done. I do feel I've already heard several chapters before. They never seem to change. Lord Nelson always dies a hero's death, killed by a French sharpshooter, but he never manages to leave the stage in a grammatical way."

Max smiled, hoping to escape meeting the poets, in particular. "It does sound like a full house."

"And a full church—so to speak. Formerly the Priory Church of St. George and now rechristened the St. George Studio. The star crime writer will have it to himself. I'm not sure if that is fitting or a travesty, but it's how Lord Duxter wanted things to be organized. Anyway, apart from Lord and Lady Duxter, it's just me and Carville rattling around that big old place. Oh, and Jane Frost, of course."

"No book reviewers this time?"

"Good heavens, no." Awena was aghast. "No more foxes in the henhouse; Lord Duxter has learned his lesson. Writers are too sensitive. Same with the editors. No, no. You can never put all sorts together under one roof."

Jane Frost was already in the library of the old priory. She thought of it as her treasure trove. A place full of surprises and long-lost gems, moldering with age and only awaiting loving hands to wipe the dust off and bring them into the light. The gloomy events of recent days at Hawthorne Cottage hadn't altered her schedule. The library was her sanctuary.

Jane was in many ways a romantic, with her head in the clouds. She loved books—adored them. The feel of the bindings, the rustle of the paper, the smell of the ink. She loved learning, and everything worth knowing—well, everything in the world, really—was in books. Her own mother hadn't known what to make of her, for her mother was a pragmatic woman, both feet on the ground, a hard-working businesswoman until the day she died—too soon, when Jane was just eight. Jane had been the third of three sisters, and both her elder sisters had been stunners—spoilt and beautiful. Wisely, she had watched them, learning from them rather than giving herself over to jealousy. When she'd met Colin he'd actually been dating her older sister—until Melanie had tired of him and dropped him. Colin had been so handsome, Jane couldn't believe her luck.

But he had wanted her, and not just on the rebound, either. Perhaps she had learned a few things from her prettier sisters, after all, about how to offset shortcomings with charm. This was something every French woman seemed to be born knowing: how to use plainness as a way to disarm, to catch people unawares, until they saw past the surface to the woman beneath.

She and her sisters were mostly raised by an aunt and her husband who had three boys already. The sister cared only about her own children and didn't give much thought to Jane and her sisters. Hand-me-down clothes, gifts for the boys but not for the girls at Christmas. No one believed her at school when she told that story so she'd stopped telling it. If anything, the aunt may have been jealous of her own sister—seriously, not giving the orphans in the household a Christmas gift? How mean-spirited can you get? How Dickensian!

So Jane escaped into books—Dickens actually was a favorite—and reading became her refuge. Her sisters were boy-mad, and only into dreaming about the clothes and makeup they couldn't afford. Fortunately for Jane, there was a lending library in her parish where she could read all she wanted for free. Auntie couldn't put a stop to that one pleasure, although she did try.

So Colin had been the one ray of good luck in a melancholy landscape, and Jane had thanked the gods for sending him to her. It was too bad he came equipped—she couldn't say saddled—with a young daughter. But it could have been worse. And Poppy would be away at school soon.

Jane further could not believe her luck when Lord Duxter had offered her this job the year before. While large swathes of the archives had been lost with the havoc of the Dissolution, a few monks with a sense of history had managed to spirit away some of the more important books and papers from the priory library onto the shelves at King's College, Cambridge. With the purchase of the property, a wily Lord Duxter had managed to have some of the archives returned to their rightful place. They were in total disarray, dusty, torn in places and with pages missing and leather bindings collapsing. Still, for a bookworm such as Jane, it was heaven to be allowed to sort through them, taking reverential, white-glove care turning the pages. She had long regarded the printed word as the salvation of mankind—mankind itself being so often lacking, in so many ways.

She looked up now to a labeled shelf and realized she'd need the library ladder to reach her objective, which was the set of ledgers dating back to the time of the foundation of the priory. She pushed the ladder over and scrambled up with alacrity. One thing they never taught you in getting a degree in information systems was that you'd better not have a fear of heights. Also, that wearing short skirts and heels was at all times a bad idea. Jane could just reach the ledger, easing it out of true with its fellows with infinite care.

She was small of stature, if possessed of a jockey's strength from hoisting about boxes of books and papers, and just into her thirties, a fact that had passed unacknowledged by her stepdaughter. Netta had said she supposed it was good that the girl wasn't a hypocrite, although Jane didn't see what was good about rudeness. Today, as most days, she wore a gray suit several sizes too large for her; she'd just dropped nearly a stone in weight on a new slimming regimen and hadn't had her clothes taken in.

She knew she was no great beauty with her sharp nose and sharper eyes, well hidden though they were behind glasses, but along with these strong features she was strong willed. She knew better than to judge a book by its cover and felt others would be wise to do likewise. She'd once had a library patron who chose books based on their titles alone, and would complain bitterly when *Sister Carrie*, for example, turned out not to be a book about a nun, and a book called *Demon Summer* turned out not to be about devil worship. Jane, with a low tolerance for this kind of thinking, had campaigned unsuccessfully to keep the man out of the place on the days she worked there.

Having descended from the ladder without mishap, Jane held the heavy volume against her hip as she burrowed into the drawer of an enormous wooden desk in search of the magnifying glass she kept there. She couldn't find it at first and wondered if Carville had borrowed it. He was always "borrowing" things and forgetting to return them.

Ah, there it was. The next half hour passed quickly as she carefully turned page after page, trying to make out the minute handwriting.

After a while her mind wandered and she began pacing the

familiar stacks, coming to a halt before the old library clock. As she wound it, she thought of her husband, anticipating his arrival. Memories cascaded through her mind as all of her thinking centered on him: Colin will be home soon—it seems an age. It seems like yesterday! Everything must be perfect for him. I'll make a list of his favorite foods before I do the shopping. It's a long flight from Riyadh—well over six hours. And then the drive from Heathrow. He'll be famished.

These busy thoughts were interrupted by the sound of soft footfall at the double doors. It was Awena Owen—well, Jane supposed, Awena Tudor was her name now. Married to the dishy vicar over the way in Nether Monkslip. Awena was always dressed as if for a festival—bright, embroidered long dresses with trumpet sleeves, often gathered just below the bust by bejeweled sashes. She should start her own fashion line. Jane suspected it would be as big a hit as her cooking books, which had turned into a bit of a foodie empire. Some people had a golden touch, and Awena was one of them.

"Hello, Awena." The two women hugged briefly. They'd been working together several weeks as Jane helped Awena locate some of the written recipes from the priory archives, as well as records of crops and harvests in the area. Jane enjoyed Awena's company: There were people you could unburden yourself to and never have the unburdening come back to haunt you. With Awena it was like that. You could be sure what was said in confidence would never be repeated. For someone like Jane, self-contained and used to self-censorship, having such a confidant came as a novelty and a welcome relief. But she had little she was willing to confide for the moment. Her anxiety about Colin's return was probably self-evident.

Indeed, nearly the first thing Awena said was, "I would bet you're getting anxious to see your husband again. However sad the circumstances that bring him back."

"I know. Something about an ill wind that blows no one good. Netta's death was such a shock, even though she was elderly; she always seemed like she might soldier on forever, you know?"

Awena nodded. "She was tough. The only time I saw a crack in her composure was when Leo died."

"And even then . . . I think the stiff-upper-lip business is overrated, personally."

"She was lucky to have you. Were you with her at the last?"

"No, I wasn't, and that's going to haunt me. She was alone in her bedroom and she may have been in some distress, according to Dr. Winship, but she never called out. I never heard a sound all night. In the morning, I found her."

Awena thought Bruce Winship probably should have spared the family knowing that, but she knew the doctor prided himself on clinical detachment. It probably never occurred to him he was being less than tactful, or helpful. She said, "Thank goodness Poppy wasn't the one to find her."

"Yes! I had the same thought. Poppy has suffered quite a lot in her sixteen years. This would have been the last straw. She slept through it all, too. Well, to be honest—I don't think she was there, Awena."

"Not in the house? Why? Wherever would she have been?"

"With that kid Stanley she hangs about with. Stanley Zither. She thinks I don't know but I do. I've tried talking with her but at that age . . . besides, I'm just the stepmother." She made a mock grimace. "I know nothing useful."

Awena smiled. "How wonderful it is to know everything at the age of sixteen. I did, too. It's amazing how much I've forgotten now."

"Too dumb to live, people over thirty, Poppy might say. 'But what is so headstrong as youth? What so blind as inexperience?' Charlotte Brontë was right. Anyway, I do miss Netta sometimes. I find myself turning to see if she wants more coffee or something and of course she's not there. She wasn't easy, but I liked her. Admired her, in some ways. For one thing, she'd never let anyone get above themselves, and that's a good quality." She sighed, turning to reshelve one of the books Awena was returning. "She used to call me her 'little toad.' She meant it affectionately."

"It doesn't sound all that affectionate," said Awena doubtfully.

"You had to know her sense of humor. She and I understood each other well. But yes, as you say, having Colin back for however long will be wonderful. I am going to try to persuade him to stay. This Saudi thing isn't working. The money is nice, but even so. We'll figure something out. Money really isn't everything."

"There's a rumor going round that he was almost killed in Saudi."

Jane nodded earnestly. "A runaway truck nearly ran him down. Or off the road, or something. He thinks it was a kidnapping attempt."

"It's like something out of a film. They've been talking about it over at the Cavalier. How dreadful."

"I keep thinking of that Rupert Brooke poem. You know: 'If I should die, think only this of me: That there's some corner of a foreign field, that is forever England.'"

"From 'The Soldier.' Yes, I suppose," said Awena, again doubtfully. It wasn't as if Colin were taking mortar fire or something. But he lived in a place that was perhaps the world's oddest mix of luxury and deprivation, as far from his upbringing in England as could be imagined. Away from his wife and daughter, there was no question he was making a sacrifice of a sort for the good of his family. At least, Awena hoped it was to their good.

"Brooke was only twenty-seven when he died," said Jane. "I find that immeasurably sad, don't you? At least Colin would have made it into his thirties—still too young. It doesn't bear thinking about. Anyway, I did start to wonder. If it wasn't a kidnapping, what was it? Could someone have it in for him? Could Poppy be next? Could I?"

"Oh, surely not."

Easier for you to say than others, thought Jane. Probably nothing will ever touch you. You with your home and your hearth and your fluffy-headed baby and your dashing husband. Some women have all the luck.

Awena looked at her friend. The standing wooden clock in the corner struck the hour, recalling her to the need to get moving soon.

Why was it Jane Eyre always came to mind when she was with Jane Frost? It was more than that they were both Janes. There was what she imagined was a physical similarity, as well. This Jane couldn't have weighed much more than seven stone, and while her green eyes—her best feature—blazed with intelligence, they were large and froglike in her small face, and set perhaps a fraction of an inch too wide. Awena wished Netta hadn't had that awful name for her—her little toad—because with the slightly bulbous eyes, magnified behind glasses, the description caught too well. "Plain and little" was Jane Eyre and so was Jane Frost, but Awena thought they also shared that spark of wit, of intelligence. And something more. That iron will and determination. Jane Eyre had been willing to risk it all rather than compromise. Awena thought the Jane before her now was cut from the same cloth.

With, perhaps, more than a trace of the romantic.

"I have the nature of a hermit," Jane had once told Awena. "What I love is to be surrounded by books, and to be sunk into a good story that makes me forget the world outside. I almost prefer books to human beings."

"I suppose we all feel that way sometimes. Books can provide a much-needed escape from life."

"From people," said Jane. "Books are infinitely more satisfying than people. And books—at least books have a beginning and an end. People seem to go on forever."

Chapter 9

JUDGMENT

"Such a shame about Netta," said Elka Garth, pushing her hair back from her forehead with one hand, being careful not to anoint herself with flour. She wore a newly washed and starched apron she was trying to keep clean, even if past experience had shown that by the end of the day it would be smeared with chocolate and raspberry preserves.

"Yes, but not unexpected, is it?" Suzanna Winship asked, peering over her stylish reading glasses. She'd taken over her usual corner table in the Cavalier, facing into the busy room. From there she had a good view of new arrivals and could best take advantage of the room's acoustics. There was tacit understanding and acceptance that this was Suzanna's table. Since the dozen or so tables sprinkled about the Cavalier were covered in gingham cloth and each held a small vase of fresh posies, it rather marred the CEO effect for which Suzanna may have been striving, but nothing could dim her steely gaze. The village was hers to command, at least insofar as the business of the Women's Institute was concerned. Miss Pitchford held the fort in all other village matters.

"My brother says he's surprised she hung on as long as she did," she added. Suzanna's brother was the village's doctor; Suzanna, as has been said, its unofficial ruler. She had won the title fair and square by seizing the reins of the Women's Institute a few years previous when the then incumbent was dispatched in an untimely manner. Whether she held on to the power fair and square was open to debate, but since no one else wanted the job, protesting voices remained still. "Colin before he left told Bruce his grandmother was sometimes acting confused, forgetting to take her doses of medicine and so on."

Elka nodded sagely, lips pursed as she concentrated on her task. She was dusting icing sugar over the pastries on a tray she was preparing to set out for the morning crowd at the Cavalier. She'd been thinking how much Netta, come autumn, used to love the tarts, made fresh from apples plucked from Elka's orchard not ten yards away.

Little Tom Hooser, the son of Max's housekeeper, walked in. Not tall enough for his head to reach the top of the counter, he stood waving a pound coin in the air until he captured her attention, then pointed at one of the chocolate-drizzled pastries in the display cabinet. The child never seemed to be in school; today he apparently had once again slipped the surly bonds of his elder sister, Tildy Ann. Elka refused the coin and sent him off with the pastry.

"I wonder how Jane is coping," Suzanna said. "And Poppy. I suppose Colin is on his way home now?"

"Yes, and hasn't Lord Duxter been marvelously helpful about all that? He stepped up and made all the arrangements. You don't just leave Saudi Arabia whenever you feel like it, you know. And wasn't he generous, too, offering a car and driver and whatever else was needed to help with the arrangements for Netta."

"I thought the men in Saudi could do whatever they bloody well pleased, whenever they pleased," said Suzanna. She opened up her purse to find a lipstick and mirror to begin touching up her makeup. It was a good thing, too, she noted. Her chin was dotted with sugar and jam from the blueberry tart she'd just devoured. Pushing her wavy blond hair behind her ears, she added, "Just not the women."

"Oh, no, no. Exit visas are strictly controlled no matter who or what you are. I gather Lord Duxter had to cut some red tape to get Colin home quickly."

"But it was for his grandmother!" put in an outraged Miss Pitchford, setting down her pen and crossword to sip her tea. As usual she had taken the table nearest the window overlooking the High, where she could keep an eye on village comings and goings. If she and Suzanna could only learn to cooperate and share information, they could rule the world, but such collaboration was not in their natures. "For a family emergency, surely, officials would understand, even there . . ."

Elka shook her head. "It doesn't matter. Urgent family business, whatever. And to attend a funeral, perhaps it is felt that there is no rush."

"They wouldn't feel that way if it was *their* grandmother," Suzanna pointed out.

"I'm sure you're right. It's a different world from ours over there."

"I guess that's why Jane didn't want to go with him."

"Too right," said Elka. "But I know she did try her best to come to grips with the idea. She did a lot of reading up, and joined a few chat groups online with women who had lived there. She thought she could manage. But in the end she said there was just no way: Colin would have to carry on on his own. And of course his employer would see that he had regular vacations so they could see each other. Jane simply put her foot down for once and I don't think Colin wanted to press her. He agreed it was no life for the wives over there, even in the compounds, where they try to make it as much like home as they can for the workers."

"And then Colin had that near-miss accident," said Miss Pitchford.

"When the car tried to run him and a colleague off the road? Yes, Colin told Jane that nearly had him putting in his resignation on the spot. Frightened him silly, it did. A cybersecurity expert might well be a target for kidnapping in those parts. Or blackmail. Extortion. All manner of mischief."

"Have you seen Poppy lately?" Suzanna asked. "How is she holding up?"

"All right, I think. She hasn't been in here since Netta . . . you know. I don't know that she was that close to her. Still, it's her great-grandmother. It's hard to say how children that age will react. I don't imagine it feels very real to Poppy. She's a dreamer to begin with, I've always felt."

"Are she and Jane getting along, do you think?" This was Miss Pitchford, who suspected they were not, but wanted her suspicions confirmed. She prided herself—wrongly, at times—on the accuracy of the gossip she spread. Not exactly a question of giving value for money but something along those lines.

"I *think* they get along all right," said Elka, searching in a drawer beneath the counter for string to tie up a box of biscuits she'd be delivering by bicycle later. "Better than most stepdaughters and stepmothers get along. Poppy's own mother was . . . well, troubled they say. Jane tells me she disowned Poppy before she died. They'd had some quarrel and words were said that could not be unsaid. The next day, the mother was dead. That will mess with your mind, won't it, when you're only just a child?"

"I didn't know Lord Duxter got so involved in the arrangements for retrieving Colin from the Saudis," said Suzanna, snapping shut her compact mirror. "What's it to him, anyway?"

"Oh, yes," said Elka. "I think he's just trying to be helpful. It seems to be in his nature, doesn't it? I mean, it was he who found the job for Colin in the first place. He pulled strings with an old friend. One of these gentlemen's club things that go on."

"He's said to be very well connected, Lord Duxter." This from Miss Pitchford, whose awed reverence for all things having to do with the nobility was widely known and routinely parodied by Suzanna, who now rolled her eyes behind the older woman's back.

"He's a hard-headed businessman," Suzanna scoffed. "That type does nothing without good reason."

Elka looked doubtful. "I suppose he must always consider the bottom line first. Anyway, I understand that in starting the writers' retreat he took advice from Lord Feathersham, and certainly that was wise of him," she said. "It was Lord Feathersham who turned Barn-stable Hall into a destination for young families on holiday, with a petting zoo as the showcase. Otherwise he'd have had to sell up and get out as so many owners of these stately old piles have had to do. Weddings and anniversary parties also keep him afloat, and now he runs the place as a five-star bed-and-breakfast."

"There was some educational connection, too, wasn't there?" Miss Pitchford, given her schoolmistress background, likewise adored all things with an educational component.

"Oh, yes. His offerings of summer courses on history and an-tiques and so on have proven to be surprisingly popular, particularly with Americans, and particularly with American retirees. Somehow he talked Tormeadle University into granting accreditation to the classes and then things really took off for him."

"So Lord Duxter took sound advice from someone running a much bigger establishment," said Suzanna. "You see?"

Elka wasn't sure what she was supposed to see, but she said, "Yes. And he hired Jane, a trained librarian, to run the old library—to file and organize and get things sorted to see what was actually in there. It's a jolly good thing she turned out to be honest, too: I understand there were a few surprises to be found in the stacks, like some rare old books that Lord Duxter immediately cashed in on. The sale at auction at Sotheby's of one old play script went for a phenomenal amount. It was thought to be written by an inferior writer, but Christopher Marlowe may actually have held the pages in his hands. That one sale helped fund many of Lord Duxter's enterprises."

"That and his wife's fortune."

This was greeted with a few knowing looks, and several women paused at this juncture for reviving sips of coffee.

"The poor woman," said Suzanna. "But I also heard he used his influence with the airlines to bump someone else off the flight to help Colin out. He has that kind of reach."

"Yes, I'm sure that's all very nice," said Elka hesitantly. "After all, if he got Colin sent way over there, it's right and proper he help bring him back for his grandmother. But what about the poor soul who got bumped?"

"I don't know," Suzanna shrugged. "Maybe he got some kind of upgrade. Perhaps a free food voucher for his trouble."

Now Elka's look was tinged with scorn. "Have you tasted airline food recently? I wouldn't consider that a fair trade, not at all." Elka's son, in a miracle of miracles, had scraped together the necessary to send his mother on a package tour to Majorca for four nights and three days. It was all she could talk about for weeks. She'd had to close the shop rather than leave it in his care—some miracles could only stretch so far. Still she was pleased to discover the world had not come to an end because she took some well-deserved time off.

"How are things going over there at the retreat?" Elka asked. "I usually have half a dozen writers in here before it's over, mewling about and tapping on their laptops. They get bored, and, one supposes, hungry, and start looking for things to do to avoid writing. The poets especially are fond of chocolate, I've noticed. But I've had no one come in lately but that Carville person."

"Yes, and *he*'s all up himself," said Suzanna over her newspaper. Carville had not responded to Suzanna's blandishments, which was unusual. Most men did, for Suzanna was a stunner.

"I would agree with you," said Elka. "I know he's a famous author but clever is as clever does. Or something."

"I liked his last book," put in Elsbeth Lincaster, a horsey woman from the next village over. She pushed aside the little vase of flowers on her table as if it was obstructing her view. "It was shorter than his usual, and with not so many characters to keep track of."

"Lady Duxter must be feeling better," said Miss Pitchford, putting out feelers for information. "She has been *look*ing ever so much better."

At that, Suzanna Winship raised her head from the printed page. Her eye caught that of Elka and the two exchanged knowing glances. Suzanna murmured something that sounded like, "She who pays the piper." Elsbeth made a little sound into her coffee that might have been a whinny.

Miss Pitchford soldiered on, never one to be derelict in her duty to inform the public. "I hear they've been getting along wonderfully," she said. "An OBE has a position to maintain, after all. A place in society. I'm sure we all look up to him. And a happy home life is part of what is expected of a man of his stature."

Elka looked unsure of this theory, as well she might. In her own position, she heard many rumors; she could hardly help but do so. The Cavalier was a major center for the exchange of village gossip, although Elka tried her best not to participate. But seeing the little cat smile on Suzanna's face, especially, she wondered again.

As so often, while Miss Pitchford was able to spread rumor at the speed of light (bypassing fact-checking for the sake of being first to break the news), often what she spread was pure fertilizer. And on this occasion in particular, she could not have been more wrong.

PART III

As It Lays

Chapter 10

DEATH

In late September, Max read in the *Monkslip-super-Mare Globe and Bugle* the news that a couple had been found in Prior's Wood in an apparent suicide pact. Miss Pitchford was down with a cold that threatened to turn into pneumonia, which was why, Max surmised, the jungle drums also were down for repairs. Normally he would have received a call from one of his parishioners about this event the night before.

Max was surprised to read that the victims were Lady Duxter and Colin Frost, although he didn't know why that came as a shock. People got up to all manner of things, in his experience, more than ever made it to the front page of the local news. But for local news, this was sensational, and the reporter (Clive Hoptingle) felt at liberty to show off his education by making comparisons with Lady Chatterley, which Max thought an absurdly odd and sensationalistic touch. Colin was hardly a working-class gamekeeper, just for one thing. He was a good-looking man, in this case somewhat younger than Lady Duxter, and there the comparisons and contrasts should have

stopped or should never have got started. But lazy scribes love a
cliché as much as they love a catchphrase, and the Monkslip scribes
were some of the laziest in the land.

He had to read nearly to the end of the story to be told that Lady
Duxter had survived and had been rushed to hospital in Monkslip-
super-Mare the evening before. There was no word on her condition. Colin Frost had soon been pronounced dead.

Max's first thought was for Colin's survivors—his wife, Jane, and
daughter, Poppy. Even though they were not regulars at St. Edwold's,
he of course knew them both, as he knew everyone living in or near
Nether Monkslip. He would pray for the two of them, for Lord Duxter, and for all the people who would be affected by this news. Most
of all, because of her youth, for poor Poppy. To lose a father, and
in such a way, mere weeks after losing her great-grandmother . . .
That poor child.

Of course, Lord Duxter might be experiencing pain of a different sort. Max had heard rumors about Lady Duxter over the years
but had paid them no mind. That was the sort of corrosive gossip
that needed to be starved of attention.

The phone on the kitchen wall jangled. It was DCI Cotton,
ringing from the police station in Monkslip-super-Mare.

"Max, hello," he said. "Do you have any free time soon when
we can meet?"

"Certainly," said Max. "I'll be over at the vicarage in about an
hour, after I lead Morning Prayer. Will that do?" Max assumed the
visit had to do with that morning's news. Since attempted suicide
had not been classified as a crime in England for many decades, Max
supposed Cotton might have some associated issue to discuss.
Max had over the years become Cotton's de facto adviser on any
number of crimes, large and petty.

Precisely one hour later he and Cotton were sitting in low chairs before the vicarage fireplace, watching the first fire of the morning catch hold. Thea rested contentedly at their feet. The wood was not quite seasoned and was full of resin. It made delightful cracking and popping sounds as the flames consumed it.

"You've heard about Lady Duxter and Colin Frost," began Cotton.

"Only what's in today's paper," said Max. "There's no question it is suicide—and attempted suicide?"

Cotton looked taken aback. Leave it to Max to get to the nub of the matter. Of course, he'd realize it was unusual for Cotton to consult him over a clear-cut case of suicide. "None whatsoever, as far as the coroner can determine at the moment. The physical evidence tallies, and what you might call the emotional history does as well. It seems this is not the first time Lady Duxter has tried to take her own life."

"And Colin?"

"And Colin what?"

"Is this the second time for him, too?"

"Not that we're aware, no. It was the first and obviously the last time. But he left a note, and there's a sad old poem. It is pretty clear what happened. At least, on the surface it is clear. It has long been rumored that she had a lover."

"It might have been more convenient to take a lover closer to home, don't you think?"

"That's just it, Max. That's the very thing. It fits the circumstances as we know them. Colin Frost was sent over to Saudi Arabia at the urging of Lord Duxter. I mean to say, he had arranged through a friend of his to get Colin a job over there. I think that speaks volumes, don't you? Lord Duxter wanted the man out of the way, perhaps in a vain attempt to save his own faltering marriage. The enforced separation may have provoked a sort of madness on both sides."

"And Colin's wife, what did she want?"

"Jane? I've no idea. We'll be talking with her once she's calmed down. Apparently she needed a doctor's attention when the discovery was first made. She's been sedated pretty much since it happened."

"And the daughter? Poppy?"

"She flat-out refuses any medical attention. She says there's something 'wrong about all this' and she wants her wits about her when talking with the authorities. Dr. Winship prescribed some sleeping tablets for her but so far she won't take them."

"Does Poppy have evidence? Or does she just have a bad feeling?"

"A bad feeling. Same as me. Max, there is pressure from on high to put paid to this one, and as quickly as humanly possible. Because of the scandal, the caliber of people involved. If Lady Duxter comes out of it, they don't want her waking to a mess, her life in tatters, to say nothing of her marriage."

"They?"

"I gather Lord Duxter had a word on the quiet with my super. These titled sorts always think they have a lot of clout with the police, God knows why. We don't actually care what they do so long as they don't harm anyone doing it."

"Or frighten the horses."

"Precisely. My super rang me the minute he'd got rid of Lord Duxter, telling me to take a closer look and make sure nothing was missed. I'd have done that on my own but it's nice to have backing from the brass."

"What is it that bothers *you* about this, then?" Max asked. "So far, I've only heard your evidence in favor of a suicide theory."

"There's something about the timing that doesn't ring true," said Cotton. "But I can't quite put my finger on it. Colin Frost came home to Hawthorne Cottage for his grandmother's funeral. He's spent the past weeks handling her estate, sorting and putting things up for sale—all the usual. And in practically the next minute, he's one half of a suicide pact. The dead half."

"Is Hawthorne Cottage going on the market?" Max asked. "I mean, before Colin died, was he planning to sell up? I'm assuming he is his grandmother's heir."

"He is, or was. I don't think the plan was to sell right away. At least while the daughter is going to school here in the area, the thinking seems to have been to keep the roof over her head, and over her stepmother's, of course. Since Jane Frost works at Wooton Priory, Hawthorne Cottage is convenient for her."

"Yes. I know Jane, if not well. Awena especially has made attempts to draw her into the circle, but she's a self-sufficient type. Let's back up a bit. The newspaper said the bodies were found by a local man walking in the woods at dusk."

Cotton nodded. "They were found before sunset by a local hunter, one Andrew Todd, who called it in at five thirty-nine."

"And what did he find, exactly?"

"A man and a woman, both in the backseat of the car." Cotton paused. "Interestingly, Todd was with old Leo Henslowe when he had his hunting accident. Todd was acting as a beater, driving game out of the bushes. He was the first to reach Leo but the old man was already dead and past any hope of saving. I'd say Todd has bad luck in that department. Anyway, Todd recognized Lady Duxter right away—she's a known figure in the area and he's lived here most of his life. Colin we ID'd from his driving license."

"I see. Describe the setting for me. Where were they found?"

"The car was parked about a mile from Wooton Priory. There's a thick woods that surrounds the priory, you know, called Prior's Wood. Almost dead center of those woods is a pond. There's an un-paved road you can take to get to the pond, and the car was found pulled off to one side, not quite hidden in the trees. The place is mostly deserted this time of year. In the summer, it's a bit of a lovers' lane. Teenagers, you know."

"When the car was found, was the engine running?" Max asked.

"No. It had run out of petrol at some point. It was Colin's bad luck it didn't run out more quickly, but death by carbon monoxide asphyxiation takes a matter of mere minutes. They were both poisoned by carbon monoxide coming in through a vacuum hose attached to the exhaust with plumber's tape and then threaded into the car. It's rigged up quite amateurishly but it got the job done. It's an old car, practically an antique, belonging to the Henslowes, or the plan may not have worked. Modern cars have better exhaust controls."

"Fingerprints?"

"Only Colin's on the vacuum hose. There were no prints on the tape. But he was wearing gloves; they both were. It was ruddy cold in those woods, even in late September."

"I suppose even when we're facing death we want to be warm and comfortable."

"I suppose that's true," said Cotton. "And listening to music, as well. All quite cozy, except . . . The lab's running a toxicology report on both of them. There was half a bottle of whiskey found beside them in the car and an empty but labeled prescription container of an antidepressant drug—hers. Quite powerful stuff, especially when mixed with alcohol. And then with the carbon monoxide on top of everything . . . well, it looks like they wanted to be absolutely sure that something worked."

"But it didn't work. They're not both gone."

"No, only Colin," said Cotton. "He was past reviving when he was found, although they tried to resuscitate him all the way to the hospital. Lady Duxter remains in a coma, and no one can say if she might recover. Dr. Winship was the nearest physician and he rushed to the scene. He tells me most people don't fully recover from carbon monoxide poisoning. After coma can come acute psychosis and melancholy—people are never the same, in other words, and are invalids for life. But some do recover, and in quite a dramatic fashion. Yes, there have been cases."

"Miracles can happen."

"I suppose it's your business to know, Max."

"Lady Duxter has tried to commit suicide before, in almost exactly this way. Her husband sent her to a sanatorium in Switzerland, a sort of combination dry-out clinic and health resort, after that failed suicide attempt. Apparently she did herself some serious damage with an overdose of pills mixed with alcohol. Then she ran the car in the garage with the door closed. He found her just in time. No one spoke of it—of course, now they will speak of nothing else. It's odd, that."

"How do you mean, odd?"

"Oh, I guess I'm thinking, she should have got better at suicide, having had prior experience."

Cotton nodded. "Practice making perfect, in a horrible sort of way—I do see what you mean. Instead, she seems to have got worse at it."

"*I* saw a man and a lady in the woods," came a small, clear voice from a corner across the room.

Only Max recognized the voice, but Max and Cotton jumped as one, startled eyes scanning the room. It was as if one of the knick-knacks on the shelves had spoken.

"Tom?" said Max. His housekeeper's son had an unnerving habit of playing quietly in a corner of the vicarage study, pretending to read one of the ancient theology tomes or taking a nap with Thea—so quietly Max often forgot he was there. He must have followed Max in. What a conversation for a child to have overheard. "When was this you saw them, Tom?" he asked gently. "The man and the lady?"

Tom shrugged, losing interest in anything requiring precise measurement. In his universe, time ran on quite a different continuum from that of adults, anyway. The days were only long when he could not manage to shake his bossy sister's supervision, and short on the days he found himself free to roam the village and beyond. "They lost their clothes," he added.

Tom was rather an authority on this subject, having routinely shed most of his clothing up until the age of two and a half during his various breaks for freedom. It had not been uncommon at the time to see him running thus unencumbered up the High, chased by Tildy Ann.

Max and Cotton exchanged looks. The child may have witnessed an assignation between Colin and Lady Duxter. Cotton sighed and made an "Over to you, Max" gesture. In his experience small children made notoriously unreliable witnesses.

"They lost their clothes?"

Tom nodded, clearly pleased to have made an impression. Max didn't doubt he was telling the truth, or some version of it that fit his limited experience.

"Did they see you, Tom?"

He shook his head at this foolish question. "I hided."

"Yes, you're quite good at hiding, aren't you, Tom? Were they talking, the man and the lady?"

At this, Cotton shot him a sardonic look: *What do you think?*

Tom shook his head, a definite no, reinforcing Cotton's sentiment.

Oh, my. Well, thought Max, in other circumstances he might tell the child to go and discuss all this with his mother, but a more disinterested mother than Mrs. Hooser was difficult to imagine. Distracted rather than disinterested, Max reminded himself. Tom's sister was too young herself to be a confidant in this sort of situation. But

Tom didn't seem in the least distressed or disturbed by what he had seen. He was simply passing along information. And now, clearly, he was done. He began pulling one of the old, fraying volumes off a lower shelf.

"Well, thank you, Tom. Do you know where your mum is right now?"

"Upstairs." And before Max could act on that information: "I like it here better."

"Yes, I know, Tom. But right now DCI Cotton and I have a lot to talk about. Please go and find your mum."

Chapter 11

THE HANGED MAN

Tom left the door to the vicarage study ajar when he left the room, probably planning a stealthy reentry once the grown-ups were again preoccupied. Max went to make sure the door was firmly closed before rejoining Cotton.

"You're not thinking murder, are you?" Max asked, resuming his seat. "Or perhaps that Colin was meant to survive, and something went very wrong?"

"I'm not sure what I'm thinking," Cotton replied, stretching out his hands to warm them over the still-roiling flames of the fireplace. "If not Colin to blame, or Lady Duxter, in a sort of botched attempt that backfired—who do we have?"

"Colin's wife, Jane, and Marina's husband, Lord Duxter."

"Colin's wife is alibied by the girl, Poppy, as it happens."

"And, in a way, by Awena," said Max. He and Awena had of course discussed the news over breakfast.

"Awena? Really? How is she involved?"

"She was having a conversation with Jane in the library at what appears to be the relevant time. I'm sure you'd agree, she is an impeccable witness."

"Absolutely. I'll get a statement taken from her but for now, I'll take it as gold. And going from there, perhaps we can count to when the bodies were discovered. Jane thinks the car had a quarter of a tank of petrol. If we can measure the amount of carbon monoxide Colin inhaled, perhaps we can make a good estimate of the time the car was rigged to asphyxiate them both. But it has to be at some time before dusk. And Jane was with Poppy well before dark."

"They alibi each other, in other words. And Awena can back that up, as she was with Jane shortly after. There wasn't enough time for Jane to leave Poppy, do what needed to be done, and get back in time to meet Awena."

"Correct. As it turns out, though, the thing was done in haste. Otherwise, whoever it was would have hung about to make sure Lady Duxter was dead, as well as Colin." He paused, thinking. "Try as I might, I don't see the pair of them—Jane and Poppy—teaming up to do away with the girl's father. I won't discount it as a theory just yet, you see many ugly things in this job, but still . . ."

"Right," said Max. "That leaves us with Lord Duxter so far as intimates are concerned. I can see him deciding he wants to be free of his marriage to Lady Duxter. That motive is as old as the hills— and a common enough motive for murder. But why kill Colin, too? Is Colin just collateral damage? That stretches the imagination rather far."

"I wouldn't discount that possibility either just yet," said Cotton. "You and I have met criminals with no conscience before. And seen many victims who were caught up in something, unawares."

"It is so hard to countenance, that level of evil."

Only for you, Max, thought Cotton. Max always wanted to believe the best of people. It was the chink in his armor, that he was always surprised by man's inhumanity. Max's Pollyanna tendencies were legendary among those who knew him well. And whereas Max was saddened and sometimes angered by the knowledge of man's inhumanity to man, Cotton was simply angered.

"You say they left a note?" asked Max.

Cotton opened the small leather briefcase that seldom left his side, and extracted a single sheet of A4 paper encased in a plastic evidence bag.

"This is Colin's note. It reads, 'I don't think I can go on. Please forgive me.'"

"It's not addressed to anyone in particular?"

"No. The only prints on it are his."

Max looked closer at the note. "I think you might find the word 'on' was added later—it is difficult to say for certain with only two letters to go on but it appears to me to be by a different hand. Colin evidently left big spaces between sentences. And someone, maybe even Colin for some reason, inserted the word 'on.' I think the original may have been, "I don't think I can go.' That is quite a different sentiment. 'Go' where? To the store? To the seaside? To Saudi Arabia?"

"So he might have written this to Lord Duxter. Or to his wife. But he did go to Saudi in the end."

"I don't think I can go on," murmured Max, casting his eyes around the room.

"Yes?" said Cotton hopefully, after a few moments had lapsed.

"I don't find that compelling, do you? Even if what he actually wrote was 'I don't think I can go on,' that does not indicate a firm decision to end his own life. 'I don't *think* I can'? And it is a very odd thing to say as one is in the very middle of ending one's life— you do see? Marina was sitting right there next to him so why not just tell her this? Why write it down? To whom is he writing this?"

"Of course, you're quite right, Max. It would make more sense to say, flat out, 'I can't go on.'"

Max nodded. "It might be a message intended for his wife, Jane. Or his daughter. But I agree he would just say so. Anyway, that 'I don't think' is more the sort of dramatic flourish a person might make in a moment of—oh, I don't know. Romantic anguish."

"There was a music CD in the car. Mahler. Dramatic stuff, that."

"That would fit the situation."

"So, you are thinking Colin's wife had something to do with this?" Cotton asked. "If not directly, since she's apparently alibied, then with an accomplice?"

Max shook his head. "No. Not necessarily. Anyone might have got hold of that note and planted it. Where's the poem?" Max asked.

Cotton dove into his briefcase again and retrieved another piece of paper.

"This was found beside Lady Duxter. You can handle this one: the original is with the lab people, already dusted, and they confirm the handwriting as belonging to Lady Duxter. Only her prints are on it. What do you make of it?"

Max looked at the photocopied page. The original page had clearly been torn from a book, a daybook or diary at a guess. He read,

So, we'll go no more a roving
So late into the night,
Though the heart be still as loving,
And the moon be still as bright.

For the sword outwears its sheath,
And the soul wears out the breast,
And the heart must pause to breathe,
And love itself have rest.

Though the night was made for loving,
And the day returns too soon,
Yet we'll go no more a roving
By the light of the moon.

He handed the sheet back to Cotton. "How sad. Lord Byron, of course. The mad, bad, and dangerous to know."

"One and the same."

"I always felt that Byron was madly overcompensating for his club foot, don't you agree?"

Cotton, who had not given the matter any thought, gave a noncommittal nod.

"That he succeeded in making people overlook his disability was commendable but he didn't quite know when to stop compensating."

"It's a theory," said Cotton neutrally. Sometimes, Cotton was baffled by Max's tendency to go off on these little philosophical tangents. Cotton now squinted suspiciously at the page through narrowed eyes, as though if he concentrated enough the writing might yield more of Byron's thought processes. "'The sword outwears its sheath,'" he quoted. "Is that some sort of sexual reference, do you think? That he was impotent?"

Max suppressed a smile, although he had to admit, it wasn't completely an off-the-wall interpretation. "He was a young man when he wrote this, as I recall," he said. "Still in his twenties, but exhausted by a period of debauchery. By one of many periods of decadence, to be precise. But still, it's a theme of exhaustion for a much older man, don't you think?"

"Hmm," said Cotton.

"A drink?" Max offered. "Coffee? I need to think about this and it helps the process when I do some mundane task."

Cotton agreed to the coffee, still not taking his eyes from the page. Max strolled out, Thea at his heels, hoping for a treat, and after a certain amount of clatter and confusion had emanated from the kitchen he returned with a tray and two cups. He poured and let Cotton doctor his coffee with cream and sugar. He sat back in his chair before the fire with his own black coffee, and said, "So what are we to make of this? That Colin was a Byronic figure to her? Personally, I find that awfully hard to reconcile with what little I know of Colin."

"That was my thought, as well. By all accounts, while he was what you might call Byronically handsome, Colin was just an affable type. Hardly mad, bad, and so on. Sort of a geek—head always in the clouds, trying to sort out some programming knot, or work out some new magic trick."

"That was always my impression. Still, there is no accounting for where we choose to love, is there? And I think Colin was a decent man, an upstanding sort. Perhaps Lady Duxter found him sympathetic and kind, whereas her husband . . ."

"Yes. Her husband was anything but, by all accounts," said Cotton.

"I do wonder if the poem isn't more aimed at her husband, come to that. 'We'll go no more a roving' is a way of saying good-bye to all that, isn't it? A sort of, 'I love you but I'm too tired to go on' statement."

"Or, 'I loved you before you turned into such a jerk.' But what are you getting at, Max?"

"I guess I'm wondering why Colin didn't have any words of farewell, for his wife, or advice for his daughter. Something like an explanation would have been nice."

"I would say that was simply not his style. Lady Duxter was the romantic here. Colin, the analyst. A very different class of dreamer."

"I'm sure you're right about that," said Max. "And then, there's the notebook itself."

"I beg your pardon?"

"The page is clearly torn from some sort of bound book. A diary, a daybook, or some book where she collected her thoughts, or at least others' thoughts and expressions that were important to her. Have your people found it?"

"Ah, I see. No, they have not, and of course they had a look through her desk and her belongings, with her husband's permission, hoping to find some clue to her state of mind."

"And that's interesting in and of itself, is it not? That it appears to be missing?"

"I suppose. She may have destroyed it, particularly if it was a diary, full of deeply personal things. Things she wanted to die with her."

"Yes, many people facing death feel that way," said Max. "Generally, they don't want their children to come across what they've written and learn how often they'd thought of giving their children away to the next passerby. Or there's just the sense of wanting to keep our most intimate thoughts from prying eyes."

"Especially in the case of suicide, when the supposition may well be that people will begin pawing through your things, looking for clues."

"Quite," said Max.

"It might still turn up, the diary or notebook," said Cotton. "It's early days."

"Quite," said Max again. He was clearly not listening.

"Wasn't Lord Duxter knighted for services to something?" Cotton asked.

"What?" said Max. "Oh, yes. For services to publishing and charity, I believe. Something along those lines. He was made a life peer:

Lord Duxter of Monkslip. Ever since then he likes to talk of globalization in the publishing industry and so on. He's hoping to be invited to Davos, I gather."

"Chance would be a fine thing; I'd say Davos is more than a bit out of his league. What sort of charity does he go in for?"

"He donates books—returns that would otherwise be shredded—to schools and worthy causes. It costs him very little—it may even be financially to his advantage—and it is useful from a public relations standpoint. He also does something with writers. I mean to say, something intended to benefit writers, especially those who appear to be struggling, which I gather is most of them. He bought the old priory and its church from King's College. The church was going to wrack and ruin with too small a congregation to justify its existence, and many of the supporting buildings had long since been reduced to just their foundations. The church had been formally closed under the Pastoral Measure of 1983. I'm sure the diocese was relieved to avoid outright demolition of the historic priory by putting it in the hands of someone who would undertake to preserve it. Lord Duxter's plans to convert the main buildings and the church itself into housing and put it all to worthwhile use as a retreat met with favor."

"But not a spiritual retreat."

"Not at all, although I gather they observe silent times each day, when presumably the writers are writing instead of talking about their latest contracts. Lord Duxter runs the place as a sort of bolt hole for writers needing quiet time away from their obligations. I'm told there is little to no internet connection out there, the better to force them to create and to get away from email and social media. Lord Duxter has been quoted paraphrasing Alfred Hitchcock, saying that writers produce their best work when treated like cattle. They just need to be fed and prodded once in a while."

"And kept away from their Facebook pages. You seem to know a lot about him."

"In some ways. He is Awena's publisher. She's working now on her next book for him: *The Pagan Vegan's Medieval Cookbook*."

"So she knows him well?"

"She's met him many times, of course, but I think she knows him more by reputation, as she corresponds mainly with her editor at Wooton Press, not with the great man himself. It is pure coincidence Lord Duxter chose this neck of the woods to settle in, unless Awena's descriptions of Nether Monkslip somehow influenced him. He and his wife did have us over for a dinner party once when they first moved in."

"And what is his reputation?"

Max made a "so-so" waffling motion with one hand. "He's to all appearances aboveboard in his business dealings, otherwise Awena wouldn't have had anything to do with him. But she came to him only when her former publisher was merged into Lord Duxter's company; she didn't have a great deal of say in that. There is a fair amount of that merger business these days and in fact the book business seems to be volatile and unstable at the best of times. He's a bit of a philanthropist, which is admirable, whatever his motivations may be. The writer's retreat is more an act of charity than a money-making proposition, according to what Awena tells me. He heavily subsidizes it out of his own pocket. Well, if rumors are true, Lady Duxter's pocket. The big money is hers. I'm sure it's what keeps the whole enterprise afloat."

"Well, there's a motive. They may have quarreled over how the money was being spent."

"Perhaps that is so. I wonder if he gains or loses by her death, and if so, by how much?"

"We've got people covering that angle."

"Anyway," Max continued, "Awena told me she was in the

archives with Jane at around five-fifteen. She stayed perhaps twenty minutes."

Cotton made a note. "That helps pinpoint the time. So tell me, how exactly are the lucky ones chosen to attend the retreat?"

"I'm not sure," said Max. "Awena would know. There must be a vetting process of some kind. A CV. Sample pages of a work in progress. Recommendations from other authors or teachers. The stipend is for a maximum of one month's stay only, and I think that's wise, don't you? Otherwise some people, once dug in, might be difficult to shift. There's one exception to the rule, that I do know."

"And how is that? Rather, who is that?"

"Poppy Frost. Awena says she's always hanging about the place, writing in her notebook."

"So Poppy as well as her stepmother has ties to the place?"

"In a way. Poppy has a literary bent. She has apparently shown such talent the lord has granted her free run of the place until she heads to university. Poppy doesn't live there at the priory, of course, but as good as. I think her home situation isn't always a happy one and so the arrangement suits and having her there does no active harm. Her mother died when she was quite young and she never quite got over the shock of that. I mean, who could? All of this is according to the village grapevine, which remains almost mythic in its efficiency."

"You're referring of course to Miss Pitchford and her minions," said Cotton. "Well, it may or may not be relevant. Certainly I'll have to have one of my people talk at further length with Poppy. She may have seen something, heard something, if she's there so much. I think Sergeant Essex for this, don't you? The woman's touch and all that. Besides, she's closer in age to the girl than anyone else on the team."

"By the way—just for your information and to aid your

researches—Lord Duxter's name before he became Lord Duxter was David Bottom."

"Then how did he come to be Lord Duxter? I mean, why not Lord Bottom?"

"It's not a requirement to keep your 'real' name when you're among the honored. You can style yourself however you want. At a guess, Mr. Bottom seized the chance to acquire a more uplifting name, if you'll excuse the pun. Ian Paisley is Lord Bannside, for example, not Lord Paisley."

"And if your last name was Lord you'd be Lord Lord—which, while easy to remember, wouldn't make a lot of sense, would it?"

"Right. So anyway, our David, Lord Duxter, got a new name and a life peerage. The title exists only so long as he lives; it can't be passed on to his children. But he has no children, so that's nicely taken care of already."

"I do think it's a nice and useful thing that in this country we honor achievement in so many fields, don't you? But I gather from my team that Sir Duxter has a bit of an ego about all this. They've taken turns interviewing him because they've been quickly worn down by all the bombast."

"Yes. If he didn't have an ego before, that came along with the title. By the way, OBEs are not 'Sirs.'"

"Good heavens. How very confusing."

"It's meant to be, I think. Keeps us proles in our place, busy figuring it all out."

"There's one more thing." Again, Cotton flipped through the contents of his briefcase and extracted a piece of paper in size about eight by thirteen centimeters. It was protected in another evidence bag. "And this is really something. Suicide notes, a poem, and then this. A sort of calling card, we're thinking. But whose?"

Within the clear evidence bag was a small rectangle of thick, brightly colored, decorated paper, about the size of a playing card. Max could see on closer inspection that it was a tarot card with a macabre depiction of a man hanging from a tree by a rope tied around one foot, his other foot crossed over behind the suspended leg to form a triangle or a number four. His hands were not showing and were either tied or held behind his back. The card was numbered twelve—XII in roman numerals—at the top, and it was labeled "The Hanged Man" at the lower edge.

"How bizarre," said Max.

"Isn't it just?"

"It was found in the car with the rest? The note, the poem?"

"Yes, but on the floor. Half tucked under a floor mat."

"I suppose someone may be trying to tell the police something," said Max. "In a childish way. That Colin was a trickster, a magician, always playing with cards and performing magic tricks. When he was around for Harvest Fayre, he would do card tricks, tell fortunes— all in good fun, nothing serious. The children loved it. They loved him, come to think of it. There was something childlike about Colin."

"Did he use tarot cards, though?"

"Not that I recall," said Max. "But he may have done. There is probably all manner of significance to this particular card: The Hanged Man. So macabre. Awena will know something about it. She sells tarot cards in her shop. Who could own a New Age shop like Goddessspell and not know something of the tarot?"

"Does she carry this exact brand? I know, or I am learning, that there are dozens of designs, different manufacturers."

Max shook his head. "I wouldn't know. But she keeps good records. If the deck did come from her shop she may be able to tell us who bought it. But also as importantly, what it means, this particular card. I'll ask her this morning and give you a ring, tell you what she said."

But he was in for a surprise when he asked Awena about it. He had returned to their cottage after Cotton left, finding her in the kitchen. She turned from stirring soup on the Aga and took the tarot card from his hand. Whatever she was making, probably soup or a sauce made from scratch, it smelled ambrosial, and Max realized suddenly how hungry he was, although he'd not long ago had breakfast. Awena hadn't invented the farm-to-fork movement but she marched at the front of the parade.

"Certainly, I remember this design," she said. "Poppy bought a deck for use as a party game when she turned sixteen. Her father was still here, not in Saudi yet, and he read the guests' fortunes."

She tapped the card thoughtfully against her thumbnail as she studied it closely.

"There are many interpretations for this particular card," she said finally, handing it back to Max. "Notice the man's expression—he doesn't look pained or hurt in any way. He looks peaceful. It's very odd, given his awful circumstances, but you could say he looks happy. This leads to the interpretation that he's hanging there by his own choice, seeking enlightenment. Which he has apparently found."

"I suppose that since Colin is dead one might say he's enlightened now."

"But there's a simpler explanation," said Awena. "And that's that someone saw Colin as a traitor. There was a time when traitors were hung upside down by one foot, particularly in Italy. If someone left this card behind intentionally, he or she may be trying to tell us why. Why they felt Colin had to die."

"A traitor," Max repeated softly, thinking. So someone may have been leaving a message for the authorities, after all. And it had to be considered, far-fetched as it seemed, that that person was not nec-essarily a murderer. It couldn't be said that only a murderer would leave behind such a clue. But why was it done? Was the message sim-ply, "Whoever killed him—even if he killed himself—he deserved to die?"

Max supposed Colin's work in a country known for repressive regimes might brand him as a traitor in some eyes. That by his work he was reinforcing or enabling a despotic regime.

But what did any of it say about Lady Duxter? That she was sim-ply collateral damage?

Just as likely, the betrayal hinted at by the card was personal. Colin had been found with another man's wife, after all—a fact that pointed the finger of guilt directly at Lord Duxter as the card leaver. Of course, it pointed the finger just as much at Jane. Or at Poppy. Or her boyfriend, Stanley. Or anyone in the village thinking that leaving ghastly clues at a murder scene was a spot of fun.

Max shared some of these thoughts aloud, adding: "I don't think we have to reach that far, do you? All the way to Saudi Arabia, I mean? He was cheating on his wife. That's a betrayal very close to home. Or if the card was intended to represent Marina, it's the same story—an unfaithful spouse. And all by the same token, it could have been aimed at both of them."

Surely Cotton was at work checking out alibis for anyone with a remote attachment to the case. The trouble was, more often than not, if people didn't know they'd need an alibi, they were doing some-thing completely unverifiable. Something innocuous; some solitary chore or diversion like watching the telly or scrubbing the sink. The fact that they could have been the guilty party under these cir-cumstances was not enough in and of itself. Still, motive and opportunity.

Looking at the card, Max realized there was still a further

possible explanation. The card may have been in the car for days or weeks, unnoticed. It may have been dropped there by a passenger, someone who had been given a lift. Someone having nothing to do with the case.

He felt that a visit to Wooton Priory was in order. Surely it was at the epicenter of whatever had transpired between Marina and Colin.

Chapter 12

THE TOWER

Her hair was tied in a knot, held in place at the top of her head by a
plain rubber band looped haphazardly around the shiny strands and
by what looked like a dozen bobby pins. A sharpened pencil pro-
truded from the resulting samurai knob of hair. He gathered from
all the reinforcement that Jane Frost was what his grandmother would
have called a real belt-and-suspenders type, but despite the precau-
tions, her hair was escaping in tendrils around her face. He could
see she'd been crying.

She stared at him out of eyes enlarged by the thick lenses of her
glasses encased in heavy black frames. Max thought a good optom-
etrist might have steered her in a better direction but she seemed to
be a woman of the practical sort (those frames would last forever)—a
person more interested in what was going on inside of her head than
in what the world made of her. She wore a suit of heavy fabric, too
warm for the season and of an unattractive shade of shark gray. No
earrings, no necklaces or bracelets, no adornment of any kind. She was
saved from irredeemable blandness by a smooth, fair complexion

that appeared to be free of makeup, and by a lovely swan-like neck that held her narrow head erect.

He knew her slightly from St. Edwold's. She would sometimes go to the Sunday service at ten where she would be pleasant to all, just managing to avoid the internecine warfare of the church flower guild or becoming ensnared by the many other volunteer opportunities. He gathered that taking care of Netta had been for her a full-time job in and of itself. Netta, on learning that Jane had worked briefly in a nursing home to pay for her schooling, had requisitioned Jane for her own use. When he and Awena had invited her over for dinner, she'd declined the invitation with what sounded like genuine regret.

She had looked up, startled, as he had entered. "Hello, Father Max. I meant to drop by the vicarage soon to see about the arrangements." Her voice was so calm, so matter-of-fact, she might have been discussing having a coat altered at the tailor's. Max reminded himself this was Jane's normal mode, calm and not much given to frenzy or outward display, and perhaps she had no other style. Perhaps for some, tragedy was much the same as happiness and the aim was to stay somewhere in the middle at all times, on an even keel. And the drugs given to sedate her were undoubtedly still in her system.

"When I heard you were here, I thought I'd save you the trouble of stopping by," he said. "I'm not always easy to find, as I have duties at two other churches to call me away. Of course I'm at your service but only when you feel up to talking. I'm a bit surprised you're back at work already." When she made no reply, he said, "But many people find comfort from grief in their work. I see it all the time. I'm the same way myself, come to that." In fact, faced at one point in his life with overwhelming grief, Max had fled to Egypt hoping a change of scene would change everything. It had. It was in Egypt that he had turned his back on undercover work—or so he had thought at the time—and begun his journey to the Anglican priest-hood. He wasn't going to mention any of that to Jane in case it gave her ideas, however. Fleeing was all well and good but not when there was the well-being of a teenaged girl in mourning herself to con-sider. And not when the police might have questions to ask about her husband's death.

Jane nodded, looking gratefully up at him. Among the many sterling qualities for which he was renowned, compassion was at the top of the list. "I'm sure tongues will wag but honestly, this is, as you say, my comfort. My work helps me cope. What would I do at home? Actually, I lasted about ten minutes at home this morning. Every corner holds a memory of Colin, or of Netta." Changing what was clearly a too-raw subject, she said abruptly, "I suppose Poppy will want me out of the house. She'll want to sell up and cash in. I don't know what I'll do if that happens. Where I'll go."

Max was genuinely shocked. "Surely not," he said. "Besides, the house must belong to you?"

"Colin was always a bit of an optimist when it came to . . . to my relationship with Poppy. He only saw the rainbows, always. A complete dreamer he was. Anyway, the solicitor has been on to me already. Colin left his property, which now includes Hawthorne Cottage, to both of us equally. To me and to Poppy. It might have been better if he'd just left it to a distant cousin or an animal sanc-tuary. Poppy can be—difficult. I don't see us sharing a home in peace, at least, not for long."

Max was at a loss. He wasn't even sure of the legality of such an arrangement. Surely the usual thing to do would be for him to leave everything to his wife, since his daughter was still a minor, with the understanding that Poppy would be taken care of in the natu-ral course of things. Had Colin had some concern that the natural course wouldn't be followed? That Jane might try to cheat Poppy out of her fair share? "I am sorry," he said. "It is one added burden on top of what you're already bearing, you and Poppy both. I'll have a word with her if you like. It's important right now that you have each other, and that she recognizes your importance to her world."

She laughed, a derisive, dismissive sound. "Very good luck getting anywhere with her, but of course you are welcome to try. Expect to get an earful of the most dreadful rubbish about me, though. She took against me almost from the first although I've tried everything to get her to see I'm not the enemy." Jane shook her head; her face held an expression of sadness and remorse. "I was stubborn as a girl, too. Thought I knew everything. It feels like payback to me now. Anyway, was there anything more in particular bringing you here today?"

Inventing wildly, Max said, "Ever since my son was born I've become more interested in my family's genealogy. Awena tells me Lord Duxter has an extensive collection of books about the Middle Ages and manuscripts and ledgers from the period. Of course, with a last name like Tudor, it's a hopeless task. I've no real idea where to start. I thought you might know."

"Nothing simpler. Perhaps you are descended from royalty, is that the hope?"

She was mocking him but it was nicely done; a small, tired smile lifted the corners of her mouth. Max leaned back against a sagging wooden bookshelf stuffed with leather-bound volumes, crossing his arms and watching as she consulted her computer. He noticed a copy of *Wuthering Heights* lying on her desk. The book may have come from Hawthorne Cottage, where he'd seen dozens of such classics on the shelves. He had assumed they belonged to Netta and they may have done. It was good to see someone appreciating the classic reads. Max regretted he so seldom had time anymore for the Brontës, who had been particular favorites of his in school. Perhaps, he thought, when Owen was a little older his parents might take him to Yorkshire to visit the Haworth parsonage where the famous authors had lived out their too-brief lives.

Jane clicked expertly through an online catalog before standing from her swivel chair to lead him with graceful steps through the stacks, her practical, low heels clicking against the wooden floorboards in a resounding echo.

"There you are," she said. "Please use the gloves on the shelf there, to page through the older books. I try to keep it all as pristine as possible. The periods of history you're interested in, I would imagine, are of the reign of Henry's father and brother, of Henry himself, and of course of Mary and Elizabeth. There's an entire section devoted to those years, although the Tudors were around in Wales long before that. It wouldn't surprise me too much if you were somehow related."

"Thank you," he said. "I'm sorry to take you away from your regular job."

"But this is my regular job," she said. "I am so grateful to Lord Duxter for it, especially now. I want just to forget." She turned her face, now a hectic shade of pink. "What Colin did . . ."

Was probably unforgiveable—he finished the thought for her. "I meant to say, the writers must require more of your time and attention than does the casual inquirer like me."

She nodded, agreeing that this was so, or perhaps not caring if it were so; it was hard to say. She was a difficult one to read and Max prided himself on being able to read people well.

"I mean, I imagine they might be a demanding bunch," he said. "Awena has some rather amusing stories . . ."

He waited for a response and got nothing but a rather shy, sweet smile, a smile of resignation. She had small, very white teeth. She stood taller, straightening her back. Finally she said, almost as if he'd wrested a confession from her, "They're not too bad. At least, not all of them. And of course Awena in particular is always a joy. She will come up with the most unusual requests, too. It's almost like a game. 'Stump the Librarian' or something. But more often than not I can track down what it is she wants. She makes the whole thing a fun challenge. And of course she's always so grateful for the help."

"That sounds like her," said Max. "And what did she have you chasing after most recently?"

"The pomegranate as mentioned by the Venerable Bede."

"I wouldn't have thought pomegranates were around much in his day."

"That's what I mean," she said. "I always learn more from her than from any of the others. Plus, as I say, she's always the most grateful for the help. She gave me a jar of pomegranate preserves as a thank-you gift."

"I'm getting the impression," said Max, "that the others are . . . What is the word I want?"

She laughed. "I think rude is the word you want. Also thoughtless."

He paused, taken a bit aback by the change in her tone.

"Preoccupied, perhaps?"

She thought about this before replying, as if weighing her words. It seemed a habitual tendency with her and he liked her for it. It was a pattern he wished more people would adopt rather than rush to explain, or excuse, or accuse.

"No," she said at last. "I mean rude. I've come across it before with writerly types—I meet them so often in my line of work. You can excuse it up to a point. Their heads are always inside their—uhm—inside their books, thinking about whatever it is they're writing. Some of them are quite brilliant, of course, and so one has to make allowances. But some of them are mediocrities at best, and a little courtesy would go a long way toward making them bearable. Carville Rasmussen, for one, only *thinks* he's a genius."

"Ah. Well. Great self-confidence is essential in his business, I suppose. As it is in any business."

That earned him another small, sardonic smile. "Is that what we're calling it, then? Self-confidence? I don't think you can have spent many hours in his company, Father Max. Then again, I suppose diplomacy is part of your job."

His returning smile was warm. "How did you come to be here, at the priory? Are you from an academic background?"

"Not in the sense you mean. My father taught at Oxford."

From her expression, a mix of confusion with a tinge of regret, Max wondered if he had been one of the mediocrities she had had in mind.

"Really? I was a student there. Years ago now of course. What was his subject?"

"Philosophy." She managed to imbue the word with the weight of centuries, of high stone walls and dusty tomes read by candlelight by hooded monks.

"Ah," said Max. "What was his name? He might have been one of my dons or lecturers. Philosophy was very much a part of my required curriculum when I was preparing for the priesthood."

"His name was Blackwood. So was mine, before I married."

Not a mediocrity, then. Dr. Angus Blackwood had been one of the world's renowned scholars and writers on the subject of existentialism. Max had a couple of his books on his own shelves back at the vicarage. The books were barely touched but they were there if he needed them. Perhaps in case of some existential crisis. Most often they served as doorstops when the spring winds blew through the crooked old building, which listed and jutted at all angles like a child's conception of a house.

"Is that where you met Colin? I ask because he seemed to be an awfully bright and talented man. He was absent so much for his work, I'm sorry to say I didn't know him that well."

"That, apparently, makes two of us." Again the smile, not bitter as might be expected under the circumstances. Max gained the impression of a woman reeling, a woman struggling mightily to cope with too much bad news coming at her at once. Humor, even of the dark kind, was a sign of a successful coper. Perhaps she was someone accustomed to bad news.

"You didn't want to go to Saudi Arabia with him?" Max was probing, but as discreetly as he could. Speaking of diplomacy, any service he conducted for Colin would have to be a masterpiece of understatement and misdirection.

"No, but not for the reasons you may be thinking. I thought our marriage was solid enough to sustain such a separation. I would have sworn to it, in fact. But Saudi—I quickly decided it was not the place for me. I also foresaw a lifetime of postings to similar places, and I'll be honest, it worried me. I wondered if I was failing him as a wife for not having the can-do, adventurous spirit of the other wives. Perhaps we were a mismatch from the start." She hesitated, and Max could see her draw back from the brink of saying something more. Instead she added, "But the fact is I hated everything I learned about it, and Colin—Colin could see how wretched I was, trying to talk myself into going. So he raised no objections to my staying here. About that time, anyway, it was becoming evident that Colin's grandmother, who raised him, would be needing more help as she got feebler. So my being here while he went away was useful and seemed to be much the best solution."

"And of course, there was Poppy."

A brief laugh. "And yes, there was Poppy. Not that she needs anyone's help—just ask her! Especially now, when she really does need someone to lean on, she's completely shut down. I suppose Stanley is a comfort but I wish she weren't so—so proud, I guess it is. She thinks it's a sign of weakness to cry but honestly, I don't think it can be normal not to cry, do you? She hasn't shed a tear over her father. She just seems angry all the time. At me."

"Does she really have no one but Stanley? I could talk with her, or Awena is awfully good with young people." Destiny was good with the very young ones of the parish, quite willing, as was Max, to surrender majesty by kneeling down to their level and talking in silly voices and playing whatever daft games they suggested, but somehow he thought Awena might have a special affinity for a teenage girl so suddenly alone in the world, being thrown much too early into adulthood.

"Thank you. But if I suggest it, you know, she won't . . ."

"I understand. She has to think it's her idea. I'll see if there isn't something that can be arranged. Seemingly by accident. You know. We men of the cloth have our devious ways."

Jane nodded gratefully. "You really are very kind, very understanding. Her mother died some time ago and, well, it's really not been working out between us. She resents my standing where her mother should be standing. And I know this—I can't pretend not to know this. I'm at my own wits' end and I feel so at a loss, I can't cope, I can't even help myself, much less help a sixteen-year-old who h-h-*hates* me." This unleashed a flow of tears, and the flood of emotion that the distraction of work had kept tapped up finally escaped. She nearly doubled over, as if in pain, reaching out blindly to steady herself against a shelf. Max put out a hand to help balance her, but she either didn't see it or she ignored it. When she recovered herself it was to talk of mundane matters, her eyes blurry and unfocused. Such was the way of grief, Max knew: it was a seesaw of emotion that would go on for months or even years.

She said, "Colin and I talked briefly of sending her away to school, she was so obviously wretched with us, with me, but to be honest, our finances couldn't sustain such an idea. After a few months in Saudi, Colin was starting to get us on our feet again. Paying down some outstanding creditors. Soon, it might have been possible. Things were looking up. Just a few more months." She sighed. "I really think a few months would have made all the difference."

Max thought that Colin's fidelity to his wife might also have helped matters but he was wise enough to know his opinion on this didn't matter. She would let that tape unspool at the rate she had to in order to survive. There might come a day when she hated Colin for his lies but right now the mourning for the loss of him by her side overtook anything else.

She seemed almost to be reading his mind. Surely something of his concern must have shown in his expression, for she said, "It will come. That day when I can forgive him. What difference does it make now he's gone? I'm just not there yet."

Max decided to take a slight risk, to try to reach her. She could always tell him to back off into his own business. A vicar soon learned to fashion a carapace of steel from constant embroilment in the troubles of others. "Tell me," he said gently. "How did you meet Colin?"

"How did we meet?" She paused, as if this were a question she was seldom asked. "We met in London. He'd once dated one of my sisters, actually, until she moved on to greener pastures. Anyway, he used to visit the library where I worked. I started to notice he was always there when I was on duty and it dawned on me slowly that Colin was there for me. To be around me. It was rather sweet, actually. Until it got to be completely annoying, but that came later. He would ask me to help him find something on the shelves and it became obvious he could have found it himself. It was just an excuse to spend time with me. Anyway, after a rather rocky courtship, we got married. The rocky part should have alerted me. We quarreled all the time, it seemed. To be honest, I think it was Poppy I fell in love with first, in a manner of speaking. She was beautiful and she could be so sweet, so trusting. Then . . . well. Anyway. Colin. He was handsome and I wasn't used to handsome men falling for me. I came to think of him as stolidly handsome—does that make sense? That cliché about the strong, silent type made manifest. And he was awfully bright. Just, well, a bit of a dork."

Apparently Lady Duxter didn't think he was a dork, but Max also kept this thought to himself.

"Did anything happen, in his last days . . . I mean, was there any sign of what was to come? Anything out of the ordinary?"

"Yes. Yes, there was, but I don't see how it could . . . Anyway, I've been remembering. Colin was with me in the archives, waiting, about to give me a ride home and idly leafing through the things on the shelves that I hadn't sorted yet. I saw him slip something in his knapsack and I sort of, you know, berated him. Nothing is supposed to be removed from this room without my approval, although it's a tough rule to enforce."

"What was it, do you know?"

She shook her head. "I asked him, later that night. He got very mysterious—oh, it was maddening, Colin in mysterious mode. Colin the magician. He wouldn't tell me. He would only say he'd found something he thought was dynamite. I've no idea what it could have been. I have to confess, I went through his kit after he'd gone to bed. I found nothing."

"You've really no idea?"

"He'd been looking through some of the old household account books, as far as I could tell. There are very few exciting mysteries to be found in there, let me tell you. Suddenly, he got all excited and worried looking but he wouldn't tell me what he'd found. He just got very nervous—happy nervous, you understand. Wound-up nervous. I don't think it was the account book itself—those things are of monstrous size. It was something tucked inside."

"Is that book still around?" Max asked.

She nodded. "I'm still going through those books and other papers that were in the box with them. Come, I'll show you."

They walked to a table laid out with aged, leather-bound books, all in various stages of decrepitude. Scattered around them were bits of paper—bills and receipts, the odd letter. But nothing that Max could see at a cursory glance was of a personal nature. No hidden treasure maps, no birth certificates, nothing to excite the casual observer.

"These are the household accounts dated from 1454 to 1664," she was saying. "The book for 1460 is the one he was looking at. Believe me, I've been through it page by page. But again, I don't think the book itself was the issue. It was something tucked inside the pages."

"And this never turned up? Not in his knapsack, or somewhere at home?"

"No. I can't say I looked every single place it could be. It may still turn up."

He would get Cotton to send someone to have a look. It might be a wild-goose chase but he couldn't ignore anything that might have been a motive for murder.

Max took his leave of her half an hour later, with a promise to see to Poppy.

He walked the priory grounds for a while, taking in the leafy scent of the air and relishing a small escape before he must return to his duties at the vicarage. He had hoped for a word with Lord Duxter but Jane had informed him the lord, after yet another talk with the police, had retreated to his rooms and was not seeing visitors. Max decided it was best to respect those boundaries for now.

As Max neared Prior's Wood he saw he'd wandered unawares near the priory's turret—a small round tower stuck onto a corner of the main building. The wooden door that led inside proved to be unlocked. Wanting a better view of his surroundings, he quickly ran up the narrow circular stairway—probably a hundred steps in all to the top. Max was in good shape but he was winded by the time he reached the parapet. He was reminded he needed to get back into his running routine.

From the top he could look far out over the woods to the pond. He had, in fact, a bird's-eye view of everything. The trees and bushes were still wearing traces of their summer foliage, faded leaves clinging stubbornly to branches until the winter winds would shake them off, leaving stark black outlines against the sky. It was a lovely view and Max beheld it in something like wonder at its simple beauty. He found himself wishing he could paint but he knew he could never entirely capture the scene.

Because of its location, the turret appeared not to be a watchtower for approaching enemies but simply there to offer a view of nature at its finest. Even in medieval times when each day must have seemed a struggle for survival, full of surprise visits from unexpected armies, there must also have been a need for undiluted beauty. As great a need as there was now. A set of binoculars rested on a ledge sheltered from the elements, but they weren't really necessary on such a clear day as this.

Max was turning away when a movement caught his eye. A splash of color moving through the trees, sunlight glinting off what appeared to be a decorated sleeve or hem. There it was again, the flow of bright cloth showing between branches still decked with foliage. Then a dark head came into view, thick hair braided with gold thread and coiled at the back of a beautiful neck. It was Awena. She was carrying a straw basket, and looking much like a character in a fairy tale. An enchanted Snow White come to life. She was evidently foraging mushrooms for that night's meal. As he watched, she set down the basket and, taking a small scarf from her pocket, dipped it in water at the pond's edge, wrung it out, and wrapped it round her neck, presumably to cool herself off. *As the deer longs for the waterbrooks*, thought Max, *so longs my soul for you*. Still oblivious to his gaze she resumed her task. Max felt like a spy, an interloper on this little domestic scene, but he stood watching until she moved out of his sight under another thick canopy of trees. He could have called out but it was doubtful she could have heard him, given the distance, and it was likely to startle her if he did.

Chapter 13

THE MAGICIAN

Max returned to the vicarage to follow up on a few telephone calls awaiting his attention, matters he didn't feel he could delegate. He had a noon service to offer at St. Edwold's, and planned after that to go and talk with Colin's daughter if he could find her.

Before Cotton left him earlier that day he had extracted a promise from Max that he would talk with a few people, ask a few questions around the village. "Work your magic," as Cotton put it. Max thought it was difficult to see what he might achieve but reminded himself that even journeys in the dark begin with a single step.

Noticing the weather had started to drizzle, he was putting on his overcoat and fedora when there came a knock at the front door, followed by the door to his study being flung open. Mrs. Hooser announced: "It's Poppy, the poor wee lamb," and, without waiting for his reply: "I'll be sending her in, then."

Max, who was used to villagers dropping by the vicarage unannounced for advice, for a shoulder to cry on, or simply for a chat, was not surprised to see Poppy there, wearing a red dress to match her name, and a distractingly glittery eye shadow. While the tie-dye dress fell conventionally below the knee, she'd offset the conventionality by wearing a black leather jacket and purple-and-black striped knee socks over white-lace hosiery. At her wrist was a gray digital activity tracker. It was an odd ensemble for a girl in mourning—for anyone, for that matter—but Max rather thought a mindfully uncurated style was Poppy's go-to presentation.

On the one hand, he found he couldn't tear his eyes from that makeup of hers, but later he would be hard-pressed to recall precisely what color eyes she had, other than that they were a shade of blue. She had exaggerated this oddly mesmerizing effect by lining both eyes completely in black. He wondered that she'd taken the time for this elaborate toilette but then realized the makeup acted as a barrier to the world, and perhaps that was what she needed most at the moment: a wall to keep people away. She'd also done something to the tips of her hair, which were a fire-engine red, and she wore long earrings that dangled to her collarbone. Max learned later over dinner with Awena that these were called chandelier earrings.

"The child looked as if she were starring in a cabaret," he said.

"Sixteen is not the age of a child," she reminded him. "Not anymore. I was out on my own and making my way at about that age."

"I would bet you had a lighter hand with makeup than she has. It's a wonder her mother lets her go to school looking like that."

"Stepmother," Awena corrected him. "And I'd be willing to bet Jane doesn't know. And as likely she doesn't care, but that's to her credit, as far as I'm concerned. More wars with teenagers are lost over makeup and hairstyling than over drugs or anything really important. Certainly Netta would not have approved if she'd known, however. Girls often wait until they're at the school to make costume and makeup changes. And then of course, they undo it all before they go home. Honestly, I'd say it's harmless. Makeup wears off; hair grows back in. As long as she's not into drugs—and I'd swear she was smarter than that—the rest is just a phase." She paused and looked at him. "Did you never have phases, Max?"

"I went through a rather horrible phase where I wore a lot of black."

"You still wear a lot of black."

He laughed. "Yes, but this was a sort of tragically glamorous and chic black wardrobe as opposed to a—well, a subdued priestly garb. I also wrote some stupendously pretentious poetry. I am sorry to have to tell you I read some of it *out loud* in this sort of cellar dive near my house. I did not, however, strum a guitar as I warned my audience of the end of the world as we know it. And before you ask, I consigned all my poetry to the flames when I reached the age of reason. Which was about when I turned twenty-one. I was afraid my mother would unearth it one day and have it bound into little booklets to hand out to her friends."

"I'm sure the girls all thought you were wonderful," she said. "Dressed all in black, with your dark hair and piercing eyes. Or were your eyes flashing?"

"I think I rather hoped they smoldered with banked passion. I'm not sure I believed the girls could possibly be in their right minds if they did think me wonderful. If there is a more self-conscious age than sixteen I'd like to know what it is." He paused, remembering. "I also wore these awful boots, with brass buckles on the sides. I can't imagine what I was thinking. I must have looked like some sort of musketeer out of a school play."

She laughed at this image of the young Max, who she knew must have been as kind-hearted and earnest and well-intentioned as the current Max.

"Actually, I think I'd rather you didn't know all this," he said.

"I would rather you always thought of me as being the suave, dashing hero of legend that you married, as having skipped right over the awkward, trying-out phases of adolescence."

"I do, and I always will," she assured him. "Anyway, what did Poppy have to say for herself?"

"She mostly talked about how butter suddenly wouldn't melt in Jane's mouth when she was around Colin on his return from Saudi. How she flattered him and 'sucked up' to him, even cooking for him, which she never had done before. Poppy implied rather than said outright she thought Jane was planning to poison him."

"Oh, dear. It's worse than I thought."

"Exactly. We can put that last bit down to a bit of teen drama, I think, and too much time spent watching true crime shows on the telly. But something else she told me I tend to believe. And it makes everything a bit worse, and certainly more complicated, than we imagined."

He came to look back on the conversation he'd had that day with Poppy as pivotal to solving the case. If he hadn't needed to rush off for the noon service, she'd have had his fuller attention.

There were few people her age in the village, and fewer still who came to St. Edwold's Church, so someone like Poppy was a bit beyond his usual experience. At least, that was the story he told himself at the time—he was simply out of his depth with a sixteen-year-old girl. He came to wish most of all that Awena with her level head had been there to ask the questions he never thought to ask Poppy that day.

Once admitted to the room by Mrs. Hooser, the "poor wee lamb" darted in, lightning fast, a red sprite flashing against the somber grays and browns of the study shelves. She perched on a chair by the fireplace and held out her small white hands to the flames for warmth. Max, taking off his hat and coat, moved to join her.

"How are you holding up, Poppy?" he asked, taking the chair opposite.

She didn't answer, but "How do you think?" seemed to hang in the air.

"I was actually just on my way to see you after the noon service," he said.

"Oh," she said. "I never go to that."

"I know. I wasn't sure you'd be home. Your stepmother is at work. Probably you know that."

"She's always at work. Jane is a drone. Or a pod person. I've never been sure which."

Max chose not to go down that path. "You spend a lot of time with Stanley Zither these days, I hear."

That got her attention; quickly she raised her head and stared at him from out of those overly decorated eyes. "I suppose *she* told you that. She should mind her own business. She doesn't approve of Stanley, you know. Because he's in a band. Neither did Grandmamma approve of him, but she didn't approve of anything in the whole entire *world*." Poppy lifted those small hands to draw a large orb in the air, to demonstrate the vastness of Netta's contempt for everything—everything that mattered to Poppy and presumably to all other right-thinking people.

Max rose to put another log on the flames. The rain, tapping softly at the windows, had quickly lowered the temperature of the room by several degrees. "Why is that, do you suppose?" he said mildly, brushing traces of sawdust from his hands. "Stanley always struck me as a very fine young man."

She nodded her head vigorously. *There, you see?* "He is an

outstanding person in every *way*. Bright. Loyal. Clever. Everything in total, you know? But Grandmamma had someone else in mind for me, and Jane, to keep the peace, went along with whatever she said. She doesn't care, Jane. But I think just having me gone was the whole point, so whoever I left with, it didn't matter. I was a conundrum to her. Just a complete burden." Conundrum was Poppy's word for the day, used slightly wrong in this context.

Max, sensing this was at least partly true, let her take the lead, now that she was off and running.

"She was jealous, too, I think. Here was Jane, stuck with my father, while I had Stanley. I mean, my father was a good guy, but you could tell she didn't think so. I would bet she thought the past months without him have been great. Total, like, freedom. And they had solidified her belief that marriage to him had been a huge mistake. Solidified as in made solid, you know. It's from the French." Solidified had been Poppy's new word for yesterday. "Certainly, it solidified mine. She practically danced all the way home from seeing him off at Heathrow. My guess was, when he came back she was planning to start loosening the ties that bind. Not right away, not all at once, but eventually."

"You think she wanted a divorce?"

"I do. I mean, *duh*. She hated it here. She always called it Sodding Monkslip. Sorry, should I not have said that? I was just quoting her. Anyway, she always wanted to be back in London, to hear her talk. The plays, the museums and galleries, on and on."

"Many people find Nether Monkslip a bit of a slower pace. And an acquired taste." Max remembered his early days in the village, when the deep silence punctuated by random, piercing squawks and the hooting of lovelorn owls kept him awake.

Poppy, who like Jane found the pace glacial and longed for the bright lights of the big city, was not to be diverted from her main topic. "I never liked my stepmother, not much I didn't. And I never trusted her. Like, never, from the beginning. What a snake that woman is. She's a witch—for real. She is! I tried to warn my father but he was besotted. I would swear she killed him, I know she wanted him dead, but . . ."

"But what?"

"But I was with her that evening. Briefly, but . . . yeah." Poppy's reluctance was palpable. She really would have liked to land Jane in the soup. "I asked if I could borrow the ATM card. My father was there with her. He'd been drinking, but he was okay. I kissed him good-bye; I'm so glad I at least had the chance. But there is no way she had time to do it."

"What time were you there?"

"About five o'clock. Maybe five after. I just stopped in for a moment and I left right away."

"And where did you go?"

"I walked to the bank in Monkslip Mallow to use the ATM."

"Did you keep the receipt?"

"No. There was no reason to. Anyway, it was five twenty-five. I remember looking at my watch. Stanley was waiting for me in the village, and wondering where I'd got to. I dawdle sometimes. It's a bad habit—my head gets lost in the clouds when I'm writing a story or something."

He'd relay all this to Cotton and have him ask the bank about the time of the withdrawal from the ATM. It was a good alibi if she needed one. Undoubtedly the ATM had camera coverage, too. Awena had been with Jane at five-fifteen, she'd said. So between Poppy's testimony and Awena's, there had not been time enough for Jane to get out to where the car containing Colin and Marina was, stage the scene, and get back to the library in time for her meeting with Awena.

Poppy meanwhile was pursuing another thought. "She's not even pretty! I said to him. He had no idea what I was talking about. And he—he was so very handsome."

"Love is blind, they do say."

She nodded. But what would Max know about it? His wife was gorgeous, talented, and genuinely kind, not phony-kind and condescending like some adults. Awena was everything Poppy wished her stepmother was or would be. Awena was vibrant and colorful, where Jane was as plain as a white plate.

Poppy pushed her hair behind the elaborate earrings, made of ruby-colored glass to go with the dress. They were nearly the only things she wore that came close to matching. "But for the sake of getting along and not upsetting my father, I pretended everything was fine. Mostly, I tried to stay out of her way. That worked—mostly. But I kept tabs on her." Poppy nodded sagely. "She thought she was rid of me. But I saw."

Max bit. "Saw what?"

"The kits."

"I'm sorry. The kits?"

Poppy sighed deeply, hesitated a moment, then clearly reached an "in for a penny" decision. "She has all these test kits, you see. Kits that measure the amount of hCG in your urine. Well, in a woman's urine. I think she bought these tests by the case—I found so many empties in the bin."

"Pregnancy tests?"

"That's right."

In his surprise, Max rather blurted out: "Why would she need so many? Your father had only just returned home."

Poppy sighed, exasperated that she had to spell this out for him. Men could be so thick, even dishy, experienced men like Father Max.

"I don't think my father had anything to do with this. It was in the summer she started buying these kits. He wasn't even here."

"Oh."

"Yes, *oh*. You see? So what was she up to?"

Having an affair was what she was up to, clearly. Max had read somewhere the more sensitive of these tests were able to detect a pregnancy as early as seven days after conception. So, who was the lucky man, if not her husband? And why test so often, come to that. Was she worried she was going to become pregnant? Or was she worried she might not? It was very curious behavior.

He had to allow, he supposed, for the possibility she was receiving in vitro treatments. Even in Colin's absence, it wasn't outside the realm of possibility, if a bit unusual for a woman in her situation. But given everything else Poppy was saying—well, if Poppy was making things up or getting things wrong, could he really rely on what she said? Still he asked, "Was she seeing a doctor or visiting a clinic routinely?"

Poppy thought a moment, then shook her head no. "I don't think so."

"How many of these test kits did you find?" he asked.

She answered promptly, "At least a dozen, just in August alone."

What madness, thought Max. To test and retest like that. If fear of pregnancy was the point, surely prevention would have made more sense. Of course, perhaps the hope of finding oneself pregnant with a longed-for child was the point. He thanked Poppy for telling him, although he wasn't sure himself what to make of this information.

"Poppy," he said. "You've suffered a terrible loss. I don't want to add to your sorrow. But there is an investigation been started into your father's death, you know."

"I didn't know. So someone else thinks it's fishy besides me. Good."

"You'll do all you can to help the police, am I right?"

"Well, *duh*. Of course. The only thing holding me together is wanting to get at the truth. But I don't know where to start. I'll do anything. *Any*thing to help."

Max rather thought that would be her response.

"You had some tarot cards at your birthday party, I hear."

She looked puzzled by this tangent, as well she might. "Well, yes. My father was here and he loved anything to do with cards. But it was just a game. Nothing to it. I don't believe in that stuff. Do you?"

"Do you still have the cards?"

"I've got them in my bag." Before he could stop her, she reached down into the tasseled brown handbag she'd brought with her and extracted a small colorful box.

"Did the police not ask you about these?"

"No. Why should they?"

He supposed DCI Cotton hadn't yet sent anyone to the cottage to look for them, or that she'd been gone when they got there.

"They might be relevant to the case." Having said that, he wasn't sure why. It was more a point of interest to learn where the tarot card found with the victims came from. That upside-down hanged man with the baffling expression. "Would you mind if I gave them to the detective in charge?"

"Sure, yes," she said, pushing the box at him. "Of course."

"Just a minute," he said. He went to his desk and retrieved a tissue. It was probably all much too late, for certainly she'd been handling all the cards for ages along with her friends, but there might be latent prints Cotton would want preserved.

She handed the cards into his now-shielded hand as her words tumbled out anew, trying to force him to see her view. She seemed to sense he was half convinced already and was determined to press her advantage.

"Did you see her at the funeral for Grandmamma?" she said. The kohl-lined eyes narrowed in remembrance. "It was enough to make a cat puke. Standing next to my father in the graveyard, holding his hand and somehow, through it all, looking *thrilled*. She was just pretending, you see. Of course she was. Pretending to be happy that her husband was back at her side. She actually had tears in her eyes. Tears of joy, one was supposed to think. I don't know how she managed that." Poppy tossed her head back, aping her stepmother as she gazed adoringly at Colin. It was actually quite a good imitation but Max felt he should draw a line now.

"Poppy . . . ," he began. "This is your stepmother you're talking about."

She waved that aside and rushed on, ignoring him. "Cooking all his favorite meals, too. 'Would you like pork chops, Colin? I know they're your favorite. How about some applesauce to go with them? More potatoes?' Pah! *That* never happened before. He ate what he was given, if she could be bothered to put some frozen ready meal from Sainsbury's in the microwave."

Was this just the expected reaction of a young woman in shock, who has lost so much and is in deep mourning for her family? Max wondered. Of all times, it was now she would miss having her own mother to turn to. As if reading his mind, she said, "I know people will think I'm just causing trouble for Jane. Out of grief for my father, for my parents, for my great-grandmother. I'm upset, sure I am. I can't sleep, thinking about it. But I can disentangle that, you know? Separate it out from the rest. I don't trust Jane and I just don't and that's got nothing to do with anything else."

"You are bound to feel two ways," Max began. "I—"

"But the clincher was," she rushed on, "that with all this lovey dovey stuff on display for the public, he slept on the sofa every night."

"Oh."

"Yes! My father was sleeping on the sofa at night. From the moment he returned from Saudi until, you know." She had captured the vicar's attention at last. That was so satisfying.

How very strange, thought Max. Surely after months away from each other, and with no apparent rift between them, the couple would at least share a bed. The pregnancy tests made even less sense. Assuming Poppy was telling the truth about that.

Poppy's face was flushed now with a sort of gratitude, her eyes shining. Someone was listening. Someone at last was trying to understand what she'd been saying. Max wondered how far Poppy's theories had been sprinkled about the village. Gossip was a horrible thing—contagious. In the village, Miss Pitchford was in charge of chatter, but she had many at her beck and call. With her advancing years and declining health, she had found it necessary to assemble an army to assist her.

"You see?" Poppy nodded grimly. "You do see, don't you Father Max? Jane was up to something. I don't know how, or what, or even who. But she was up to something. And my poor father, he never saw it coming. And now Marina . . . she was kind to me. She always had time for me. I'm so worried about her."

What she told him next he wasn't sure he believed. But he felt he had no choice but to act as if he did. He knew he'd never forgive himself otherwise.

The telephone rang soon after Poppy left. It was Adam Birch phoning to say the book he'd ordered for Max had arrived. Adam's shop, The Onlie Begetter, was on Mermaid Lane off the High, and as Max would be passing nearby on a promised pastoral visit to old Mr. Greeley, he told Adam he'd be right over.

The bell over the shop door rang and Adam emerged from the back carrying a load of books he'd found at an estate sale. "Hidden treasures in here," he assured Max, adding that he'd scoured the world to find the book Max had wanted: *At Home with the Buddha*.

"It sounds like something Awena would read," Adam commented, placing the book inside a paper bag printed with the shop's name and logo, a copy of the Droeshout engraving of Shakespeare.

"I've promised to let her read it when I'm through," said Max. "How have you been, Adam? It's been a while since I've seen you about."

Adam's face flushed rather pink above the brown cardigan he habitually wore. Max hoped he hadn't been too obviously prying. Adam had long been rumored to be seeing something of Elka Garth, although they both seemed to feel no one in the village was aware of their by now well-established and talked-about connection. The only question in everyone's mind was when the two would get around to tying the knot. Susanna Winship had been taking bets it would be within a year, while older hands at the game like Miss Pitchford held out for something closer to six months. Elka had begun wearing an engraved band on her ring finger that she maintained was simply a ring that did not fit any other finger on her hand, and since Elka was incapable of dissembling, the villagers had to be content for now with what was surely a signal that she was "taken."

Reminded of his own courtship with Awena, which had set the village grapevine alight for months, Max was reluctant to press Adam on such a sensitive topic.

"I've been rather busy, Max," said Adam. "Writing. You know."

He pushed his thick glasses further up his nose. The brown eyes magnified by the lenses were soft. Adam was one of the gentler souls of the village, along with Elka, and Max for one applauded the fact two people so deserving of happiness had found it.

"Hmm," said Max. Even though he suspected Adam was more busy visiting with Elka when both their shops were closed than writing, Awena had told him that the worst thing you could do was quiz a writer about his writing habits. Writers were always, she had assured him, writing, even when it didn't much look like they were. Well, *most* writers, she'd added.

Adam, like many members of the Writers' Square writers' group, which met in his shop, had been laboring over some kind of manuscript or other for ages. Max might have asked him how his book was progressing but he was rather afraid he'd tell him at length and put Max off his schedule for the rest of his day.

"So you were not signed on for Lord Duxter's writing retreat?" Max asked.

"Oh, not I," Adam replied. "I have to keep the shop open, you know. And Lord Duxter has rather raised the standards of the retreat to published authors. To keep out the riffraff—the wannabes like me."

"I don't call that raising the standards," said Max. "People sincerely working on their books are writers, surely."

"Well, God bless you for thinking so," said Adam. "That's my thinking, exactly."

"Tell me," said Max. "Has this 'raising the standards' business made anyone—oh, I don't know. Disgruntled with Lord Duxter? Would anyone be holding a grudge?"

Adam peered shrewdly out of those basset hound eyes of his, smoothing his thinning hair. "You're referring to what happened in Prior's Wood, aren't you? Of course, I've read the news. But that would mean—surely, you're not thinking that was some sort of attack on Colin and Lady Duxter, to get even with Lord Duxter? That it was all somehow staged?"

For someone not writing a crime novel—at least, not the last Max had heard—Adam was quick off the mark.

"Really, I'm just wondering aloud, Adam. It would be best this conversation not be repeated. If it got out through the village grapevine, you know—I was merely talking. There's no proof th—"

"It's much too late for that, Max," said Adam cheerfully. "Madame Cuthbert was in earlier—she'd just come from Miss Pitchford's—and apparently there is a groundswell of rumor already. Miss Pitchford had had a word on the telephone with the man who found Colin and Lady Duxter."

Of course, thought Max. The story in the newspaper would be enough to get the conspiracy theorists going immediately. Why wait for proof?

"He didn't say anything to her he hadn't already told the investigators?"

"No, no. It's just that Miss Pitchford likes to get her news from the horse's mouth, whenever possible."

"Yes. Very sensible of her."

"It's an odd thing," Adam began.

"Yes?"

"Well, I was in Prior's Wood on a few occasions over the summer—it was so hot, you know, and the shade of the trees was most welcome. So I'd pack a picnic lunch . . ."

"For just yourself?" Max asked lightly, pretending a sudden keen interest in a display table of gardening books. He picked up one on gardenias and began leafing through the pages.

"Well, no, of course not. Sometimes—well, every time, if I'm honest—Elka would come with me."

Just when it didn't seem possible Adam could blush a deeper red, he managed it.

"So, what was odd?" Max asked.

"Well. Erm. You know the entire place is rather a meeting spot round these parts. A lovers' lane, for some. That area where Colin and Lady Duxter were found, especially. Rather secluded, hidden. You know. Elka and I actually found a bra hanging from one of the tree branches one time we were there. In the dark, I suppose Lady Duxter or someone just forgot to retrieve it. It was gone the next week, when we came back."

"Hmm," said Max.

"Should I—should we—tell the police?"

"I don't suppose it's important, do you? But I'll be seeing something of DCI Cotton, and I'll be sure to pass that tidbit along. Could you describe it for me?"

"It was lacy, you know how women's things are."

"All right. Any particular color?"

"It was red."

As red as your face? Max wondered.

He spent a few minutes browsing before taking his leave. Max could never resist a bookshop, particularly this one. A small fireplace lent a cozy glow along with two Tiffany-style lamps. Books were organized according to a code only Adam understood, but he liked to prominently display his own favorites, on every subject imaginable, in the front window. Used books tended to be put to utilitarian purposes—to hold up a table or prop up a lamp. Adam had acquired a stained glass window from a church about to be demolished and had it installed. It represented the patron saint of writing, St. Francis de Sales, and shards of colored light spilled from it onto a display of mystery novels in one corner. St. Francis, Max noted, looked quite serene, and no goats were anywhere in sight.

As he was leaving, he saw Jane at the foot of Mermaid Lane on her way to the High Street shops. The sun had made an unexpected appearance, turning the day freakishly warm, and she carried her cardigan slung over one arm along with her shopping bag. She wore a sleeveless dress too large for her; Max thought she might be losing weight from the strain. She raised her free arm high in a friendly wave, but walked briskly on, clearly not wanting to be waylaid.

Max's own steps slowed as he turned over in his mind his conversations with Jane, and with Poppy.

Chapter 14

TEMPERANCE

Max was pondering what best to do later that day when Miss Pitchford interrupted his thoughts.

Every village has a Miss Pitchford. Every town, every city, every hamlet, without exception, has a Miss Pitchford. There is never more than one, for the Miss Pitchfords of the world can never tolerate competition. Nether Monkslip's Miss Pitchford happened to be the prototype, the mold from which all the rest in every place were made.

Since she seemed to be immortal, however feeble she might become, there was never any talk of finding her replacement. Once the time came, such a person would emerge to take her place, like Athena emerging from Zeus's skull, fully grown and geared for battle. A Miss Newcastle or a Miss Wychwood would appear, armed with knitting needles and with a preternatural ability to suss out scandal.

Miss Pitchford had come that afternoon to beard the lion in his den, as she so often did. She had blown open the door to his study with such stunning force Max's MI5 training had automatically kicked in. He shot up from the desk and made as if to fling himself upon the frail old woman wrapped in her hand-knitted shawl, recalling himself just in time from an ankle tackle that would surely have shattered her bones.

"What is it, Miss Pitchford?" he demanded, exasperated, and tapping his heart to make sure it still beat safely tucked under his ribcage. Then, more politely, breath restored, he added, "How may I help you today?"

"The question is how I can help *you*, Father Tudor," she replied. She marched in with that *"ah ha!"* gleam in her eye that Max had often noticed when she had spotted a typo in the parish newsletter. Whether or not Max was strictly accountable for the typo, he always came to hear of it. Suzanna was in fact the editor and it was true the newsletter became progressively more interesting the more she enjoyed a glass of wine or two in the evening. But also strictly speaking Max had to allow he was responsible for all the content. He was the publisher, answerable, as Miss Pitchford liked to point out, only to God. And, presumably, also to Miss Pitchford.

She wasted no time in getting to her point.

"You went to Wooton Priory today," she announced. Max didn't trouble to enquire how she knew that. Of course she just would know that. "I believe that while you were there you spoke with Jane Frost. It would be only natural you would console a grieving widow such as she. But of course she would be at the priory, and not at home, as she should be. It wouldn't have happened in my day, I can tell you *that* much for a fact."

"What is that, Miss Pitchford? What wouldn't have happened?"

"Why, all this gallivanting about, of course. Running all about the village, when she should be at home, making preparations." She pushed back a rogue wave of marcelled hair that had dared escape a tortoiseshell comb.

"Oh. Of course."

"And I felt I must warn you."

Max, still processing what Poppy had told him, found himself reluctant even to talk with the gossipy woman carrying her usual tale of gothic woe—whatever it was this time. He would have asked Mrs. Hooser to help him dodge her but he disliked involving his housekeeper in these deceptions. Besides which, she was hopeless at deception.

"You think she's plain, don't you?" demanded Miss Pitchford. "A 'plain Jane'? Well. You've never seen her dance at the Harvest Fayre or the May Day festivities. I have. It's *scandalous*, that's what it is— an absolute scandal, all that jitterbugging about, and it's an open invitation to . . . to . . . all manner of . . ." Max waited, rather hoping she would say "fornication"—being with Miss Pitchford was so often like talking with a throwback to the Victorian era or someone from the temperance movement—but in the end she settled for something less Biblical.

"To *extramarital* relations." She finished strongly, and Max felt he had to hand this one to her. She had navigated those tricky rapids with barely a slip of the oar.

He was wondering if someone had attempted to revive the jitterbug at one of the village festivities, but then decided the jitterbug was probably the latest style of dance, apart from the waltz, with which Miss Pitchford was personally acquainted. "Yes, yes, I'm sure you're right, but I—"

"I'm not finished," she said.

Again Max waited, an expression of polite expectation and hope pasted on his face. It took all his strength not to glance at his wristwatch or at the clock on the mantelpiece.

"Why else was she always going in to Monkslip-super-Mare?" Miss Pitchford asked scornfully. "To shop? *Pah!*"

Max, who had the clearest picture of Jane being generally in the archives at the priory, blowing dust off the old volumes, was intrigued. In spite of himself. For if Miss Pitchford said Jane often went to Monkslip-super-Mare, it was likely true. Her spies were everywhere.

"Now I know you think I'm an old foolish woman," she began. She waited for the bleat of protest, which Max duly offered. *Baa*. "But I have lived a long time and I have kept my eyes open and my ears to the ground." Max, waiting for her to get to the point, kept himself occupied trying to picture Miss Pitchford posed in such an anatomically challenging way.

"And I know a lie when I hear one," she continued.

"Oh? What lie is that?"

"Why, Jane Frost never in her life canned a nectarine. For one thing, I don't know a young woman her age—a Londoner, no less— with the first inkling how to do such a thing. Nectarines are tricky. You don't want to use the raw pack method—the results are unsightly, to say the least."

Max, who had no idea what the raw pack method might involve, nonetheless managed to look suitably aghast.

"Besides, and more to the point, it was far too late to be canning that variety of nectarine when she said she was. The Terrace Ruby is ready in July, especially given the warm weather we had this past summer. That's how much *she* knows about it. She was *always* lying about where she was and what she was doing. I just don't know why. If she was lying about that what else might she lie about?"

Max, puzzled by the implications of what he was being told, said nothing for a moment. Surely all would be revealed in good time. To Miss Pitchford the subject was clearly sacred, so it was hard to tell if anything she was saying carried weight in a world beyond canning.

"Anyway, wherever she was at the time of my gardening talk to the Women's Institute, for example—'Mulch Ado About Slugs'— she wasn't at home canning nectarines. You do see that, don't you? Unless canning is a metaphor for something else. Something risqué. I would not care to hazard a guess *what*. Would you?"

"When did she tell you this, Miss Pitchford?"

"Why, she told her tale to all who would listen. At the Cavalier, a few days before Netta died. But I tell you, she was not at home canning, not then or at any other time. Unless I miss my best guess, she was out there in those woods again."

To mention your doings at the Cavalier was much like shouting them from every village rooftop. Jane's homey alibi, if it was meant to be an alibi for what she was actually doing that day, appeared to be false. But could Miss Pitchford be believed, or was she fallible, as she so often was? There was a time when her gossip could be relied on absolutely, but her powers might be fading now with age. And spite, of which she had a wide streak, so often colored facts to suit the carrier of that information. He would ask Awena, the go-to person for all things having to do with canning or pickling, to make sure Miss Pitchford's nectarine information was accurate for this region. But if Jane weren't canning—never the tightest alibi, anyway— what was she doing? More to the point, why would she lie about where she was and what she was doing?

Unless it was a polite excuse for missing the mulch-and-slug lecture—a strong possibility. Still, Max felt he'd been taught a resounding lesson in humility and in the dangers of dismissing the testimony of the old and querulous. Of the busybody who, after all, tended to see all in such a small place as Nether Monkslip and environs. He'd been dodging Miss Pitchford pretty much since he had come to the village, and he should not have done so. She may have held the solution to many a case all along. It was an odd little clue and he wasn't sure what it meant, but it was decidedly . . . odd. More odd behavior in Jane's column.

"And as for those people at the priory. *Well.* David—Lord Duxter as he now styles himself—was in his youth a philandering rogue, so I hear."

"I think most men go through a stage of sowing wi—"

"Balderdash," she said. "Once a rogue, always a rogue."

"Yes, in his youth, perhaps he was."

"He's only fifty-two now—hardly too decrepit to get up to all manner of debauchery. He was not born in the purple; his nobility was acquired. It makes an enormous difference, you know."

"I hadn't realized," said Max. "Fifty-two? He looks older. He's older than I am, certainly." He wasn't sure why he'd said that, and clearly Miss Pitchford wasn't sure, either. She looked at him suspiciously with her steely, accustomed-to-command gaze (she was a former headmistress, after all). Max felt as if he had somehow admitted to some scandalous personal failure that would cast Nether Monkslip into the tabloid headlines. "Vicar Admits All Manner of Debauchery."

As there seemed to be no way to back out of the predicament he'd created for himself, he said quickly, "Of course, you're right, Miss Pitchford. But moral character has nothing to do with age. Look at Moses."

Now she looked at him as if he'd taken leave of his senses. "What are you talking about, Father Tudor?"

Honestly, I've no idea. "Moses is a good example of a man who throughout his lifetime behaved with integrity. And he lived to be one hundred and twenty. I just don't want to condemn Lord Duxter on no evidence except that his age permits him to run around."

"I've just given you the evidence."

Max sighed, the sort of small, inaudible sigh that punctuated most of his conversations with Miss Pitchford. There was, he knew, no point in telling her that what she had shared with him was her opinion. The lord was perhaps not the most popular man but he was always friendly—there was that to be said for him. Although civil might be a better word. He was known, also, for his charitable contributions to good causes. When St. Alphege's in Monk's Crossing had needed its roof repaired he had offered to match funds for the drive. Not to mention the fact he'd been honored with that OBE. The Queen didn't hand out prizes like that lightly, one would assume. Although it had to be said, Mick Jagger was hardly a poster boy for the contemplative life, so perhaps that wasn't the strongest argument to use. Wisely, he kept these comments to himself, saying mildly, "Let's wait and see, shall we?"

"Wait and see. We'll all be murdered in our beds if that's the attitude the authorities take."

"DCI Cotton is looking into things. You can rest assured it will be all right in the end."

"It's not his first marriage, you know. Lord Duxter has been married be*fore*."

"I didn't know that. Well, thank you, that's very interesting, but surely not germane."

"He drove the wife to madness with his infidelities, his casual cruelties. It is said."

Max was not taking the bait labeled "It is said." Surely now they were in the land of rampant speculation.

"No one has ever seen the lord's first wife, you know. No one. They assume she's dead; he tells everyone she is dead. But she is really in an asylum. He divorced her, for madness."

It was news to Max that was grounds for divorce, but probably she meant some legal term related to incurable insanity. How horrible for her, if true. For Lord Duxter as well.

"She was removed from his house, never to be seen again. He

had her removed. There was madness in that family. Everybody knew it. Except the lord, poor man. He was duped into marrying her for her money. No one really blamed him if he had a roving eye. I know it's wrong, but the villagers felt he deserved some happiness."

Well, gosh. There was all of Jane Eyre condensed into digest format. Still, Max was astonished that Miss Pitchford could countenance such a liberal attitude toward these things. It was unlike her to look the other way over this sort of carry-on. Max marked it down to the lord's famous charm with the ladies—all ladies of any age, apparently.

He supposed he'd have to ask Cotton if any of it were true. The bare bones, probably. Just the bones would turn out to be true.

Chapter 15

WHEEL OF FORTUNE

The next day Poppy officially went missing. Max barely had time to open the study door in the vicarage before Jane burst in.

"Max!" She wore a long-sleeved dress of a striking color of blue, and it looked as though she'd recently had her hair professionally done, probably again at the Cut and Dried Salon. But her face was a hectic color, and her eyes looked swollen and red, practically bruised, from crying. This dress also looked as if it needed to be taken in. "Poppy has disappeared. Please, you must do something. I don't know—" She shook her head in confusion. "I don't know what I'm going to do. Without her." The last word was expelled on a sob. But Max sensed fear rather than sorrow in her aspect. This was a woman frightened half to death.

"Try to stay calm," said Max. "Here." And he directed her to one of the low chairs by the fireplace. "Tell me what happened. When did you last see her?"

"That's just it. I don't know, you see. I don't—she left for school at the usual time, I think, but she hasn't come home. I got back from the salon—" At this she looked guilty, as if she'd been caught in a pub crawl. "I just felt I needed a break, you know? With all that's been happening. A break! But now none of her friends have seen her."

"Stanley?"

"I rang him first thing. He says they had a fight. He claims he has no idea where she is now. I don't believe him."

"Have you told the police?"

"Well, no."

"No? But you must."

"I didn't like to do that. She'll be so upset and angry to know there's been a fuss made. She's like that, you know. So proud. Prickly. She would never l—" Jane dabbed at her eyes with a handkerchief, only making matters worse. Her eyes looked completely inflamed now. "She would never listen to me. But I know a thing or two about the trouble a young woman can stumble into, thinking she's invincible."

"But you are assuming she's alive and well. Just that she's taken off on a break of her own, to think things through."

"I don't know, am I?"

Max was recalling another girl who had gone missing in the woods well over a century before.

"We must let Cotton and his team know. They'll find her. She has a mobile phone?"

"Everyone that age has a mobile phone. They issue them at birth, it seems."

Max, reaching for a pen, said, "What's the number?"

She dug around in her purse and came up with her own phone. She pulled up Poppy's number on her screen and rattled it off.

Max thought it interesting that she didn't know the number for her stepdaughter off by heart, but then again, it was so easy to hit "reply" and not have to have memorized anything these days. Unlike spellcheck, the reply function reduced rather than increased the chance of errors. But Max didn't have any impression the two were close. Certainly not into exchanging text messages except to transmit essential information about expected arrivals and departures.

Max picked up the heavy Bakelite telephone on his study desk. As he dialed Cotton's number, he asked Jane: "You'll need to speak to Cotton yourself, but try to remember now: When exactly was the last time you saw her or heard from her?"

She was vague. "This morning perhaps? I tell you, I leave her to her own devices. She prefers things that way. There's less friction. Anyway. When I got home I could see she had taken some clothing and makeup but left her favorite posters behind. All these stupid band groups she likes."

"She could hardly travel with posters," Max observed. "Too awkward unless she folded them, ruining them in the process."

"She would never be separated from those posters voluntarily," Jane insisted.

"I understand your concern," said Max.

"You seem very complacent," Jane said. She crossed her arms and began vigorously rubbing her upper arms, as if to warm herself.

"Not at all. I'm very concerned for the child's safety. But let's not worry needlessly. I am sure she is quite safe. Quite sure. I can practically guarantee it: Poppy has all the sense needed to take herself out of harm's way."

But Jane clearly was upset, and now closer to hysteria. He would have said this was atypical behavior, and he could see it was not an act.

She got on the phone with Cotton, telling him what she knew. He seemed to have the same reaction as Max to her comments about the posters, for at one point she wailed, "But, they're her favorites!"

After a few minutes she turned to Max and said, handing him the receiver, "He wants to talk to you."

He took the phone, still warm from her hand, and listened as Cotton said, "Tell Jane we'll get search-and-rescue volunteers out in the woods to look for her stepdaughter."

Max turned to Jane and said, "They'll be starting the search right away. Before we lose the light." To Cotton, he said, "With dogs?"

"Certainly with dogs. Trailing dogs and air-scenting dogs."

"Thea would love to be part of that. Perhaps I can take her out with the searchers."

"I didn't know Thea was trained. That would be helpful—the more the better. And I'll see if I can't requisition a helicopter. We can't have a child go missing in the middle of all this, Max."

"Before you do that, let me call you from my mobile with some more information. All right?" He listened and added, "If the circumstances were different, perhaps we wouldn't be as worried. She's a teenager and rather a headstrong one. But with her father dead and her great-grandmother, it's too much . . ." He looked over at Jane, who nodded.

"I know," said Cotton. "The timing is not accidental. It couldn't be."

"We're assuming she just wandered into the woods." Again he looked at Jane, as if to make sure she was listening. "But of course she could have taken a train into Staincross Minster. From there she could have gone anywhere."

Jane mouthed the word "London." Max nodded.

"I know," Cotton said again. "Of course, we'll be looking into that angle."

"It's possible she just—I don't know. Felt it best to keep a low profile for now."

"Why do you say that?"

Max, who had turned away to look out the vicarage window, stole another glance over his shoulder at Jane.

"Really, I'm not sure I can say right now. I suppose I'd rather think Poppy is in hiding or even off on a sulk than think she's—you know. Rather than assume the worst. Again, I'll ring you back in a few, all right? And of course let us know . . ."

Max rang off after a few minutes. He turned to Jane, who was pacing the floor in front of the fireplace, and he offered her the usual British panacea, a cup of tea. She accepted distractedly and after a few minutes had collected herself enough to sit before the fire, staring unseeing into its flames. She sat in the very chair Poppy had vacated not all that long before.

An hour had passed, and as there had been no word of Poppy, Jane had grown progressively more distraught. "Oh, this is all my fault," she had said, more than once.

Everything in her behavior seemed unmoored and out of character. She stood up several times, saying, "I really must go. She might be at home." Max, wanting to keep an eye on her, persuaded her that Cotton would be more likely to call the vicarage if there were news. She seemed to be coming unglued before his very eyes. The tissues Max had handed her, several times in fact, were in shreds, used less to dab fiercely at her eyes now than as a sort of stress ball.

She spent part of the time wandering the room, perusing the shelves of the study, her mind clearly elsewhere. It had to be said there was little on those shelves to interest even a professional archivist. Max had inherited most of the musty old volumes from his predecessor. He wondered if she'd notice the Blackwood books.

At an earlier point he had excused himself to ring Cotton as promised, from another room. He had also rung Awena to fill her in. He had then returned to his study to resume fitful work on his sermon but in truth she was such a distracting element in the room, he finally put the pages aside—yet again.

"How is it your fault?" Max finally asked her. He rose from his desk, rejoining her at the fireplace where she sat in a dejected pose, literally wringing her hands, rocking herself back and forth, lightly keening. A quickening wind made a haunting sound, too, as it whistled round the top of the chimney. Max spoke in measured words in a low tone, hoping she would match her mood to his own. In the silence she might realize how out of true her behavior was. She hadn't mourned for her husband like this.

She looked up at him, somewhat in surprise, as if she was not used to anyone taking time for her like this. She stared at this solemn, well-intended vicar for a long moment, seeming to reach a decision. She said, "I—I wasn't honest with you when we spoke before. I considered it all to be no one's business but my own. This village—well, you know how they are in the village. Busybodies, all of them. Busybodies. But now, if we're to find Poppy, I have to say. I have to be clear and tell what I know about—things. Things that might have set Poppy off. It's the only way. I see that now."

"And what is that?" he asked. "What is it you want to tell, Jane?"

"It's just this: I knew . . . I knew about the affair, you see. Colin's affair with Marina. Well, to be completely clear, I suspected there was something between them. The way she hung on his every word. But with Colin gone so much, it was hard to see it as ongoing, you know. I think—no, I'm certain; I know—Lord Duxter sent Colin away to put an end to it. To their being together. It doesn't appear to have worked. Absence making the heart grow fonder and all that." She looked at Max intently, willing him to understand. As if this were a burden she had lived with for too long, and she welcomed the chance to free herself of the worry. Or at least to share what had been bothering her.

The one thing we all want most, Max reflected, is just that. Not so much fame, not so much riches, but to be understood by at least one other living soul. It had been obvious to Max that something had been going very wrong in Jane's world, and in Poppy's, and for some time.

"I wasn't worried about it, you see," she added. "And for Poppy's sake, I should have been."

"What do you mean?" he asked. "You didn't see Lady Duxter as a threat to your marriage?"

"If I'm honest, no. Perhaps I should have been less complacent, less egotistical—less whatever it was that shielded me from the truth. But so far as I knew, Colin was planning to quit his job in Saudi, just as soon as he'd built up some savings, and we were going to move away once he did. Especially since his mother was getting so old, and then of course she died . . . well, there was nothing keeping us here."

"How did Poppy feel about these plans? She would have had to change schools. And then, there's Stanley she'd be leaving behind."

"I don't think she was aware of our plans. We treated her like a child in that respect. And now I regret not taking her into my confidence about things that affected her. Do you know, in spite of everything, in spite of all the nonsense with the hair dye and so on, Poppy is basically a good girl. We just assumed she would fall into line—for her father's sake. How arrogant of us! But we told ourselves we'd take care not to move her in midterm or anything too upsetting like that."

"What does all this have to do with her disappearance?"

"I think she knew, too," said Jane miserably. "About the affair."

Max, remembering all those pregnancy kits, was tempted to ask, "Which one?" but he kept his own counsel along with a bland expression on his face. He allowed himself a small lift of the eyebrows and said merely, "Did she have any suspicions? About Colin's—let's call it a proclivity for suicide? When a child is given to hero worship, as I gather Poppy was, it can be an extra letdown to learn . . ."

"To learn a father has feet of clay?" Jane asked. "Yes, I know what you mean. With Colin it was a bit hard to tell what he was thinking. Still waters, you know. His mother's supposed suicide really messed with his head. Actually, there was not a lot of question that her death was a suicide. But apart from that, apart from the sort of emotional void inside him, he was as clever as could be. In fact, he was a genius, everyone said so. And for that reason, he was perhaps a bit hard to follow. A bit hard to live with. What he didn't know about cybersecurity just hadn't been invented yet. But depressed? If he was he kept it well hidden. Keeping his feelings buttoned up—well, that was just second nature to him. I blame his mother for that, as well."

"And how so?" Although Max thought he knew the answer.

"She was cold, distant—very secretive. She made a secret of the silliest things, he told me. Where she was going, and who with, and when she'd be back. She never talked about her past, completely shutting him out. I never got any impression that her children— Colin had a sister; she lives in Devon somewhere . . . Oh, dear, I suppose I must phone her about Poppy now. It flew right out of my head. I don't think I can cope with any more of this!"

"If that news would be better coming from a sort of disinterested party, I'd be glad to call on your behalf."

"Oh, would you? It's that—I barely know her. She was at our wedding, and we exchange Christmas cards and the like, but I don't have a real sense of her. Just what Colin told me—that they endured a fairly wretched childhood with a superficial woman not really cut out to raise children. Colin said once they were her props—just as everyone said Netta made props of her own children. But he was angry at the time and that just came out. He never said anything like it again. I do know he thinks—sorry, thought—his sister was sort of damaged and he avoided her. He felt sorry for her but he couldn't cope—he said he had his own problems. I don't think I can either, if she falls apart at the news—she couldn't even pull herself together to make it to Netta's funeral. So, yes, I'd really appreciate your help."

Since helping people was ostensibly why he was there, help he would. But his conversation with Jane had raised more questions in his mind than answers. If the affair between Colin and Marina was real, was their suicide attempt real, too? Had he and Cotton set off on the wrong track altogether?

Cotton would soon supply some answers that only muddied the equation.

Chapter 16

THE CHARIOT

The night passed without news of Poppy.

Later that same evening, Jane finally had insisted on returning to Hawthorne Cottage, quite alone, refusing further offers of help. Also offers of dinner and breakfast invitations from Max and Awena. "If Poppy calls or comes home, that is where I need to be," she'd said. "I am quite used to being on my own, and I would prefer it now. Please don't let's make a fuss."

Nonetheless, Max rang his curate as soon as Jane left the vicarage, asking Destiny to stop in at the cottage and check on Jane that evening, on whatever pretext she could dream up. "She can't be alone," said Max. "Keep an eye on her, please. But for the moment, let's do more or less as she asks. In a few more days things should look a little brighter."

"How can you know that?" Destiny asked. "With the child missing?"

"I suppose," said Max, "because for Jane, things couldn't look much worse, now could they? And I actually think it's as well Poppy is out of the way for the moment." Max peeked out from behind the curtain to where a biscuit moon kept watch over the village. "Until we know what's going on."

The next morning DCI Cotton appeared at Max and Awena's cottage as they were taking turns feeding Owen his breakfast. Cotton stopped to ruffle the soft, downy hair on Owen's head.

"I've got something I want you to see, Max," he said. "Morning, Awena."

Max invited Cotton into the sitting room, carrying in coffee mugs for both of them.

"We've got some new evidence," said Cotton without preamble. "Evidence captured by CCTV."

"CCTV? There are no security cameras around the priory."

"No there aren't, worse luck. But this footage didn't come from the priory. Our robbery team was scanning footage in connection with some recent holdups outside the Sainsbury's on the High in Monkslip-super-Mare. One of the sharper lads noticed something else—rather, someone else. They'd been captured on film in a nearby alleyway that the team thought was being used as an escape route by the robbers."

"Yes? And?"

"Well, wait for it." He paused. Cotton had spent much of his childhood backstage in theaters where his mother was performing. Sometimes, this early exposure to drama showed.

"I'm waiting," said Max.

"It was Lady Duxter."

"Marina? Taking a shortcut to the parking garage, perhaps." Max knew that particular Sainsbury's well. If a shopper didn't exit at the back there was an alternate route to the car park via the alley

Cotton described. That store was where he and Awena generally did the "big" shopping for dry goods. Even Awena had sometimes to allow the convenience of paper products, so long as everything they bought was of a recycled brand.

Cotton shook his head. "That's as may well be, that she was on her way to the garage, but where she was headed was beside the point. She was with a man. And it is evident from the footage that they were lovers."

Well, thought Max, *we knew she had a lover.* But from the look on Cotton's face, that wasn't his news. He had been saving a surprise for Max—a surprise he wanted Max to help him pick apart. "When was the footage taken?"

"About a week before she was found with Colin."

Taking it from the look on Cotton's face, Max said, "And it was not Colin she was with in the CCTV footage."

"No, most definitely it was not. It was not Colin Frost. It was Carville Rasmussen."

Ah. The writer staying in the old church at the priory. Ostensibly "polishing his manuscript."

"Interesting," said Max. "Have you spoken with him yet?"

"I was just on my way. Do you want to come with me?"

"Are you serious? Of course. Let me grab my coat and say good-bye to Awena and Owen."

Unorthodox as it was, Max had sat in on dozens of interviews with Cotton or a member of his team. He was by now considered to be a sort of unofficial mascot on many an investigation, bringing luck in apprehending the bad guys.

But luck, Cotton knew, had nothing to do with it. Max had an uncanny ability to notice what others missed, and to draw out of suspects things they'd rather were kept undisturbed. Or things they knew of great importance that they didn't realize were important.

"All right," said Cotton. "Let's go."

Cotton drove expertly through the narrow lanes of Monkslip Mallow on the way to the priory.

"Apparently this Carville person rated his own separate accommodation," he explained, slowing as he drew up behind a tractor. "It's a bit of a secluded spot but not far from the main priory building."

"I know," said Max, settling his sunglasses case on the car's console. The day, which had started out sunny, had turned overcast.

Like everything else in Cotton's world, his car was spotless. No junk or random papers thrown about. No empty paper cups or wrappers. He probably wiped it clean of prints at the end of every working day, before returning home to Patrice and their daughter, Alexis. How Cotton managed with an infant in the house Max couldn't begin to guess. He probably walked around the place with his feet covered in crime scene booties. His love for Alexis was immense, and he never complained about the upset to his routine.

"Most likely," Cotton continued, trying to peer around the tractor, "Carville made a contribution to the upkeep of the place. These crumbling old piles cost the moon in maintenance, or so I am told. Even Lord Duxter of Monkslip probably finds making ends meet to be a bit of a challenge."

"When did people stop reading?"

"They never stopped, not really. They just started reading on screens and no one quite knows how to turn a profit from that. E-books seem so ephemeral. Here we are."

Cotton slowed the car to a crawl as they neared the front door of the old church, less to conceal their arrival than to stem the waves of gravel being thrown up by the tires. The author apparently heard their crunchy approach, for before long he stood waiting at the entrance. Indeed, he looked delighted by the distraction, an impression he confirmed by saying, once introductions had been exchanged, "I am very glad of your company at the moment. Philip Delaplante is the biggest ninny ever invented and I regret every day having invented him. Do come in."

"That is your series character, is it?" Max asked, looking about him at the cozy interior nestling inside the old stone walls. The pews and altar had been removed, of course, and what was left was a large, imposing space with a soaring ceiling. The area was broken up by various rugs and sitting groups and tables scattered about. In the middle, in pride of place under a skylight fashioned from the sides of the central steeple, stood an enormous refectory table currently in use as a desk, with papers, pens, and other implements of the writing trade on display. Max saw no laptop or computer, which surely was unusual in this day and age. Carville seemed to rely on writing with the old-fashioned ink of the days when the church originally had been built. Max never ceased to wonder at the masterpieces that had been composed using only quill and ink.

"I understand you are here working on a new novel," said Max, adding, with more than a twinge of envy: "What a perfect setup you have for that."

"That's the idea, but you've caught me on a slow day. So much going on—it's hard to concentrate. That girl gone missing, and all the rest . . . At least, that's been my excuse today. Tomorrow there will be another."

"You've been here how long, sir?" Cotton asked him.

"About a month."

"And no laptop to distract you?" said Max. "I'm impressed." He himself wrote his sermons and saw to parish business on a computer that had been state of the art perhaps ten years previous. Sitting as large as a small refrigerator on his desk, the computer smugly rejected all invitations to update itself, however couched in dire warnings those invitations came from its maker. Max felt there was safety in knowing that only the most inept cyber thief would attempt to hack such a crumbling relict and probably would not have tools old enough even to attempt it. He still used the oldest viable version of Word available and so long as it allowed him to highlight key passages of his narrative and use different-colored fonts he told himself he was content. He also relied heavily on the backspace key when his sermons wandered too far off the path.

Money for office upgrades always seemed to end up being spent on food or shelter for a parishioner in some temporary distress and so, he felt, it should be.

"The conditions are ideal, actually," Carville Rasmussen was saying. "There's no Wi-Fi signal that reaches out here to the church, which is a blessing. I do have a laptop, but I've largely set it aside. People have forgotten what it is to use a pen and paper to write. It slows the thought processes and, I believe, makes for a better book. The people staying at the house all have access to Wi-Fi, and I see them on their phones all day, wasting time that should be devoted to listening to their Muse."

"Ah," said Max, wondering if it also made keeping the book at a manageable size more or less difficult. But they were here on other errands. Cotton, apparently feeling he had used enough soap to soften Carville's ego by this point, asked bluntly, "When, sir, were you planning to tell us about the true nature of your relationship with Lady Duxter?"

Carville dropped into a chair, as if his legs suddenly could not hold him, and all the small talk in the world could not shield him from his new reality.

"How did you find out?"

"I'll be happy to share the police report with you if you'd like to read it, sir," said Cotton. Seeing Carville's expression, he added, "That was a joke. The point is, we know all about it. You were seen by what I'll call a reliable witness. The evidence is irrefutable. I would advise you to tell us what *you* know about this tragic situation. Anything else at this point will be obstruction. Certainly when my sergeant interviewed you, you said nothing about your connection to Lady Duxter."

"Of course," said Carville. "Of course I want to help. I'll do anything. But you see: I said nothing in the first instance because this suicide business with Colin stunned me. It also just plain confused me. I couldn't believe she was having an affair with both of us, running two men at once. But was that just my ego talking?" He tugged at the rollneck collar of his dark Hemingway jumper as if suddenly it constricted him.

It was a self-aware comment from a man who was hardly known for self-awareness, thought Max. But if Carville had known he had a rival for Marina's affections, how would he have taken it? Probably not well.

"I said nothing also because it would upset Lord Duxter to no purpose," Carville continued, "and it would make it sound as if his wife were just, you know, sleeping around all over the place. Why would I want to ruin her reputation and his image of her in that way?"

"That was considerate of you, sir," said Cotton, still unfailingly polite. "But your silence wasted police time. We have apparently been haring after the wrong, well, hare."

"I know. And I believe that, too: she would *not* have been with Colin *and* with me. And furthermore, more to the point, she had just been shopping in London."

"I beg your pardon?"

"She had just been shopping in London for new shoes and makeup. What woman does that as she prepares to kill herself? She showed me the shoes. I couldn't believe what she paid for them, but that's beside the point. It proves she was not planning to end her own life. No woman would go out and buy extravagant items one day and then try to kill herself in practically the next instant." Carville visibly puffed his chest as he said, "I'm an expert on characterization and I tell you, no woman would do that. A *Telegraph* reviewer said my books leap off the page because of the lively characters, and Kerridge is a man who knows characterization when he sees it. He called *Scott's Bungalow* 'brilliant' and 'a staggering work.'"

Carville warbled complacently on in this fashion, reliving his career highs and lows. He seemed to be able to quote verbatim from every positive review he'd ever received, while questioning the intelligence, morals, and antecedents of anyone who had given him a less-than-glowing review. He seemed to have a particular grudge against some Dubrovnik-based publication called the *Publishers' Clarion*, which he condemned as "jingoistic tripe."

While he waited for Carville to run out of petrol, in a manner of speaking, Max was thinking that depression was a strange animal. If Marina was bipolar, he supposed she might have done something just that illogical: spend too much on shoes and then, in an emotional crash, kill herself. Illogic might be at the core of the symptoms. But he was willing to admit he was no expert on this topic.

He also doubted that Carville could possibly be as certain of her motivations as he claimed—author with keen insight into character or no. What worked in a novel might be miles distant from the nitty-gritty facts of real life.

"What color were the shoes?" Cotton wanted to know.

"They were blue," Carville replied promptly. "Blue suede with a very high heel and red undersoles. As I say, hideously expensive."

Max knew that Cotton asked the question as a sort of double-check, because Marina had been found wearing such shoes.

Max noticed that Carville spoke loudly and rapidly, like a man making an awards acceptance speech who was afraid someone was going to come and rip the microphone and the award out of his hands. Possibly he'd had a bad experience or two with this very sort of thing in the past. He was often winning or being nominated for awards for his page-turning, characterization-stuffed novels. And for every author who spends most days toiling alone, such occasions offer a too-brief spot in the sunlight before the author is once again consigned to months of solitude and drudgery. Not to mention the opinions of jingoistic rags.

"Some crime writer," said Cotton, as the two men walked away, leaving Carville Rasmussen with head in hand, contemplating the twists in the plot of his own life and finding them, presumably, satisfyingly complex.

"That may be part of the problem," Max replied once they were safely out of range. "Carville's always seeing plots where there are none. It's his job."

"A sort of professional paranoia?"

"Yes, indeed. I saw it all the time in Five. When you live your life jumping at shadows, suspecting everyone . . . it's not healthy, and the tendency sort of bleeds at the edges into your real life."

Max rarely talked of his former career. Cotton gathered he was much happier away from those constant shadows. Although it had to be said, the county of Monkslip was shaping up to be as full of shadows as his old life.

"I go round and back to how Colin and Marina ended up in that car together and I just can't see it," Max said to Awena on his return home that evening. Cotton had dropped Max off at the vicarage with a promise to ring him later. He was keeping tabs on a few things and Max asked to be kept informed as much as possible.

"Here," she said, setting a cup of tea before him. "Have some tea while I finish this chapter. I made it from eyebright. It's an herb that clears the thinking. And it helps you trust in what you already know."

He took a sip. "It tastes nice, anyway."

"The beta-carotenes in the brew help your thinking processes. You'll see. Literally, you'll be able to see."

Finishing the tea a few minutes later, he put down his cup and saucer and said, "I think I'll pop into the church for a minute. I want to make sure all is secure for the night."

It was a fact of modern-day life that churches, even St. Edwold's, could not be left unlocked all day, as once they had been, so people in need of a quiet moment could stop in on impulse. The risk of vandalism was too great, even in Nether Monkslip, which was no longer the tiny backwater it once had been.

"Yes," she said, not looking up from her work. "Someone might break in to steal that new stained-glass window."

"Please," said Max. "I'd almost forgotten about it."

Max made the short walk over to the church, thinking how grateful he was that despite the village's small population, St. Edwold's continued to thrive, at the same time so many churches across England were being closed to worship each year. The Priory Church of St. George where Carville now churned out his masterpieces was a perfect example. Dwindling numbers of British identified as Christians, but in Nether Monkslip the church was a social center as much as a place of spiritual rest and renewal. Max was more than happy that so many of all faiths felt they were welcome there.

Besides, who would deny the power of belief in healing—mind, body, or spirit? If an hour of contemplation or a visit to any of the world's shrines heals the believer, what doctor would call the cure bogus? A cure is a cure. Awena's powers were—he hesitated to use the word supernatural. But they went beyond the reach of most of humankind. He had seen it for himself, experienced it for himself. He disliked the term applied to her beliefs—neo-pagan, an umbrella word covering a wide field of nature- or earth-based beliefs and practices. Certainly she didn't belong to a group or cult; her beliefs were her own—private and, he gathered, as idiosyncratic and individual as she was. She maintained a dedicated meditation space in their cottage, a space Max regarded as sacrosanct. However, as Awena herself said, there was nothing "neo" or new about the connection to beliefs that predated Christianity. For his part, he cherished her because she was a person nearly devoid of negativity, and her belief in another, better world beyond this one was absolute and unwavering. Unlike Max's own. He aligned more often than not with those who prayed, "Lord, I believe; help thou mine unbelief."

Max unlocked the church door, which had duly been locked by the verger, and walked up the nave of the tiny church. It rested gleaming and immaculate in the jewel-like glow cast through the windows by the setting sun. The offending glass was still there, of course, leaning against the wall, waiting for him to deal with it, but he felt he was becoming somewhat reconciled to the artist's vision. After all, goats were God's creations, too, and there was nothing firmly against the idea of Christ being a shepherd of goats as well as sheep. The entire story of the Good Shepherd was simply a metaphor for God's caring, of course. Max even began to see that what had struck him as malevolent in the creature's eyes now looked all-seeing and wise.

However, having learned that lesson about the need to be less dogmatic, he still planned to have a word with the artist Coombebridge.

Perhaps something could be done. It seemed a far lesser priority at the moment.

He sat in a pew to the left of the altar and composed himself, giving thanks for what he recognized as his many blessings and replaying in his mind all the events of the day. Autumn flowers adorned the altar in many shades of yellow and gold and orange, all part of the stately procession that marked the seasons. Some of the flowers had been left over from Netta's funeral, the formal arrangements harvested and refreshed with new blossoms. It was in the spring that the women of the altar guild outdid themselves, bringing flowers from their own gardens, turning the place into a riot of colors. Max had started offering Taize services every spring, at Awena's urging—meditative singing prayer.

Last season's robins had looked harassed, Max remembered: They'd been tricked into spring because winter, like an overstaying guest, would not leave. Instead it came and went, came and went. And then summer arrived seemingly at once, with a cloying heat. Nether Monkslip, usually the most temperate of places, had suffered greatly.

A phrase from a Shakespearean sonnet came to him: "From you have I been absent in the spring." He recalled the past spring when he had been absent from Awena, helping Cotton solve a case in Monkslip-super-Mare, and how it did seem like a dark winter, to be yearning constantly for the sight of her and Owen, and to be shot through with a haunting dread he might not see either of them again.

With the remembrance of spring his thoughts circled round to his sermon, still in half-completed stage; he was beginning to think he needed to put it aside for one of his standby sermons, a sort of generic good-versus-evil evergreen recap that he wheeled out for emergencies. The story of Bathsheba haunted him, being as it was about an essentially good man succumbing to temptation, for no good reason than because he could, power corrupting absolutely. The tale of Bathsheba began in the spring, when the kings went out to battle. Only King David had stayed behind . . .

His sermon needed a stirring conclusion about how easily we are misled when we obey only our desires. About the pure selfishness of David, which was so out of character for him, really. And the steep unhappiness his selfishness, his lapse from grace, had brought him.

Absent in the Spring had also been the title of one of Agatha Christie's books, one of her rare departures from writing mysteries. In it, a woman briefly discovers her true nature, only to in the end— probably—lapse back into forgetfulness and routine, losing the insights so painfully gained. As Max recalled, whether or not the truth of the discoveries would stay with her, changing her forever, was where the mystery lay. It was a mystery of the heart, then. Of human nature. And mankind's endless capacity to deceive itself. All of her books concerned the mysteries of the human heart, but none so strikingly as *Absent in the Spring*. Agatha had said it was the one book she wrote in which she was entirely satisfied with the result. And she'd written it in three days.

Max, who had struggled endlessly with this Bathsheba sermon of his, could only envy her.

These reminders of spring pulled him up short. But why now? It was autumn now, and spring had been unremarkable except for the changeable weather—which had become the norm in England, as around the globe. The summer following that unstable spring had been blazing hot, a recent and unpleasant memory Max had no problem calling to mind. How his dark shirt had seemed to smother him, and how his clerical collar had chafed at his neck. But how, too, his happiest moments had been spent with Owen in the swimming pool in Staincross Minster, teaching him to swim. The child took to it naturally, splashing about like a dolphin in no fear of the water, while some of the other children had screamed down heaven at getting their toes wet. Max had been rather smug about his son's ability, as he so often was bursting with pride of his beloved offspring, but he made up for it by telling the small lie to the other parents that he had been training Owen at home in the bathtub.

So, spring, summer, now autumn. Suddenly last summer . . . had something changed with the summer? So far as people attached to the murder investigation were concerned, the biggest life change had been Colin's, with the move to Saudi Arabia—adapting to a new job in a new culture, and no doubt missing his familiar surroundings. Lady Duxter had gone about her business much the same as always, to all appearances. A bit wan and drifty, nothing obviously startling happening in her day-to-day. The summer was when the writers' center began opening its doors to what Lord Duxter rather inanely called the deserving poor—the writers who came to him for peace and succor in their labors.

No, try as he might, Max could not get to the bottom of what was troubling him, but he believed Colin's sudden absence and equally sudden return in the autumn for his grandmother's funeral might be the only events of any moment in the otherwise sleepy village.

Colin's return had been time sensitive, to be sure, and Lord Duxter had had a hand in making the complicated arrangements for a foreigner who needed quickly to leave Saudi. Netta having died, arrangements had to be made, yes. But his wife Jane was here handling things. Why the hurry to get Colin home practically the next day? People, Max reminded himself, all dealt with grief in different ways. Certainly, if his own mother died, God forbid it, he would want Awena and other members of his family at his side, as quickly as could be arranged.

One member of his parish had actually organized the funeral of her mother in great haste, so that her brother, who lived at a distance, would not have time to make arrangements to attend. He never understood that—had there been some old score to settle? Some bitter rivalry for the mother's affections? But ever since Max had fallen for it and gone ahead and held the funeral (the woman had not told him she had a brother), he had been acutely sensitive to relatives who were in any sort of rush over the funeral arrangements.

In the end he decided he might go and have a talk with Jane tomorrow, to try to get a sense of what her husband had been feeling about the changes in his circumstances. What his life in Saudi Arabia had been like. Had he been doing well at his new job? Had he adapted to the place or had he found it all to be too big a culture clash? The death of his grandmother must have been upsetting, if not unexpected. How any of this could lead to death by his own hand, however, Max wasn't able to decipher. Or to murder, for that matter. What was odd was that Colin had been away so much—hardly ideal circumstances in which to conduct an affair. Perhaps that had been part of the problem, the vast distances, once love had struck.

Max wondered when the affair had begun. *If* it had begun. That was hardly something he could come right out with and ask Jane Frost, was it? Not if he expected an honest reply.

Luther the church cat came padding out from where he'd been hiding and did something he seldom did: he came and sat by Max, as if to offer comfort. Together they sat staring at the altar flowers, those flowers in remembrance of Netta.

Chapter 17

THE DEVIL

The next day Max was at his desk balancing the parish accounts, but within five minutes into the "outgo" columns he was interrupted. It proved to be one of those days when he felt he needed a revolving front door on the vicarage.

It was Lord Duxter—the man, it seemed to Max, at the very heart of what had happened. *Up pops the devil.* The thought rose unbidden in Max's mind.

David, Lord Duxter, had blown right past Mrs. Hooser to enter the room unannounced. Mrs. Hooser got her revenge by making a rude gesture at the lord's back. She left without offering to bring tea and somehow Max thought it better not to ask her for any.

He and Lord Duxter quickly settled in the low chairs before the fireplace. Max had come to think of the place as his confessional.

"I am deeply troubled, Max," Lord Duxter began. "And I don't know what to do."

"Over your wife's situation, of course. Naturally, you are. But there is hope, isn't there? There is always hope. I pray daily for her full recovery. What do the doctors say?"

Lord Duxter ignored the question, rushing on to pour out what was in his mind. "Yes, of course, but more—I'm more upset at the manner in which she was found. The circumstances."

Found with another man dead beside her, her apparent lover—yes, that idea would take some getting used to for a grieving spouse. But Max sensed that was not entirely what was on Lord Duxter's mind.

"My wife was . . . a very disturbed woman, Max. Highly strung, given to these episodes of depression for which there seemed to be no cure. I say episodes but really, they were epic plunges into despair. There is no question that she was a challenge to live with. But do you know, I loved her in spite of it all."

"Of course you did," said Max. "Do," he corrected himself.

"No one will believe that, especially now, but it's true. She was a romantic, but quite intelligent with it—someone along the lines of Virginia Woolf, I always thought. But solid underneath it all, do you understand? Underneath all the, well, the drama and silliness? And quite, quite loyal to me. I never doubted her on that score: her faithfulness."

Max, who had had quite a different impression of Marina, held his tongue. This was the man's wife, and his view might be as valid as anyone's, if not more so. But Max having been her confessor, in a manner of speaking, this entire conversation rather put him in a spot. She had never confessed to an affair, to be sure, but her unhappiness in her marriage was no secret, certainly not from her vicar. Wan and wraith thin, she had sat where her husband sat now, using Max as a sounding board as she debated how to cope with what she perceived as her husband's titanic indifference. She knew, or believed, that her husband had married her for her money. That he had in fact been forced into the match by his father, "the greedy old sot"—her words.

"So when she was found with Colin," Lord Duxter went on, "I was flabbergasted. Absolutely floored. I tell you, I never saw any sign that anything like that was going on. She was devoted to me *utt*erly. So this affair with Colin—what nonsense. It can't be true, you do see. Because, she would never do that to me. Not to *me*. The scene must be staged somehow."

"Staged."

"Yes, man. *Staged*." He pounded the arm of his chair for emphasis, turning red and looking like Owen when he wanted to be released from his high chair. "He was murdered and someone attempted to murder my wife, and that's all there is to it. Or Colin murdered her or tried to or thought he had and then took his own life."

Well, that was a theory, and it was not without some interest to Max or the police, who had got there long before. But as evidence or proof of anything it was a theory full of holes. For here was Lord Duxter's ego on full display. It was almost as if another person had come into the room, someone dressed in cloth of gold and a cloak of peacock feathers, like some potentate from a bygone day. His wife could not have killed herself because she adored her husband. And she adored her husband because he was so adorable.

Max didn't discount altogether what Lord Duxter was saying, but it would need a lot more "proof" than that this man's ego had been bruised.

And didn't this ego business sound familiar—didn't it just? Why do women always seem to fall in love with the same type of man, over and over again? But at least the writer Carville had had the humility to wonder if his ego had been involved in Marina's downfall. Unlike David, who seemed to assume his very wonderfulness shielded him from the charge.

Now Lord Duxter was saying, "And there's something more. We were told at the inquest that Marina and Colin had been listening to music in that car, but later I was told it was Mahler. Marina hated Mahler, and no matter how depressed she got, she would never choose that to be the last sound she would hear on earth. And I doubt if someone like Colin had ever even heard of Mahler. I knew something was up but the cop I was talking to was a bit of a booby, and I wasn't sure he'd pass along the word. So I rang DCI Cotton. Sound man. He said he'd look into it, that they were considering every angle."

Max thought this bit about the music was a telling point but difficult to prove after the fact. He was almost afraid to ask, but: "Why would Colin do that? Stage a suicide?"

"Oh, I don't know, do I, dammit?" Lord Duxter thundered. "Do you think I haven't asked myself that over and over? That's for the goddam police to sort out. The man liked doing magic tricks. Maybe this was just one more. He was an IT type, a techie—their minds work that way. Never the straight path, oh no, not when some circuitous route will do. I'm just telling you what I know is true. And you can believe it or not. But tell your friend Cotton from me: my wife certainly did not have an affair with Colin"—his voice dripped with distaste at the name: *Co*-lin—"and she most certainly did not try to commit suicide, either."

Max had noticed before that Lord Duxter could not bear to have anything he said questioned. And to do so was to provoke this sort of explosive reaction. Poor Marina, having to live with this. He remembered the rumors had gone round—still were going round at Elka's, like sifted flour floating in the air—that Lord Duxter had "sent" Colin overseas to get rid of him. In fact, to get him away from his wife. That the pair of them had been found together in a suicide pact certainly lent credence to the rumors. Their love had been thwarted. Colin had had no choice but to accept the job, having been unemployed for so long. But it meant distance from her for long stretches at a time. As Cotton had theorized, they simply saw the futility of their liaison: Lady Duxter had access to little of her own wealth, thanks to her husband using her money to keep his publishing empire afloat. So for the two lovers, for the time being, for the foreseeable future, these long separations would be the norm. And that had tipped an already unstable woman over the edge.

It didn't entirely explain Colin's tipping over with her, but according to his known family history he had his own issues with instability. Which was why he had lost his job and been unemployed for so long in the first place—if those rumors were true. That downward spiral that caught so many in its coils.

Max thought it through. According to what Cotton had told him initially and in later conversations, the two lovers were found to have been drugged by one of Marina's many prescription drugs. The coroner had determined they had attempted to commit suicide, one of them successfully, using the drugs and the carbon monoxide to make sure one or the other, or both factors together, would prove fatal.

The lord stood abruptly and, placing his hands on the mantelpiece, stretched his arms out, standing back to view the flames. Turning suddenly, he said, "Truly, I am flummoxed. I suspected my wife was slightly infatuated with Colin, if you want the truth." That would be nice, thought Max. "But I didn't realize it was reciprocated to this extent. Not at all."

"This came out of the blue, then, did it, sir?"

It was here that Lord Duxter stumbled from his former barbed confidence. "I can't say it was a complete surprise—the affair, I mean, not the—you know. The attempt. Not all this."

"She never said? Never asked for a divorce, expressed her unhappiness, demanded that you pack and leave?"

"I? Why should I go anywhere? It's my house." Paid for with her money, but never mind, thought Max. "Oh, she expressed her un-happiness all the time. It was a sort of generalized thing. My wife was a depressive, I tell you. It's an illness like any other, like gout or hives or something. I learned to live with it as best I could. I did love her in my way. I *do* love her. But it wasn't always easy, living with someone like her, with an illness like hers."

"Who was treating her? Dr. Winship?"

"No, no. She was a private patient of Dr. Prothmeyer in Monkslip-super-Mare. He's a specialist in treating diseases of the mind."

Max decided to go for broke, watching carefully for the man's reaction. He had only Poppy's word to go on, and Poppy was hardly a disinterested witness to her stepmother's goings-on.

"Is that how your affair with Jane started?" he asked bluntly. "When Lady Duxter appeared to be slipping into madness?"

He braced himself for a barrage of disavowals, but those preg-nancy tests needed an explanation, and Lord Duxter was in close proximity to Jane every day. The man who, like King David, had ar-ranged to send her husband away. There weren't any other candidates that fit the bill so precisely, and Carville was out of the running. But Max was still puzzled by the lord's attraction to Jane. Max berated himself for thinking in clichés, but since Max had first known her, Jane was no one's idea of a femme fatale. She only recently seemed to be coming out of her chrysalis, taking extra care with her appear-ance. That blue dress, the hair appointments.

He watched as the lord struggled with the easy denial. Full of bluster at all times, he was at the same time a terrible liar, his face reflecting a cascade of emotions, with embarrassment finally win-ning out. Lord Duxter had certainly been put through the wringer by recent events. Would he emerge a changed man? Or would he, like Agatha's character Joan in *Absent in the Spring*, soon forget the insights gained?

There are, Max reflected, liars who lie to make themselves or their children—extensions of themselves—look good. Then there are liars who lie to damage others. The false witnesses—these are the most destructive. Although the first brand leave a mark, too, especially on their children. Max thought Lord Duxter was of this first brand of liar. Faint praise, indeed.

"Tell me how it started," Max prodded, realizing he'd hit the bull's-eye. "You and Jane."

Slowly, the truth came trickling out. Lord Duxter's face was the red of a sunset as he said—quietly, for him: "Perhaps I was bewitched. Do you believe that is possible? Well, perhaps you do. Not that your wife is a witch, not exactly, but you know what I mean."

"Awena is a Wiccan," said Max steadfastly. "She does *not* practice witchcraft. Wicca is a pagan religion, an earth-based faith." So many people had harebrained ideas about what that meant in reality. Any religion that wasn't strictly mainstream, that didn't involve steeples and temples or mosques, was dismissed outright, which always made Max bristle with annoyance.

"Anyway," said Lord Duxter, "if you saw Jane at night beside that lake, you would understand my reaction." His expression was that of a man entranced at the memory. "I saw her by starlight, you see. From the turret."

Starlight. Well, that explained it. "Go on."

"She was in Prior's Wood, by the pond. It was a clear, moonlit night and she was kneeling by the water, as if in prayer," said Lord Duxter. "I had the odd conviction that was exactly what she was doing—praying, or performing some sort of incantation, making some offering. Perhaps reviving some ancient rite that had long been banished by the forces of Christendom. I know that sounds . . . odd, but that was the effect this had on me. She wore a robe of deep blue, some shiny material embroidered with arcane symbols in silver thread. She scattered about some leaves or herbs she took from a bowl and plunged her hands in the water three times. All I knew was that it was something pagan, a ritual from prehistory. I became convinced—I still am convinced—that before writing or representational art, before the Church or any sort of sanctioned religion had taken hold in Monkslip, women had come to this forest to perform this ritual. And later, much later, when it was dangerous to do so, they came in secret. At least, that was my fanciful thought. I tell you, I was bewitched."

"What sort of ritual was it?"

He shook his head. "I've no idea. I've never seen anything like it and she never would say. Does it matter? It was some sort of hocus-pocus. She had that much in common with Colin. Colin and his parlor tricks.

"Anyway, I was mesmerized. Hypnotized by the grace of her movements—she has the most beautiful way of carrying herself, you know, her steps as graceful as a dancer's. Her movements force the eye to follow. And the stars shone in the sky around her. *Only* around her. It was as if she were an actress on a stage. I was transfixed. The light from the moon had an almost greenish tinge to it that night—it was a full moon that first night I saw her, and it fell in a stripe on the water, did I say? It was at the comet end of that strip of light that she made her offering or whatever it was. Meanwhile one star, one star in particular—well, it was so bright it had to have been not a star but a planet, and it seemed to crown her in glory. To anoint her.

"She took down her hair and it fell in wavy curls around her shoulders and down her back. Mermaid hair, she has."

Is he serious? Max wondered. Apparently he was. Lord Duxter continued, caught up in the glorious, transformative memory: "And then she stood and let the robe slide from her shoulders. She stood naked underneath that canopy of stars, and she held up her hands to the sky in some sort of—I don't know. A benediction. I was captivated, besotted—whatever you want to call it. I'll admit it. She was gorgeous. Stunning, I tell you."

Ah, thought Max. *I believe we've reached the core of the matter now.*

"I know it sounds absurd and rather sordid and voyeuristic but it wasn't," Lord Duxter rushed on, anxious to be understood. Max thought he understood all too well. "Night after night for a week this went on."

"And you just watched her."

"Yes, at first. I didn't plan to—you know, do anything about it. I hadn't sought her out, but I also didn't chivalrously turn my back once I saw her. I fell under her spell, right then and there. To think this lovely creature had been before me all along, hidden in plain sight. Her model's figure hidden under shapeless suits and dresses, her eyes behind those hideous glasses, too big for her face. I asked her—once we were lovers; so quickly we became lovers—and I asked her why she hid herself. Why she didn't flaunt herself more, she was so gorgeous. And the answer she gave made perfect sense—once you realized what she really looked like. 'I grew tired,' she said, 'of the attentions of men.' But then she added, 'Until you.' What man could resist that sort of thing? It's the oldest story in the world, isn't it?"

Oh, thought Max, yes. It certainly was. There were many variations to this story, too.

"And then the spell was broken, when she . . . when she . . ."

Max wasn't going to force him to finish the sentence: when she became pregnant. All this put what Poppy had told him under a clear light, and it was looking more and more as if she had been telling the truth—allowing for certain embellishments based on her dislike of her stepmother.

Lord Duxter added fuel to Max's theory of Poppy's veracity when he said, practically spluttering in frustration, "Jane told me she was on the pill, and now I think—oh, God. I should have realized, with Colin gone so much, the pill wouldn't really have been the logical choice. The first time we . . . you know . . . she told me not to worry, it was all taken care of. I took her word for it. She had always been nothing if not reliable—hyper-reliable, neurotically so, if I may put it that way. I depended on her entirely. So when it came to this—this quite different matter—I didn't draw a distinction. She must be telling the truth."

"Perhaps she was."

"Oh, come on, Max. You don't really believe that, do you? This was no accident."

"We could argue the point either way, but what you are left to deal with is that you may have fathered a child on Jane. Those are the facts now. So the only question is, what do you propose to do about it?"

Lord Duxter stared at the floor, shaking his head back and forth in frustration. He was not entirely a bad person, thought Max. Few people are bad through and through. But despite his business acumen he was a silly man and a weak one, easily blinded by his immediate wants.

Talk about being a romantic. Starlight, indeed.

"I'm damned if I know what to do," said Lord Duxter.

In the end, Jane saved Max the trouble of a trip to Hawthorne Cottage to hear her version of events. Soon there came a knock on the vicarage door, and Mrs. Hooser ushered the young widow into Max's study.

Today it was a bright yellow dress she wore. She must have

been on a bit of a shopping spree. He offered her coffee, which she accepted, as before. But she stirred the brew unnecessarily, never tasting it, finally dropping the spoon to the floor with a clatter. She put the cup on a side table, where it stayed until the coffee grew cold.

Max retrieved the spoon from the floor, saying, "Actually, I've been hoping to have a word with you for some time. But . . . is there something you'd like to tell me first?"

A blush rose from her chest, covering her face. It was like watching a wildfire take hold.

"About Lord Duxter. Yes, of course."

"Well, yes. But I had much more ordinary questions on my mind for the longest time. I am wondering now if I haven't been a bit of a fool about all this. I had wanted to talk with you about practicalities, such as your husband's final resting place. About the date for the service. About flowers and readings. I was assuming you would want Colin to be buried out of St. Edwold's."

"Aren't there special rules? About suicides?"

"There are if you want them. I don't draw such distinctions. A loss of a human life is an incalculable loss, however you look at it. But you would prefer to discuss Lord Duxter now, would you?"

She actually laughed, a high, nervous trill. "I don't know. I mean, does it matter now? Does anything matter? To Colin, or to anyone?"

Oh, no, thought Max. *It's only your husband. And presumably, he once meant the world to you.* Max didn't think he could bear to hear again that funerals are for the living.

"But I thought—well, of course you've guessed," she ran on. "And I felt it best to make a clean breast of things. Of everything. I'm not much good at hypocrisy, you see."

"I hadn't guessed," he said. "Lord Duxter told me. And you're saying you want to get in front of the story, as they say in the media." Had Lord Duxter given her a heads-up?

"If you wish to put it that way," she said coldly. Her enthusiasm for making a clean breast of things was clearly fading. "I'm in love with Lord Duxter." The tone was defiant, anticipating outrage. "And he with me."

Max, with every reason to question that last statement, merely nodded. "I know about your affair." If he'd had any doubts, even after Lord Duxter's confession, at every mention of his name Jane blushed anew like a teenager, the way someone Poppy's age might have done.

The best way to get the full story out of someone was to let them assume you knew every detail anyway, as Max had learned conducting interrogations in his MI5 days. By keeping silent you often got a fuller story than might have been offered otherwise. People, especially people under pressure, loved to fill the silence with the sound of their own voices.

Now Max merely added, baiting the hook, "But I don't know when or how it started." Which was true enough. A shade of truth he would reconcile with his conscience later. He hadn't heard things from her side yet. In all fairness, he told himself, he must do so.

"We met on a plane, of all places. Not in the village. It was the merest coincidence. I was flying back from seeing my sisters in France. He was flying back from Switzerland via France."

"Yes. He would have been returning from visiting his wife." Max may have placed an unneeded emphasis on the word "wife," but it wouldn't hurt to remind Jane that this was a marriage already on the rocks, and her interference was precisely that—interference.

But Jane nodded, eager to share her story, her love affair for the ages. The missing Poppy seemed quite to have fled her mind for the moment. "He was returning from that asylum or whatever they were keeping her in."

"It was a mental hospital." Honestly, thought Max. She was making it sound as if Lady Duxter had been tied up in chains in a place for the criminally insane, when in fact she was recovering from a coma. That the coma was self-induced, the result of a suicide attempt—well, it still didn't make her a raving lunatic. Max quelled these thoughts and again pasted a neutral, interested expression on his face, as Jane continued.

"She was there because she tried to kill herself with carbon monoxide gas in the garage of Wooton Priory—the garage at the back of the main house, you know. It had been converted from the horse stables. It was a miracle she was found in time. He found her. David. Can you imagine the horror of that?"

"I know the story," said Max. As did the entire village. It had happened not long after the WI had staged a reprisal of *The Deep Blue Sea* in the Village Hall, with Suzanna Winship miscast as the troubled and sensitive Hester Collyer and an emotionless local estate agent, Randolph Peckover, likewise miscast as her daredevil lover. A theory was bandied about at the time that Lady Duxter might have been influenced by seeing the play. Max thought it doubtful that such an unconvincing and unintentionally hilarious portrayal of psychological distress as Suzanna's could have driven anyone to thoughts of suicide. "It truly was awful."

"Anyway, because I was so late for the plane they were just in the process of shutting the doors, so a flight attendant practically threw me into a seat in first class and told me to buckle up. The plane was mostly empty so it didn't really matter. That part was fairy tale enough, getting all the first-class service on an Air France flight. Do you know they give you little warm towels to wash your hands with? It was ever so nice. And the plane was just *slosh*ing with wine and soon we all were. And while the flight was too short for food service they gave us these lovely little appetizer things. I can still taste how rich they were, how full of butter. They're French, after all."

"Yes, yes," said Max, trying to keep the impatience he felt out of his voice.

"Anyway, they sat me next to David—across the aisle from him. I didn't notice him particularly at first, nor he me. I just sort of registered 'Well-dressed older man wearing trendy glasses' and thought no more of it. What he was thinking—well, that only became clear as time passed. He acted like he didn't register me at all, and that was very likely true—then. I talked about my training as a librarian. I told him a little—a very little—about Colin.

"Then the stewardess or whatever you're supposed to call them now—the flight attendant—came by with a tray of little cups of water. We were sitting toward the back of first class and by the time she got to our row only one cup was left. He took it—I thought he wanted it for himself, you see. But he turned and handed it to me across the aisle. That's the sort of manners he has. It meant nothing to him; it was a normal thing to do.

"But I nearly cried. I was in a state from seeing my sisters, which is always a mixed bag of emotions. We had this awful upbringing, you see. And now they're successful and with rich husbands and I'm . . . I only had Colin, scraping by. I—well, anyway, I remember thinking, clear as can be, 'It has been so long since anyone has been nice to me.' I must have sort of teared up, or there was an expression on my face . . . I don't know. But he saw it and asked if I was all right. How to explain? A stranger offers me a cup of water and I go all to pieces. Anyway, we started to talk, really talk, and when he told me his name, I knew of course who it was then. I'd never seen him nor even seen photos of him, and he didn't take part in village life much, did he? But on that short flight something took hold in me. I saw that I could change my life. I didn't have to settle anymore. He told me he was coming back from a holiday in France. That turned out not to be true, not entirely. He doesn't always . . . he isn't always truthful, David. But it's to spare people pain. He didn't want the world gossiping about his wife, you see.

"I told him my husband worked in security for Earnest and Oldfield. That job was another that didn't last. Somehow, Colin has—had—trouble sticking to things. When he got the job in Saudi Arabia, doing something similar for one of the oil companies there—it was such a godsend. It was actually David who got him the job."

Max said, "Yes, I recall hearing that."

"I don't know why I should feel guilty. I haven't killed anyone. I haven't stolen anything. David—well, he pursued me and I suppose I should have resisted. But I'm human, like anyone else."

Especially since she knew—the village knew—Lord Duxter and his wife were often at odds. She may have known the lord's marriage was in trouble because of his wife's depression—a depression that probably worsened as the marriage soured. Had Jane perhaps initially refused him, saying no because of Colin, using Colin as an excuse, which would of course only increase David's determination to have her? Had she played him from the first, determined she would have him?

"I know what you're thinking. *Typical* male thinking. You're thinking the lord is someone suave and successful, someone who would never fall for someone like me."

Actually, I was thinking he was married—as were you—and you should have left him alone to begin with, thought Max.

So, thought Max, to recap: Lord Duxter shares a plane ride with Jane but doesn't notice her particularly. Not long afterward, however, he hires her to work in the archives at the priory. He's been wanting to hire such a person and Jane seems tailor-made for the job. Perhaps she also talks to him about getting Colin a job, telling him something of their financial woes. But late one night he sees her stop at the pond on her way back to the village, and he sees her there for several nights after that. She doesn't realize it but he can see her from the top of the manor house. Or—does she realize it? She knows the layout of that house well. She knows the lord's habits. Those binoculars. Did she set out deliberately to seduce him? All that dancing in the moonlight? Or is it all as innocent as it seems, on her part?

Is she victim or victimizer?

Had she tired of Colin, who was never around, anyway? And seen her way clear to getting what she most wanted?

But she had an alibi, from the most unimpeachable source. Awena. And there were, in his reckoning, at least two other people who could have done this horrible deed. Who had plenty of time and no alibi.

But Max's mind reeled away from the thought.

"What would you know about it?" Jane stood over him now, fuming. He looked up at her and suddenly was overcome by a wave of sorrow at this sordid affair that most certainly had not been worth the risk and the cost. Was this carry-on in the woods between her and Lord Duxter what little Tom had seen? Most likely it was. "But you are missing the point. To him I am like the heroine of a novel. He said so. He said I had such grave dignity. He said that."

It sounded like a great line to use on a romantic, a woman not securely attached to earth.

But maybe—just maybe Jane had something Lord Duxter wanted that she was not aware of. Who was playing whom, here? He plays to her ego, talks to her with great affection, praises her beauty. The part of her story Max believed was that David's small act of kindness melted her heart, made her want him.

But was there something else he really wanted from her?

Like help ridding him of an unwanted spouse?

Chapter 18

THE HERMIT

The phone rang and he was going to let it go unanswered, as he wasn't nearly finished talking with Jane. But Mrs. Hooser came pushing through the study door a moment later. She had picked up on the upstairs extension.

"Call for you," she said. "Says it's important." It was always important. Someone had probably let his geese run free into a neighbor's garden and Max was being called in to act as arbiter. His days were filled with refereeing such important issues as this. When they weren't filled to overflowing by conducting a murder enquiry.

"Who is it, Mrs. Hooser?"

"I don't know, do I? Wouldn't give a name."

"Very well. Thank you."

"He was rude, I'll tell you that much. Some people have no manners. Why, in my day—"

"Thank you, Mrs. Hooser," he said again.

She was still grumbling as she left the room, slamming the door behind her.

Max picked up the heavy receiver of the Bakelite phone. It was, of all people, the artist Coombebridge. What he said caught Max's full attention. He put his hand over the receiver and said to Jane, "I'm awfully sorry but I must take this. Might I come and seek you out later at Hawthorne Cottage?"

Jane, who looked as if she were already regretting being so forthcoming, merely nodded, standing to leave and smoothing the skirt of her yellow dress.

Once Jane had left—and Max had waited until he saw her pass in front of the study window on her way to the High—he gave Coombebridge the all clear to continue.

Without preamble, the artist said, "Like I was saying, I've got information about Netta you'll want to hear. But you'll need to drive out to my cottage. I don't have all day to natter on the telephone. Tell your housekeeper for me she's bloody rude."

"Netta? But why—?"

Click.

At any other time, when he was less busy, Max would have welcomed the scenic drive on the narrow road that spooled out to where the surly artist lived in his rustic cottage by the sea. The sound of the waves and the sight of gulls soaring overhead always restored Max to his soul. For him it was a form of meditation. So he decided to treat this summons from Coombebridge as a chance to test the saying that the busy man should meditate twice as long as the man with lots of free time.

Lucas wasn't alone when Max came to call. Max imagined he seldom was alone or without female company. The blonde who opened the door to his knock introduced herself with a wide smile as Chantalina. She was probably half Lucas's age and wore too much shiny makeup, with distracting, whitish highlights layered on beneath her arched brows and high on her cheekbones. She'd painted the apples of her cheeks a hectic red to match her lips; with her fair curly hair, stiff with hairspray, she looked like a porcelain doll. Still, the smile was welcoming if coupled with an off-putting, "Changed his mind, he did. Says he really doesn't want visitors today, after all. Except, he says, from his muse."

Max tamped down his annoyance. "I'm sure he'll find this visit inspiring. May I sit here and wait my turn, then?"

He chose a chair with a little coffee table before it and sat happily looking out the open cottage door onto the stunning seascape. Coombebridge had made the scene from the cottage his own, producing countless paintings of sea and sky at all times of day and in all seasons and climates. The prices for his paintings were astronomic, yet he lived like the poorest fisherman in the region. Max couldn't even guess what he spent his money on, but allowed himself the faint hope—very, very faint—that the man might one day be induced to make a gift or bequest to St. Edwold's. The church roof was taken care of but everything else was always in need of repair.

Max could overhear a conversation in the other room that seemed to consist of Chantalina softly arguing Max's case and Lucas gruffly arguing for his muse. Finally, "Well, bring him in, then. I guess I did invite him. How was I to know he'd take me up on it?"

Chantalina led him into the inner sanctum with its floor-to-ceiling windows. She tactfully withdrew.

"Good to see you, Max," Coombebridge said, his eyes barely leaving the canvas on which he worked. "Chantalina tells me you're involved in investigating these murders."

"There's only been one murder," Max told him. "And it's not entirely clear it wasn't suicide, as it appears to be."

"What are you talking about, man? I think this green is just oily looking, don't you? I can't seem to capture the play of light on those far waves." He glared at Max. *This is all your fault.*

"Colin Frost. I'm talking about Colin. His death."

"Oh, well that's as may well be, but that's not what I meant." He turned, again briefly casting a look in Max's direction. "I don't generally do portraits, not of men or women and certainly not of children, but I'd make an exception in your case. There's more than meets the eye with you, Max, isn't there? Beneath that smooth-if-tousled exterior. I'd be willing to bet you were a bit of a lad in your day, weren't you, Max?"

"Colin Frost?" Max prompted—smoothly, he hoped. He and Coombebridge had had this conversation many times before about painting Max's portrait. It was an offer Max had managed to resist.

"I don't know anything about Colin Frost," Coombebridge said. "But he was probably murdered, too."

"Too?"

"Of course, too. Are you playing dumb? You know as well as I do, Max—you're a man of the world: he was no more in love with Lady Duxter than I'm the man in the moon."

"I would tend to agree." Even without the CCTV footage to set them straight, the psychology of that union had been wrong from the first, thought Max. On the surface Colin looked good, but there was no *there* there. Lady Duxter might have fallen for his looks alone, it was known to happen, but—as a pairing, it never sat right with Max.

"And clearly," Coombebridge was saying, "they need to raise taxes to get a proper police force together if they have to keep dragging you into things. Don't you have a baby to baptize somewhere or a wedding to perform? Instead, here you are, up to your knees again in a murder investigation. Anyway, I thought you'd like to know what happened to Netta. What I know is worth sharing, especially given what happened to her grandson. She was my patroness, you know, back when I didn't have two coins to rub together. I'm sorry to lose her. She was a battle-axe but she was *my* battle-axe, if you follow."

"I'm all ears," said Max.

"You always are. Well, I had a phone conversation with Netta before she died. About the stained glass for the church, you know."

Max, while anxious for a word on that subject, held his peace.

"In the middle of the conversation," Coombebridge continued, "she said something about having a visitor. I could hear a knock at the door, and she said, 'Just a minute, Lucas,' and she put down the receiver. She must have gone to open the door because next I heard her say something like, 'Oh, it's you. The door's on the latch. Did you get the preserves?' And someone probably nodded because I didn't hear the response. Or perhaps it was a rhetorical question. Then Netta said, 'They had better be an improvement over the last batch. I was taken *ill* from that jar, I tell you.' Then she rang off."

"That's all she said?"

"Well, I think she said good-bye, or see you around, or something like that. This wasn't like in film or on the telly where people simply ring off without a by-your-leave."

Which was exactly what Coombebridge had done, after having demanded Max's appearance at the cottage. But with Lucas Coombebridge, rules were meant for other people.

"And she said the door was on the latch," Max said slowly. "As if to say, you could have just walked in, the door was closed but it wasn't locked."

"Do you know, I never stopped to think it through. And that's because I thought it couldn't possibly be important. Not until she was killed. I've no time to waste, Vicar. Not like some I could name."

Max ignored this. He was used to the man's brusqueness. His

running joke was that Max didn't work for a living if, as Max claimed, everything was already in God's hands.

"Why do you keep saying she was killed?"

"Perhaps because she was living with two women who wanted her dead?"

That was opinion that barely rose to the level of hearsay and tittle-tattle. Netta was given to paranoia as she grew older, as all the village well knew. And Coombebridge's misogyny would certainly extend to stereotypes about three women living in the same house. Still, Max found he couldn't dismiss this information out of hand. Perhaps all three women—Netta, Jane, and Poppy—found a lot to quarrel about, living in close quarters as they did. Leaving the cap off a tube of toothpaste or repeated failure to put the dishes away were the sorts of crimes that could have fatal consequences.

"So the day before she died someone brought her preserves because the last batch made her ill. What more do you want? If she thought someone was trying to kill her, she was right, as it turns out. Even paranoids get it right sometimes, you know."

"All right," said Max. "Perhaps. But from what you say, this sounds as though a stranger may have come to the door. Jane and Poppy would have no need to knock. It was their house, too."

"You're the detective," said Coombebridge, turning away, losing interest. Talking to Coombebridge was sometimes like talking to a four-year-old. "Figure it out."

Max was realizing that, on second thought, the simpler explanation was that Poppy or Jane had not been able to open the door because their hands were full of packages from their shopping.

"What time of day was it, this visit?" Max asked.

"Around six or six thirty. I was losing the sunlight so I was anxious to get off the telephone and back to my painting. And I could hear the news going off on her telly in the background. That silly introductory music they play, like the world's coming to an end every night."

That would be six o'clock straight up, then, thought Max—if the time mattered. "You gained no impression of who her visitor was?"

"I didn't think about it at the time, no. *Is* it important?"

"Male? Female?"

"Really, how would I know? She called whoever it was 'poppet.'"

Poppet? A term one would use for a young girl, but not exclusively for a young girl. Max supposed a woman Netta's age might say it to a young man. It was simply a term of endearment.

"Are you sure she didn't say 'Poppy'?"

Just last week at St. Edwold's Max had asked Mr. Ferrar if he would help out and do the offering during the service—pass the collection plate, in other words. Ferrar had misheard him. "Would I do the *laun*dry?" he'd said, understandably confused by the request. Coombebridge was getting to an age where many people start to have trouble with their hearing. He might have misheard "poppet" for "Poppy." Max hoped he was wrong in thinking that.

"There's nothing wrong with my hearing," said Coombebridge. "She called whoever it was 'poppet.'"

But even if it had been Poppy, Max wondered, couldn't she simply have been making a delivery on behalf of someone else?

"I didn't hear a voice, if that's what you mean," Coombebridge continued. "There was no way to be able to tell if it was male or female. Although, if we can stereotype for a moment, it would be more usual for a woman to carry around a jar of preserves, wouldn't it? It's just not something men do, is it? So I guess I assumed it was one of the old biddies in the village come round for tea, her shopping basket swinging from her arm. Maybe she was returning a jar she'd borrowed."

A used or opened jar of preserves? That seemed to Max unlikely in the extreme. Max would of course ask Cotton if a jar had turned up when his team turned out the house. Although it sounded as if Netta was suspicious enough of the contents of the original jar she may have thrown it away herself. Anyway, there were probably half a dozen such jars in the house, so it might be a pointless exercise. Still, prints on the jar might mean something. And poison or drugs in the jar would mean more.

Max passed along Coombebridge's words to Cotton, pulling over on a byway to use his mobile as he headed back to Nether Monkslip.

"It wasn't being treated as a crime scene, so of course there are no photos," Cotton told him. "And if she was poisoned or doped somehow, surely the killer has removed all traces from the house by now. Nothing would be easier than to drop by for a condolence visit and have a rustle through the fridge on the pretext of making tea or something."

"I know," said Max. "It's just one more piece of the puzzle. We don't know if or where it fits in. I could ask Awena or one of the women at Elka's about preserves and such, but it seems a very long shot anyone would know or remember anything like that in connection with Netta. If anything, she generally would make her own preserves—she was famous for it. I doubt she'd be much interested in someone's bringing her their own jar. Although . . ."

"Although what?"

"If these were store-bought preserves, might she not have returned them to the store? Sent Jane or Poppy out to exchange them for a new jar? I can almost hear her saying, 'Waste not, want not.'"

"Well, that's easy enough to check into," said Cotton. "I'll get someone on it. It would have to be the village store or Madame Cuthbert's shop, wouldn't it? La Maison Bleue?"

"Most likely," said Max. "Almost certainly."

But that night, a new concern stepped on the heels of the old when Max was awakened in the early hours by the phone ringing beside his bed. It was Lord Duxter, and he was in a state, his voice booming down the line like an explosion in Max's ear.

"Someone's set fire to the old church, Max. Look out your window and you might even be able to see the flames from there. What in hell! What the devil is going on? Marina, and now this?"

Max quickly pulled on some clothes, kissed an alarmed Awena good-bye, and raced down the stairs. Thea trotted hopefully beside him but, not knowing what he was headed into, he told her she must stay. He left her by the front door, a dejected heap of brown-and-black fur.

When he pulled up to the St. George Studio in the Land Rover, Cotton and his team were already there, standing with a wretched-looking group of six or so poets and other scribes from the writers' retreat. They stood huddled in blankets to watch the firemen dowse the flames of the old church, no doubt already mentally composing sonnets or essays about the conflagration. Despite the hour, people from nearby villages started to arrive and showed no inclination to move on until they, too, had extracted every last drop of drama. They were not disappointed by their wait. Before long, they saw Cotton's team removing a body from the embers, a human form covered head to toe by a white cloth.

Standing at the edge of the crowd and peering through the blinding smoke, Max turned at the sound of a familiar voice. It was Jane Frost, once again crying hysterically.

"Oh, no, not Carville!" she cried. "No!"

Why on earth, Max wondered, was she that upset over Carville?

PART IV

The World and the Flesh

Chapter 19

THE HIGH PRIEST

To round off Max's frantic morning, at ten on the day of the fire Mrs. Hooser threw open the door to his office to announce that "his bishop" was on the telephone, meaning the Right Reverend Bishop Nigel St. Stephen. "He sounds annoyed," she assured him. She looked at Max suspiciously, this renegade priest who was always in some form of trouble, ecclesiastical or otherwise. The days when he had been dating Awena paled by comparison for scandal.

But whenever people pointed out the murder rate in Nether Monkslip had shot up alarmingly with Max's arrival in the village, Mrs. Hooser defended him with a blind devotion. He was her vicar, and despite her many failings and shortcomings as a housekeeper, he had shown her nothing but kindness. She would not hear a word said against him. There was surely a good explanation for the trail of corpses he left littered behind. Her reasoning was that there would have been more murders without Max around to solve them.

Max was hopeful. With any luck, he thought, the bishop was only calling because he'd heard about the stained glass. Miss Pitchford or one of her associates surely had got wind of the goat situation by now, in a manner of speaking.

But Max soon realized he should have known better. It was unlikely the bishop would embroil himself in such a matter. A depiction in glass of a nude Adam and Eve, perhaps. A goat with a crazed-looking protector the bishop would let Max sort out for himself.

The bishop had clearly been reading the news in the *Monkslip-super-Mare Globe and Bugle*. Clive Hoptingle, reporter, had come to specialize in coverage of Max, whom he had dubbed "the sleuthing priest," among other things. Clive, with his bombastic writing style and loose acquaintance with truth-telling, was clearly a fan of Max's investigative outings with DCI Cotton. He had taken to following Max about with a camera during investigations, popping up at the most inconvenient times before scuttling off to make his nightly deadline. Max had not seen him in recent days but that was not to say he wasn't even now planning an ambush of the vicarage.

"Not another murder, Max? And now a fire?"

"I'm awfully afraid it is so, Bishop. And the church didn't make it. I mean to say, it burned to the ground."

"With no one inside, it is to be hoped?" Without stopping for an answer, he added, "Max, I've lost count of the number of murder investigations in which you've been involved. Have you . . . I mean, has this always been . . . Have you always been so surrounded by murder?"

"Have I always carried this cloud around with me, like Pigpen, do you mean?"

"Well, yes, something like that."

"I suppose I have, yes, now that you mention it, Bishop. At university, there were a few instances, a few occasions, where I felt I could point out some clues the authorities seemed to be overlooking." He didn't like to remind his bishop that Nether Monkslip had been a peaceable little backwater of a place until he had come along. He supposed he was afraid the bishop might pull him from the area and give him another church in another village. Whether that wouldn't simply be spreading the problem like malaria to a new location Max didn't dare speculate. Surely all this was just coincidence, this spike in the murder rate around these parts?

Or was he in fact becoming a clerical lure for murder?

"So, tell me what is going on," said the bishop. In the background, Max could hear a state-of-the-art printer spitting out pages at fifty per minute. The bishop was calling from his office at Monkslip Cathedral, a place that was an homage to high tech gadgets and the tenets of Marie Kondo, the famous Japanese organizing consultant. The bishop was using his stern voice, but Max discerned more than a touch of avidity in his tone. Like Max, the bishop was a fan of the golden age of mystery, in particular the books of Agatha Christie, and in truth he took a vicarious pleasure from Max's involvement in these cases.

"So, what is it this time, Max?"

There was much that he might have kept back to shorten the tale, but not from his bishop. It was the only way Max could reconcile the dichotomy of his life. Tinker Tailor Soldier Spy. Priest.

While Max was not officially the Bishop's Eye, he seemed to be serving as a sort of conduit. Most fortunately, the bishop had never come near saying, with Henry II, "Will no one rid me of this meddlesome priest?"

"I'll know more after I hear from DCI Cotton," said Max. "But here's the gist."

The bishop listened closely. At the end of Max's recital, he said,

"Well, buildings are replaceable. Only humans are unique. Still, I'm sorry to see this one go. You know of course that for centuries it was ours, before Cambridge got hold of it. There were modern-day protests when the church was deconsecrated and the lot sold to Lord Duxter. Letters to the editor—'Whither England' and so on. But the Church is cash-strapped and many fine old properties that cost the moon to maintain have come on the block. It's often the only way to save them from demolition: find a buyer with deep pockets and an abiding love of the old architecture."

Or, Max thought, find a buyer whose wife had deep pockets.

"So the arsonist was someone not connected with the retreat, is that the thinking?" Max asked Cotton. "Someone not staying at the main house?" It was later in the day and Max had made short work of his clerical duties, determined to focus on the apparently escalating crisis taking place so nearby. Poppy's absence made him feel the clock was ticking; he couldn't suspend animation indefinitely while the investigation proceeded. The child's absence put a special pressure on investigators; the press couldn't leave it alone, of course. Readers were treated daily to hand-wringing interviews with her school companions. Without exception, they described her as "lighting up every room she entered."

"Not necessarily," said Cotton, speaking from his mobile. "Although the writers for the most part alibi each other."

"In the middle of the night?"

"Precisely. Apparently they've been having a high old time over there. Passions ignited or rekindled into the wee hours—that is true of at least one couple that met at a book fair. It's a wonder any of them gets any work done, however. The rest say they sat up drinking into the wee hours. The old church where Carville was staying was tucked well away from the main house, hidden behind some trees. That was the attraction, that the writer could have some peace and quiet in which to work. But that also means no one was particularly aware of Carville until he turned up for meals. I gather that on those occasions, he could scarcely be avoided, try as one might to avoid him. He would show up waving his bookmarks and going on about the size of his latest book contract. No one believed him on that subject, apparently, or perhaps it was that they didn't want to believe him, but that didn't shut him up."

"Are we certain that Carville was the intended victim?"

"Well, yes. What is it you're saying? Who else might it have been? He was no more or less annoying than the other writers, or so I'm told, just more successful and well-known."

"Fire is a—well, an indirect way to kill someone," Max pointed out. "With guns and knives, you can be fairly certain you've hit your target."

"I do see what you mean. It's the same with poison, isn't it? There's no guarantee it will work when you want it to. Well, it's difficult to say who else may have been the target. Carville had been living there alone, quite blamelessly—no overnight guests so far as anyone was aware or will admit to knowing. So unless whoever set the fire thought someone *else* was in there asleep, or asleep with him . . ."

"A case of mistaken identity, perhaps."

"It could be," admitted Cotton. "Or perhaps someone had simply had it up to there with Carville and his bookmarks and his bonuses and awards. They tell me he's also known at writers' conferences as a bit of a microphone hog but that would be a rare reason for wanting to kill someone, don't you think?"

"I'm sure I couldn't say with any certainty. Returning to the case of Lady Duxter and Colin: By the same token, perhaps the police should look at separate motives—meaning, someone wanted only

218   G. M. MALLIET

one of them gone—Lady Duxter or Colin. But in order to achieve
the death of one, both had to die."

"Okay," said Cotton. "That's very possible. What happened in
Colin's life recently that might account for this? What changed?"

"Apart from his grandmother's dying? Not a lot. Except . . ."

"Except?"

"Well, interestingly, Colin apparently had a near escape from
death over in Saudi Arabia."

"Really?" Cotton was already thinking that getting Interpol in
on this one would be uphill work.

"Yes, we had the story from Elka Garth and the people who like
to hang about the tea shop," said Max. "A car tried to run him off
the road. He thought it was an attempted kidnapping. I suppose it's
just possible someone followed him to England from there, to finish the job properly this time."

"A stranger in the village would be noticed," said Cotton. "Within
five minutes. Most particularly a Saudi. They'd bring it in under
thirty seconds with a Saudi."

"I don't think Colin said it was a Saudi. Still, we can't discount
the incident, although trying to follow up on it would be the very
devil. But his colleague was with him at the time and confirms it
happened: a car came flying out at them from nowhere and tried to
force them off the road. Fortunately, Colin's driver was trained in
evasive driving. But in the panic of the moment no one could iden-
tify the car or the driver."

"They didn't report it, I suppose?"

"They felt it was better to say nothing," said Max. "It's not a
country where you'd jump at the chance to get involved with the
bureaucracy, if you get my drift. Or to find yourself detained until
their inquiries were complete. Jane told the crowd at Elka's that it
made Colin desperately want out of there. And she was relieved to

have her instincts validated like that. She had taken flak from some of the villagers for not being at his side over there."

"And then his grandmother died. Do you see some sort of conspiracy here? A conspiracy against Colin?"

"We can't discount the idea, I suppose. Far-fetched as it seems. Some wide-ranging, lingering grudge?" asked Max doubtfully.

"Didn't Jane hint that Colin might have found something hidden in some ledger in the archives?"

"She did. But unless it was a long-lost Shakespeare play or something, it's difficult to see such a find resulting in a plot against his life."

"Colin was a cybersecurity expert," mused Cotton. "That alone might make him a target. But Lady Duxter?"

"Collateral damage," said Max promptly. He had known that sort of tragedy to happen often enough. "If we put aside the suicide theory, then she was in the wrong place at the wrong time. If someone really had it in for Colin, Marina was simply in the way. Professional kidnappers and assassins wouldn't have any scruples about that."

"Was Colin really that important?"

"He didn't act as though he was important, but it's hard to say. Certainly what we've learned from his employers doesn't indicate he was anything out of the ordinary, but I doubt they would admit he was more."

"A spy of some sort, you mean."

"Yes. In the employ of—God knows. Or, he was just the humble and unassuming man he appeared to be. But we can't forget that in his head were all the secrets to evading detection if someone were plotting sabotage of the oil fields. Who would choose to try to kidnap him, as apparently happened that day he was run off the road, we can only imagine. Politics in that region are even harder to grasp than those in Whitehall."

"And investigating a crime out of that region? I wouldn't know where to start, if I'm honest. This might be a case for MI6."

"I wouldn't," said Max, "bring them in just yet."

An hour later Max could be found sitting in the front pew of St. Edwold's, watched closely by Luther from his usual resting place on the altar.

How old was the cat? No one knew. Luther had been hanging about at least since the day Max took over as vicar of St. Edwold's. He seemed no older, no slower in his movements, if perhaps he was getting a bit gray around the muzzle. Certainly he was able to jump on and off the altar with alacrity, although Max also had watched him fail to stick the landing on the altar cloth and slide clean across to fall off the other side, quite unharmed. It was like watching a cat in a cartoon. Max wished Luther wouldn't leave the mice he caught for Max to find in the vestry, but he supposed it was a blessing Luther was only in it for the kill, not for the meal. Max would find the little bodies laid out almost reverently next to the altar vestments.

Max had slipped into the empty church—empty save for Luther—for a quiet moment of prayer. He saw that the Carson twins had been drawing on the backs of the pews with crayons again. He knew it was the Carsons because they'd helpfully signed their names to their artwork. GERALD and LILY—that "GERALD" written with a backward-facing letter "E."

He'd baptized both children soon after they were born. Gerald had been as good as gold in his father's arms, seemingly fascinated by the proceedings; Lily had fussed throughout, her desperate screams reaching a crescendo as Max drizzled baptismal water on her forehead. As he'd handed the child back to her mother, she'd said jokingly, "You keep her."

He opened the *Book of Common Prayer* he'd brought with him.

He tended to use the book as a sort of day planner and holder of random scraps of paper. Out from its pages fell the scattered notes for his Bathsheba and King David sermon.

The sound of the door opening pulled him from his reflections.

Destiny came to sit beside him, the light shaded by stained glass catching the tips of her hair. They glowed as if on fire, turning the strands multicolored. "I've been thinking about the sermon you've been working on. The one that's given you so much trouble."

Max, his mind still sifting through the clues in the case, emerged slowly into full awareness. "What's that you said?"

"I was talking about your sermon. I said, when all is said and done, David was not always the hero of legend, was he? He couldn't live up to all the hype, I guess. Imagine the pressure: king, poet, athlete, musician. But he became ruthless in taking what he wanted."

"He certainly paid for it when his son died."

"Yes." She looked closely at him. "What is it, Max?"

"'The Lord gives everything and charges / By taking it back.' That's Jack Gilbert."

"Oh. Nice. It's a poem, is it?"

"'Like being young for a while,'" Max continued thoughtfully.

He wasn't really there with her at all, Destiny could tell. She gave him a minute before prodding him to continue. "That's quite sad, somehow."

"Yes. 'We are permitted / Romantic love with its bounty and half-life / Of two years.'"

"Oh, my. Do you think that's true?"

Max, again struggling to rejoin the conversation, said, "Of romantic love? Oh, yes. It has a short shelf life. Then it becomes something deeper, something finer. Or it vanishes altogether. There doesn't seem to be a middle way."

"I have a feeling you're saying all this for a reason."

"Oh, yes," said Max.

A beat, as she sat with hands clasped hopefully at her breast. Then, "I don't suppose you'd like to tell me what the reason is?"

He smiled. "I'm not sure. Better to say nothing until I'm sure."

"Very well." She sat another moment, still hoping to break him. No luck. "Actually, I came in to tell you we've run out of gluten-free wafers again."

Max sighed. "If we can't get a better supplier, let's go back to having Elka bake them. She was more than happy to—"

"What is it, Max?"

The cat, playing with something on the altar, suddenly caught the object in his claws and batted it high into the air. Whatever it was went sailing onto the floor nearby. Max went to retrieve it before Luther could pounce, saying, "Luther, scat." Luther's green eyes glowered, but reluctantly he obeyed. Like an obedient dog, thought Max, only . . . not.

It was, Max could see now, a tarot card. He picked it up carefully, using his handkerchief. It was labeled "The Moon" and it illustrated a night scene with a wolf and a dog sitting near a body of water, howling at the sky. A sea creature with claws was half submerged in the water. The moon wore an angry expression.

"What does it mean?" Destiny asked him.

"No idea. I'll ask Awena before I hand it over to Cotton. It h—"

"Max?"

He had stopped talking, midsentence. Grimacing, he placed a hand against his cheek.

"What's wrong?"

"I'm afraid it's my tooth. It's been acting up. I don't think I can ignore it much longer." Of all the times, he thought. Although, there was never a good time for a dental emergency.

"Oh, dear," she said. In truth, while she was upset to see a friend in any discomfort, however small, she was more upset to see Max, whom she regarded as somewhat superhuman, suffering from something so ordinary, so mundane, so very human and boring, as a toothache.

"Just when I'm so busy."

"Isn't it always the way? 'Because I could not stop for death, he kindly stopped for me,'" Destiny quoted.

"I'm not dying," said Max. "At least, I hope not."

"Of course you're not. It's just . . . I think we all hate going to the dentist so much because it reminds us of our mortality. Decay and all that. Even more so than a routine visit to the doctor, don't you think?"

In general, Max agreed with her. But he liked Dr. Denton and the only drawback to going to him was that his office was in Monkslip-super-Mare, some distance from the village. Being in the care of such a jovial person, it was impossible to think of the statistics that placed dentistry at the top of the lists for suicide risk. Dr. Denton was fun loving, good at his job, and in the main happy with his chosen profession. He had told Max that fishing was his hobby, and when the stress of his occupation got to be too much—demanding patients, the extreme perfectionism the job required—he'd cancel his upcoming appointments, hang a sign in the window, and go fishing. He always, he assured Max, threw his catch back in the water. They served as therapy, not as food.

There had been another dentist not many years before who had not been so wise as to develop an innocuous hobby. He had instead turned to adultery and murder to occupy his off hours.

The memory of that old case nagged at Max as, minutes later, he picked up the telephone in the vicarage to make an appointment.

Chapter 20

THE MOON

A week passed with few advances in the case, except that the fire had been confirmed as arson with petrol used as an accelerant. Max spoke daily with Cotton but there were no new developments, no solid clues, no fingerprints found where they shouldn't be, no confessions made. The case would soon grow cold.

There had been one major lead but as things stood, investigators were unsure *where* it led. Max had been right in one of his theories about the jar of preserves. They had been purchased at Mme Lucie Cuthbert's shop and returned there when Netta found fault with them. They were grape preserves made from special vines grown only in France.

"Our now-missing Poppy returned them," Cotton told him. "And Mme Cuthbert was very huffy about the whole episode. I happened to speak with her myself. She was insulted to be accused of selling shoddy goods.

"'Poppy,'" Cotton relayed in a passable French accent, waving his hands in an expression of indignation, "'was at the mercy of that querulous old woman. Not to mention at the mercy of her step-mother. I felt sorry for her. Such a sweet, pretty child. She will out-grow the silly outfits and then we will see emerge *une belle femme*. But you must find her. This outrage cannot continue!'" And more words to that effect. Anyway, Mme Cuthbert had agreed to replace the of-fending jar with a new one but she held on to the opened jar Poppy had returned to her. "'But of course I kept the jar. There was nothing wrong with the preserves no matter what anyone said, so of course I kept them. That Netta, she liked to stir trouble.'"

"And you've tested the contents, of course."

"Yes," Cotton replied. "Laced with sedatives, they were."

"Enough to taste bad, then, but not enough to kill Netta out-right. Not if she was still around to have Poppy return the jar. It is lucky Mme Cuthbert didn't do a taste test herself on her morning toast. Were there fingerprints?"

"There were, mostly smudged," said Cotton. "They may turn out to be only Lucie Cuthbert's but the lab is taking care to preserve them. If you had tampered with the jar, wouldn't you have the sense to wipe your fingerprints off of it?"

"Yes. And, of course, Poppy's prints are sure to be on there. We know now she handled the jar in returning it to the shop."

"Right. And Jane's prints could be there, too, since she lived in the house. And those of any number of visitors to the cottage, I suppose. It may be pure luck Jane and Poppy didn't sample from the jar."

"Still, it's revealing. It looks as if there is no question Netta was drugged—poisoned. The drugs in the jar may not have been enough to work well, but someone may have tried again, with greater suc-cess, having figured out the better dose to use."

"We'll have to find out for sure."

"Of course."

Then finally, the word they had been waiting for came from the hospital. Cotton stopped by the vicarage to deliver the news.

And Max rang Jane Frost right away.

"I am headed for the hospital," he said. "It seems Lady Duxter is coming round, but slowly. I want to be there if and when she does come to. And I wonder if I could ask you a rather large favor. Could you come with me, and drive my car back so Awena will have it in the morning? I can't leave her and Owen without transportation and this may be a long night for me there at the hospital. They keep a guest room for visiting clergy and such, and I may end up staying the night."

She didn't hesitate. Had Lady Duxter truly been Colin's paramour, her response might have been different, but Max had assured her that was not the case. Her husband was a victim and almost certainly a blameless one.

"Of course," she said. "Whatever I can do to help. And with everyone gone—I'm so glad of the excuse not to be here. I just start to stew and worry about Poppy, left on my own. I'll just grab my purse and I'll be right with you."

"I thought you might feel that way. Good. Thank you."

"Is she going to be all right? Lady Duxter?"

"They don't know. They say the last thing Marina remembers is going to meet someone. In the forest, she thinks—she can't remember who and she can't remember where. She may be remembering a different day entirely. It's going to be a long road back but the doctor is optimistic."

Max thought back to his conversation with Cotton, who had told him, "Lady Duxter is starting to remember everything."

"*Starting* to remember?"

"As usual in these cases, it's a process of small flashbacks growing into larger flashbacks that paint a more coherent picture.

Right now she says she remembers 'someone' ringing to ask her to come over. She remembers being in the woods, so she thinks someone wanted to meet her in the woods. She also thinks she remembers being driven somewhere in a car. After that, it's a blank."

"And she doesn't know who it was? Male, female? Old, young?"

Cotton shook his head. "As Dr. Winship told us from the beginning, she might recover in quite a dramatic fashion, and recall everything. Or there may be gaps in her memory that last forever. There was the shock of someone's having tried to kill her—that's one element. The other is the carbon monoxide itself. The experts don't really know how deep the damage may run."

"Of all the rotten luck," said Max.

"I know, but at least there's this. She's alive. And she is adamant she didn't go into the woods to kill herself. She's not entirely sure she went out there to meet Colin—or to meet anyone else for that matter."

"Like Carville."

"Precisely. But in this case, where there's life, there's a great deal of hope. The doctors are working with her, not pressuring her, letting her recover on her own."

"And not planting any false memories, one would hope."

"They've got a specially trained psychologist making sure that doesn't happen. One of the best around, I'm told. Lord Duxter insisted and has been most generous in making sure his wife is well cared for."

The two men looked at each other and as one said, "Guilty conscience."

"I would imagine," said Max, "he feels horribly guilty. For not having seen the setup was all wrong. For doubting her. For—for a hundred reasons."

"We'll get at the truth, Max."

"The truth—as elusive as the moon on a cloudy night," said Max, who thought he knew the truth now but was unwilling to face it. As always, the perfidy of his fellow man astonished and dismayed him. What people would do for love or money. "It's there, the truth—it's always there—we just can't see it."

He thought of that card in the church, that moon that looked so peeved, the dog, and the wolf. Awena had told him, "The moon card is always about illusion and deception. Things that are not what they appear to be."

"Well, I think we knew that much already."

"Yes. There's been a great deal of deception and misdirection, hasn't there? Someone is playing games with you, and with the authorities. With Cotton."

Max said, "To leave this on the church altar for me to find is a sort of sacrilege, don't you think?"

"I don't, but you would be expected to think so, Max. At a guess, you're looking for someone with no religious background in the traditional sense. Or someone who has rejected religion outright. Perhaps someone angry with God, for prayers that went unanswered."

"Or prayers that were answered."

"As in, 'More tears are shed over answered prayers than unanswered ones.' Saint Teresa."

"There could be another interpretation, and that has had me worried all week. It could be a sort of calling card. Giving notice that there is going to be another killing."

"It might be a woman who is to be sacrificed, then."

"Why is that?"

"The moon always represents a goddess, not a god."

Max's heart skipped a beat with anxiety, thinking of Poppy.

Was someone planting these cards? he wondered. To implicate someone else?

To implicate Poppy?

Wasn't it Alan Kay who had said the best way to predict the future was to create it? Colin would have heard of the brilliant computer scientist. He might have idolized him. Poor Colin.

As if tracking on the idea of predictions, Awena said, "But all any of this tarot business means is that while fate and fortune play a part, we are still the ones in charge."

Well, thought Max, someone needed to come right out with it because he was not getting this obscure message. What he needed was solid proof to catch a murderer. And he also thought that, with Cotton's help, that could be organized.

He drove over to Hawthorne Cottage to collect Jane as fast as the law allowed, rehearsing what he might say to her. For Cotton had told him an exhumation and autopsy would be performed on Netta's body as soon as could be arranged, a fact Max thought he would spare Jane knowing for now.

It was a large private room where Lady Duxter lay, drifting in and out of consciousness, her aristocratic, proud features pale against the white pillowcase. Max had a word just outside the room with Dr. Martin, the man overseeing her case.

"A complete recovery is always possible," the doctor said. "We just don't know with carbon monoxide poisoning. She is lucky to be alive. The rest of this we can put down to miracle."

Jane walked over to them as they stood talking in low voices in the hospital corridor. "I'd like to sit with her if I may."

"I'll join you," said Max. "It is likely to be a long vigil. Let's go and get some coffee to bring back. I just need to pop outside first to make a phone call."

As they stood in line for service at the hospital canteen, Jane said, "When I thought Colin and Marina had been having an affair, I was fairly broken up. I can admit it now. I know, you're thinking I'm some major brand of hypocrite. But Colin and I—we were young together. We loved each other; it just didn't last. But because it was over for me doesn't mean I wished him any ill. Certainly I didn't wish him *dead*—murdered no less, if what you say is true. Thank you for helping put my mind at ease—at least Colin didn't die hating me. But now more than ever, we *must* find Poppy. When we do, I think we'll find Colin's killer, too. Don't you?"

Max could only nod noncommittally.

They returned with their coffee to the hospital room where Marina lay hooked up to tubes and IVs and the entire panoply of the best that modern medicine could offer. People imagine that a person in a coma is at peace, a sort of sleeping beauty, but Max knew how far that often was from the truth. Anyone could see Lady Duxter's mind was agitated, her hands tugging at her blankets, her handsome face crumpled in distress. She was extremely lucky to have survived at all. She was beyond lucky if she suffered no permanent brain damage from her ordeal.

Max felt his phone vibrate in his pocket. It was the signal he had been waiting for.

He left the room.

And the moment Jane Frost was alone, or thought she was, she tried to unhook the IV. It was DCI Cotton and one of his larger sergeants who stopped her, the two men emerging from behind a hospital screen.

Following close behind, having first made sure the police had Jane securely in custody, was Carville—a fully alive-and-well Carville Rasmussen, untouched by fire and enjoying his role as one of Marina's rescuers. Later he would testify in court to what he had seen while standing next to Max Tudor, from the safety of the corridor. With every retelling following the trial, Carville's participation got bolder and more heroic, until he had placed himself squarely in the room, keeping Jane in a chokehold.

But in court, for once, he would not give in to the temptation to embellish. He had seen with his own eyes, from a safe distance, Jane Frost's attempt to end Lady Duxter's life.

Jane did not go quietly. Cotton had to forcibly drag her out of the room.

Poppy and Stanley stood in the hospital corridor and watched her go.

Chapter 21

JUSTICE

"Max, you may want to come out here and see this." Cotton's voice was puzzled. Another week had passed and something had again happened to jar Cotton out of any sense of complacency. Just as the police had been tying up the loose ends of the case, getting ready to move on to the next, some thread kept threatening to unspool.

"The fire damaged one of the trees near the old church," Cotton told Max. "Well, it damaged many trees, of course. But this was a particularly old and vulnerable oak, and it fell over, splitting open—it just cracked apart, like an egg. And as men were working to remove the debris from the site, they saw the roots of the tree were actually growing around some old bones."

"Human bones?"

"Without question. There's a complete skull. And there's little doubt it is human."

Holy . . . "I'll be right there."

"How old, can they say yet?"

The two friends, the blond policeman and the dark-haired priest, stood some distance from the area where a forensics team of two men and a woman stood discussing the best way to extricate the bones, their hands and arms waving in illustration of the finer points of the many problems presented to them by the discovery of the remains. In the end they agreed they had to remove the bones intact without disturbing the roots that grew around and through them, lacing a delicate pattern in and out of the rib cage. To try to separate the bones from the roots on site would quite evidently destroy both.

"Not yet, not with any certainty," said Cotton. "It is strange: Someone had put her body inside the base of that enormous tree trunk and covered her up with dirt, moss, and leaves, tamping it all down and tightly sealing the hole. She was left undisturbed, even by animals, eventually becoming part of the tree's root system. If the fire hadn't been extinguished when it was, we might never have realized she was there—the fire would have consumed her, the tree, and all."

"Her?"

"Yes. Dr. Winterbottom decided at a glance the bones were those of a female. Something about the width of the pelvis. He thinks she was young, too, when she died. Not a child, but an adolescent."

They watched a few moments as the forensics team attempted to brush away as much dirt as possible without disturbing all the evidence of the girl's resting place. She had been put into the tree in what looked like a fetal position.

Something like that, thought Max, could so easily have happened to Poppy, and to Stanley for that matter—if Max hadn't had them taken to a safe house in London, calling in a favor from his former boss in MI5. It wasn't the first time Max had used such a ruse in his agent days. He was just starting to understand that he would never be permitted to leave those days behind him.

"Nothing simpler," George had said when Max rang him. "I'll send someone to fetch them now. Just tell them to keep their heads down meanwhile." Max hadn't been sure at the time what was going on, but his every instinct told him Jane was somehow involved, alibi or no alibi. Even if he turned out to be wrong, there was nothing for it but to make sure Poppy was out of harm's way for the duration. Stanley's disappearance at the same time, with the willing complicity of his family (more like their complete indifference) and the cooperation of the police went to further ensure someone caring was around to keep an eye on her.

"The girl's bones have to be carefully excavated, packed up, and sent to London to the forensic guys with the big Bunsen burners. We don't have the facilities in Monkslip-super-Mare to manage this sort of affair, when what is needed is a dedicated forensic anthropologist running the tests. Or in this case I suppose I mean archaeologist, if we're right in thinking the bones are very old indeed, and a preliminary look suggests that they are. In any event, it may be months before we know more.

"But it's odd," Cotton added, "how these old tales often turn out to have that kernel of truth to them."

"Just as Awena said. In this case it's more than a kernel. A girl went missing long ago, and songs were written and sung about her, and her legend, as they say, never died. The villagers seem to have suspected foul play was involved even if they were a bit sketchy as to her exact final resting place, just that it was somewhere around the woods area they called 'the Girl's Grave.' Otherwise they'd have dug her up for themselves years ago and given her a proper burial."

"Nether Monkslippers always seem to know, even if they do get a few facts wrong," said Cotton. "I suppose some equivalent of a gossipy Miss Pitchford has been disseminating misinformation about the village for centuries."

"And viewing it as a vital service to the community. Yes. So, what happens now?"

"As far as the girl is concerned, of course, we wait." Cotton looked about him pensively. "The poor thing. I think we have to assume this is the missing young woman. A girl who couldn't escape her fate. The lords and landowners in those days would have held all the cards. There was no Angela-type system that might have saved her."

"Angela?"

"Yes. Women have taken to asking after 'Angela' in pubs and bars—'How is Angela?' or 'May I speak with Angela?' It's a code to the bartender to say the guy they're with has turned out to be a problem and they need a safe way to escape from him. An escort out to a car, or a cab brought to the door, or even the police called in. In the U.S., it's called asking for an 'angel shot' and there are variations of wording to indicate how bad the situation is. An angel shot with lime, for example, means 'call the police now.' It is something that originated with the Lincolnshire Rape Crisis people. They've posted signs explaining the meaning in ladies' rooms all over Lincolnshire."

"It's one of those ideas so clever and long overdue you wonder why no one ever thought of it before. Certainly, you're right: our Victorian girl was out of reach of any help like that."

"Who do we like for this one?" Cotton asked. "What rogue long dead, himself?"

"Oh, the son of the lord of the manor at the time was always a favorite for this, once it became clear she hadn't just taken off to be with the gardener. Since someone took the trouble to hide her so well, I'm going to guess that someone was responsible in some way for her death. It may have been an accident of some kind and the guilty party panicked for unknown reasons. If this turns out to be our missing village girl I'll see if I can't get her bones interred in the vault at St. Edwold's. Members of the family are still around; they might agree to a DNA comparison." He paused to peer through the canopy of dying leaves on the overhead branches being thrown about and shuffled by a raw breeze coming off the pond. The sky had begun to roil with clouds.

"Anyway," he added, "we have a modern-day problem to wrap up."

"Lady Duxter," said Cotton. "Yes. It's lucky for her she made it but . . . Now she's on the mend, I suppose I'm wondering—will she forgive her husband? Can they just go back to the way they were before?"

"Will he forgive *her*? With an ego his size, it's doubtful. No one leaves Lord Duxter, no matter how unfaithful he's been. Anyway, I should think that's the last thing she'd want, to go back to the way things were before. Because the way things were before was awful. Bad enough to drive her to attempt suicide the one time, and making her vulnerable to Jane's murderous plot. Think how close Jane came to getting away with this. Even though Lord Duxter began to suspect her, he had no proof she was other than the efficient, docile woman she presented herself as being to the world."

"Right," said Cotton. "There was no physical evidence against her. It was her car, too, so of course her prints were everywhere. In the end we had no choice but to, well, test her."

Max could tell Cotton had rather enjoyed that moment, proving that some measure of actor's blood coursed through his veins, inherited from both his parents.

"As for Lady Duxter: Miss Pitchford reports that she's handed him an ultimatum, finally realizing how much of her depression came from her inability to speak up for herself, and from spending so much of her energy maintaining the status quo. I would say if the lord shapes up, she'll stay with him. She likes the glamour, if you will, of being Lady Duxter—*that* Lady Duxter of publishing fame. They've been together so long, and I think she's a loyal sort at heart, even if she's not the strongest of women. It's strictly up to him to appreciate that quality of loyalty. But it may be too late. Now there's Carville."

"Oh, surely those two won't end up together," said Cotton. "Carville is . . . well he's . . ."

"A self-serving, egotistical, basically dishonest man with an inflated sense of his own importance? Yes, but don't you see, that also describes Lord Duxter. To end up with Carville would be jumping out of the frying pan into the flames."

"I guess horrible men are her type," said Cotton. "Really, that's the tragedy. That the poor woman has such poor judgment she can't see what others around her see so clearly."

"Every couple is different. We just can't know." Max took a last look at the team huddled around the bones in the tree. "Come round to the vicarage when you're finished here," he said. "We'll have a drink."

Chapter 22

THE WORLD

Time passed, and Lady Duxter's condition improved with each day. Physical therapy, mental therapy, nutrition, drugs, and a good deal of luck combined to bring her round nearly to where she once had been. She would have phases of weakness and blurred vision, and according to Dr. Martin, she would never return to robust health. But she was *here*, still alive on the planet, and her husband claimed to be elated, although not everyone believed him (Miss Pitchford, on hearing the entire story, forever would brand him as an upstart cad and a scoundrel).

Lady Duxter had begun to remember and she had begun to talk.

"If there ever was any doubt," said Cotton, "we know now it was Jane who did this. And she acted alone. Up until near the end, I thought she might have a partner in crime. Carville or Lord Duxter or even a third person we never suspected." Cotton sat back in his chair by the vicarage fire and crossed one leg over another, first ensuring the crease in his slacks would remain knife sharp.

"But now in addition to the attempted murder we all saw at the hospital—our sting operation—we have an eyewitness to the murder of Colin Frost. Jane is the last person Marina remembers seeing before she passed out. She came to her senses briefly in the back of the car. There was Colin beside her, already nearly gone. And Jane was at the wheel. None of it made sense to her. Now it does."

Max slumped in his chair across from Cotton. He crossed his arms over his chest, a look of profound disquiet on his handsome face.

"This was pure evil. When will I learn to spot it?"

Privately, Cotton thought the answer was, "Never." One of Max's strengths was that he didn't see evil everywhere he looked. It allowed him to assess people without the inbred paranoia Cotton so often saw in the police force. When everyone you meet is a bad guy, the real bad guys can slip through the cracks. "When did you know, Max?"

"I didn't know for certain," he said slowly. "This case came near to defeating me, which is why I had to resort to, well, to some MI5 tricks I swore I'd never use again. I thought Jane had had no direct hand in the murders herself, because she was with Awena at five fifteen. Poppy's evidence created a sort of bookend effect to the timing: She said she was briefly with Jane at five or a little after. That's less than fifteen minutes. Poppy said she popped in to the library to ask if it was all right for her to use the ATM in the village. Her father was there, having a drink with Jane. Poppy kissed him good-bye."

"She didn't notice if his car was there, if he'd driven over, but he had."

"Yes. But all this meant Jane could not have done it all in fifteen minutes, however she went about it—subdue two people, somehow get their bodies into the car, drive them out to Prior's Wood, set up the hose for the carbon monoxide, wait several minutes to make sure they were not going to come round, and sprint back to the priory on foot.

"But Jane had altered the library clock, giving herself an extra twenty minutes. The times we were given to work with are irrelevant. Poppy's testimony in particular, as we now know, is irrelevant.

"You had Sergeant Essex run that mile, and for good measure, you had her run it back. She is of a similar build and age to Jane and like Jane, in good shape. When Miss Pitchford complained of seeing Jane running about the village, she meant that literally. Jane is a runner—not at a professional level, but fast enough to suit the purpose. In total it took Essex a little over twenty minutes to get to and from the Girl's Grave—there and back, over terrain that is not flat. And she stopped there for ten minutes and sort of moved about "committing the crime" in pantomime. If Jane ran it both ways we have to figure she needed at least thirty minutes. Add at least ten minutes to "manhandle" the victims in the first place—to subdue them with drugs and alcohol, and get them to the area where they were later found. From the start of the crime to the finish of the crime we were looking at forty minutes for her to do it all. There's no way—that did not fit what we knew of the timetable.

"The bodies were discovered very soon after, and just in time, or Lady Duxter would have been dead as well."

"Yes, that put an end time to the deed. Jane had forty minutes, tops, and even then she was lucky the hunter who found the bodies—an illegal poacher, really—didn't see her leaving the scene.

"I kept thinking Jane would need an accomplice—that for such a small person as she is, there was no way she could lift dead Colin's weight into the car. That would be nearly impossible for someone her size. Not even with that adrenaline rush that surges through you when you kill someone."

It was news to Cotton that Max had ever killed anyone. Cotton suspected that he'd never learn the details, although that wouldn't stop him from trying one day to pry the story out of Max.

"If she acted alone, I wondered, how did she manage it?" said Max. "If she had an accomplice—the only way I could see for her to shave time off the proceedings—who was it? With an accomplice to help her shift the victims, she could drive them out there and then run back, giving her that much-needed seven or so extra minutes. I thought of Poppy . . ."

"As someone who would lie for Jane. Someone she could manipulate, perhaps. Threaten or bully. Right."

"Unlikely, knowing Poppy's spirit, not to mention her dislike amounting to hatred of Jane, but not impossible. It would also go a long way toward explaining that dislike, if Jane had something on her. But I also wondered if Poppy might have done it, acting alone. She also could not do the heavy lifting by herself, but she was clever enough to convince two people to drive off and meet her in the woods. Time would be largely irrelevant if Poppy were the guilty party. Certainly, it would be easy for Jane to frame her for this murder if need be. But time mattered greatly in the case of Jane. She relied absolutely on our taking Awena's word for the time she was with Jane in the library."

"But Awena never wears a watch."

"That's right. Awena never wears a watch. Jane knew this very well. It goes against Awena's spiritual practice of living in the moment and not allowing herself to get too caught up in time constraints. Awena went by the old clock in the library—Jane would find an excuse to point out the time if Awena failed to notice it herself. But Jane had altered that clock to allow herself time to commit murder and provide an alibi for herself. This took careful planning. Almost nothing could be left to chance."

"What if she had failed, I wonder?"

"If she failed in this attempt, she simply would have tried again. She is relentless. And she was already into murder so deep."

"That would make a great title for a book," said Cotton, who was always planning to one day document his exploits with Max.

"Possibly," was Max's only acknowledgment. He knew full well how Cotton's mind worked. "Anyway. Jane invited Awena to come over to the library that afternoon, on some pretext of showing her something Jane had found in the archives. The next day, when I spoke with Jane, she was again at the library, pretending to work off her grief. More likely, hoping for a word with Lord Duxter. The clock's time was correct when I saw it. Of course, the first thing she would have done once Awena left would be to reset the clock to the correct time."

"She'd been planning all this for ages, hadn't she? Not just this closely timed murder, but the longer strategy."

"Yes," said Max. "Certainly for weeks and months. There are a few gaps where we have to make an educated guess, but it went pretty much like this: Colin is sent to Saudi Arabia, with the help of Lord Duxter. Either David wanted Colin gone because he wanted him out of the way so he could seduce Colin's wife—unlikely—or he was simply and unwittingly doing Jane's bidding, thinking he was helping an unemployed man get a job. She had been complaining rather loudly that Colin was underfoot all day and needed to be put to work. So one day at his London club Lord Duxter runs into a man he knew who said he needed a cybersecurity expert in his Saudi Arabia office, and Lord Duxter at some point puts in a word for Colin.

"Colin probably thought this was all Lord Duxter's doing and all his idea. The lord in his rather fatuous way thinks it is his idea, too. He is rather like that, seizing credit from Marina for her work in establishing the writers' retreat, for example. But I think it was Jane who instigated the whole plan in order to get her husband sent away.

"That may have been all she had in mind at the time—a little freedom—but I believe she dreamt of more. Much more. Anyway, the benefit for her of being such an unremarkable woman was that she could do as she pleased most of the time, with no one the wiser, no one taking particular notice of her whereabouts. We have all noted her quality of blending in behind the scenes and seen it as a virtue. But in this case she used her wallflower qualities to help her carry out a particularly cruel plan.

"Colin had been unemployed nearly a year—he, his wife, and daughter had been living off the good graces of Netta, his grandmother, and the situation was becoming untenable. Netta had been grateful for the company at the start of her widowhood but soon enough she wanted her privacy back. Besides, they were a larger financial burden than she'd counted on. It wasn't until her health began to fail and Colin went overseas that Jane, and Poppy, started to become permanent features in the household. Meanwhile, Jane chafed at being a sort of unpaid companion to a difficult older woman. Jane wanted out.

"Again, Lord Duxter may not have had designs on Jane in getting rid of Colin for her. He may have had only the motive of helping her financially by helping her husband. It was certainly less expensive than offering to help support her and her family by giving her a huge rise in pay.

"Anyway, by August the affair between Lord Duxter and Jane was in full swing. But what had changed from the spring into the summer? Very simply, he saw Jane bathing *au naturel* in the pond from the roof of his manor house. Do you remember how hot that summer was? It reached thirty-one degrees one day. If you recall how unseasonably warm it was it comes as no surprise that Jane and possibly others in the village would choose to go skinny dipping.

"Jane did what people have done for centuries when they were tempted by that pond. She took her clothes off and went for a swim.

And I gather that there is nothing plain about Jane in the nude. Lord Duxter, able to spy on her from the tower of Wooton Priory, was mesmerized. She played him to spectacular effect.

"And he was smitten—overcome with lust for this woman he had long ignored, seeing her as a plain, dull Jane. As someone in his employ who knew her way around the Dewey decimal system— nothing more. By the way, I think she knew full well she was on view by that pond—that she was well aware of her beauty and the effect she could have on men. But I only think that because I am certain she was the instigator from the start. It was she who wanted to be Lady Duxter, and she who orchestrated this whole series of tragic events."

Max mused, "The Bible's David went to great lengths to rid himself of a rival. He effectively sent Bathsheba's husband out to be killed. He ended up marrying her, although that soon came to grief. Anyway, our own David, Lord Duxter, was infatuated with Jane for a fleeting second and then woke up to see how unsuitable she was to someone of his age, his married state, his station in life, and all the rest. His feelings may not even have risen to the level of infatuation. No, we are probably looking at a simple case of lust, which has even a shorter shelf life than romantic love."

Max said, "What we had here, I finally realized, was the story of Bathsheba and David—but with a twist. On a hot summer day a woman bathes in the nude in the pond by Wooton Priory. The lord of the manor—Lord Duxter—sees her from the rooftop through binoculars that he kept to hand. Let's assume for a moment an innocent reason for those lenses. Possibly he was into bird-watching, right? But there was no other way to observe her from a distance, except from that roof. In any season, she would have been able to hear someone's approach through the forest. But at any time but high summer, she would not have gone swimming in the nude. We can practically pinpoint the time when the affair started from these facts alone. We also have Jane's subsequent pregnancy to narrow the time frame.

"One could argue that Jane may have thought she was alone and unobserved in those woods. That she was the victim here, or at the least, that she was swept off her feet into a situation beyond her power to control. But she knew that house and surrounding grounds well—she treated the place as her own and was free to roam. She would have seen the binoculars up there on the roof just as I did, exploring the place on a whim. Guessing what they were for, or at least how she could put them to good use, she set a trap for the unwary. For Lord Duxter. Knowing she was being watched, she put on a show for him. She went bathing at a spot and time of day when she knew he would be on the manor rooftop and would see her. She knew he went there with his nightly nightcap when the stars were out and the scene was spectacular. How spectacular David, the poor sap, was only coming to know.

"Day after day, throughout that warm spell. Within a week, he was by his own admission completely smitten. Jane in her quiet way was a knockout. The old cliché of the librarian letting down her hair and revealing the beauty hidden behind the heavy spectacles—it all happened to come true for Lord Duxter."

"Until reality struck."

"Correct. The affair lasted well into the autumn, and continued up to the day Jane's husband was found dead. Then she had to go into 'mourning'—briefly. Her plan of course was to take up with Lord Duxter again at the earliest opportunity. The part of her plan that went wrong was that Lady Duxter was still alive. Well, *that*, she must have thought, could easily be remedied.

"Anyway. That is when Lord Duxter's foolish infatuation began, as he watched Jane from the tower of the priory. Much as David spotted Bathsheba bathing, from the roof of his palace, and was overcome with desire, leaving common sense behind. Really, I should start paying closer attention to my own sermons.

"Their baby was conceived that summer. Now, thinks Lord Duxter in a panic, this woman has thrown them both in it. We may never know if the pregnancy was deliberate on her part—I think it was, but I would take it as one hundred percent given it was not part of Lord Duxter's plans.

"Still, she believed that given time she could convince him to marry her—she'd had her own way from the start, after all. But this was quite a different equation, and quite obviously, Lord Duxter wanted to wash his hands of her. He did not get into this affair for the long term. He convinces her, or he thinks he does, that she must get her husband home immediately so that Colin can be tricked into thinking the baby is his.

"She may have anticipated this would be the lord's initial reaction, so she stayed calm and pretended to do as he asked. She would work him round to her way of thinking in time.

"And what does she do? She gets her husband home by *killing his grandmother*. But not so she can make Colin think the baby is his—no. She gets him home so she can rid herself of him once and for all. It's an insane plan, which leads one to wonder how sane Jane actually is. She may be quite mad, not knowing right from wrong."

"I think so, too," said Cotton. "But of course, I just don't like her, so that colors my view. Jane wanted Lord Duxter to herself, and step one in that process was sending Colin off to a job in Saudi Arabia. Step two was killing him and Lady Duxter. Step three would be marrying Lord Duxter. The woman has ice in her veins."

"I pray for her, now she's been sent to be mauled about by the court system. It's all I can do."

Pray for her? Cotton thought he would never understand Max.

Cotton personally wished Jane Frost put away for a long, long time in the dankest prison Her Majesty could provide. The prison system always needed librarians.

"Anyway," Max continued, "when by September, Jane tests pregnant—she's been using pregnancy test kits repeatedly, according to Poppy—Jane has to get Colin home, stat. She assures Lord Duxter she'll pin the pregnancy on Colin, but again, I don't think she had the least intention of doing that. She wanted Lord Duxter for herself and this was her way in. Any maternal consideration for the child was, shall we say, noticeably absent. Jane saw it as a minor inconvenience that her intended was already married to Marina, and that she, Jane, was married to Colin. That, she thought, was easily taken care of with a staged double suicide."

"A twofer," said Cotton. "Problem solved."

"Precisely. The two people standing in the way of her happiness done away with at once, in one fatal blow. There was a case not long ago of a British dentist who did something similar—he set up his wife and his lover's husband in a fake suicide pact. I believe the pair didn't even know each other. And he got away with it for years, until guilt got the better of him. After a run of bad luck he broke down and confessed. I was reminded of it when I had to make an appointment with my own dentist in the middle of all this. Those things are always most inconvenient in their timing, aren't they? Or maybe, they are heaven-sent."

Cotton, who had no opinion on this fine theological point—to him a toothache was just a toothache—smiled encouragingly, waiting for Max to continue.

"Anyway, immediately Jane knew she was pregnant, she swung into action, killing her grandmother-in-law—eighty-year-old Netta."

Cotton nodded. "Once we exhumed Netta's body, an autopsy revealed an overdose of sleeping tablets. No doubt a high dose of her own prescription. But she actually died of asphyxiation. The coroner now believes someone simply drugged her into submission, and held a pillow over her mouth until she was dead. Smothering someone is not as easy to do as it looks in films. You have to be determined, ruthless, and utterly without a conscience. It does help if your victim is a feeble elderly woman who is passed out from an overdose."

"The poor woman had probably over time come to trust her 'Angel of Mercy,' for Jane was the consummate manipulator," said Max. "Suspicious as Netta was by nature, she'd have taken whatever Jane told her to take, and eat and drink whatever was prepared for her. Probably Jane played up to Netta's tendency to treat her like a servant. The role came to be useful to Jane.

"Colin had told Dr. Winship that his grandmother had been getting confused and forgetful about taking her doses. Poppy, and of course Jane, confirmed this when Netta died. Nowhere in the world does anyone look closely at the death of such an elderly person unless their body is riddled with bullet holes and stab wounds. It is assumed the person died of natural causes."

"So," said Cotton. "Jane did all of this in her cold-blooded way to get her husband sent home by his company on some sort of hardship leave. Netta died simply because Jane found she was pregnant and it was necessary—from Lord Duxter's standpoint—to get her husband home and into her bed quickly so he would think the child was his. Colin, the poor mug, duly returns to attend to arrangements for his grandmother."

"Poppy told me her father slept on the sofa each night," said Max.

"I'm going to suppose Jane thought it might be helpful if Poppy could testify to that, if any questions of paternity ever came up. Jane wanted there to be no doubt that this was Lord Duxter's offspring."

Max nodded. "So, that's the nutshell version. The lord is guilty of adultery, of course, but not of murder. Besides, he was in London at the crucial time."

"We were asked to believe that Colin took up with Lady Duxter, or resumed a relationship with her, and became involved to the extent that weeks later he became her partner in a double suicide attempt. Jane tried to spread the word at Elka's that he and Marina had been together for ages, but in fact, there is only her word for that. For a lot of things."

"And in this area, believe me, Miss Pitchford or someone very like Miss Pitchford would have picked up on news of an affair of long standing," Max said. "I think Jane put that about because it was very hard to believe Colin would kill himself over a woman he'd been involved with such a short time."

"She was clever about that."

Max said, "Jane was clever about a lot of things. She never claimed that Colin suffered episodes of full-blown depression, like Lady Duxter. But she hinted to all who would listen at a rather dark, Dickensian childhood for him, with a neglectful and possibly suicidal mother. I see now she was saying that Colin was so damaged he was a clear candidate for suicide himself, and that however surprised she claimed to be by his death, she was not all *that* surprised. That Colin's uncle had died of an overdose which most thought to be deliberate played wonderfully into her planning, suggesting as it did an even stronger case for an inherited tendency. Jane made sure to scatter references to that ugly event, to remind everyone, and to keep it planted in everyone's mind that there was a history of mental illness in the family. To include Poppy, of course."

"You think Poppy was next in her planning?"

"I do."

"It's all just so ruthless. And then of course Lady Duxter's struggles with mental health were widely known."

"Yes. That Marina had a well-documented history of depression and had in fact attempted to end her life just the year before—it all folded in nicely. Jane had found two perfect victims for her awful plan. They'd been handed to her, in a way. By being around the priory all day, she had access to that diary of Lady Duxter's. And then there was the note Jane left beside Colin's body."

"It was authentic," said Cotton. "Our examiners said the handwriting was almost certainly his."

"It was no doubt something he'd written to Jane during one of their frequent breakups when they were courting, or that he'd written following an argument about his going to Saudi. She'd saved it, who knows why or for how long. That is how her mind works; it is a sort of by-product of her training. She is a librarian, an archivist, and nothing written ever goes to waste. She may always have been thinking long-term about getting rid of Colin."

"She may have kept the note as a tender keepsake of their courtship."

"But that doesn't sound much like her, does it?" said Max. "Knowing how she really felt about Colin. Poppy actually told me she wondered if Jane planned to poison Colin too—if that's why she suddenly starting cooking meals for him—or trying to: Miss Pitchford distrusted very much her knowledge of food preparation. But the double suicide plan was much neater and much less likely to arouse suspicion, since Netta had just died and no one yet suspected that death involved a poisoning or overdose. With two similar events in a row people were bound to ask questions. So Jane came up with a new plan."

"And how near she came to getting away with it."

"'The world, the flesh, and the devil,'" Max quoted. "Here were all three, a trifecta of temptations: Jane's hunger for status; Jane's physical lust for David and his for her, overriding all good judgment;

and some devil whispering in her ear, oh so convincingly, that she could have it all, she could have everything she wanted. All she had to do was kill, or attempt to kill, three innocent people."

"And then Carville makes four. Or would have, if he'd stayed at home at the St. George Studio that night."

Max nodded. "One wonders where she would have stopped. *If* she would have stopped. Poppy was afraid for her life, and with good reason. Poppy knew too much about what went on in Hawthorne Cottage. She also stood in the way of Jane's inheriting everything Colin left behind. That was why we had to get Poppy out of the way to a safe house in London—with Stanley along to make it look like a true runaway situation. Just in case."

"And the case proved true."

"Yes. And there was that business of the bra Adam Birch told me he and Elka had seen, hanging from a branch in Prior's Wood. Just as I was leaving his shop, Jane happened to cross my field of vision. She was wearing this shapeless dress too big for her and when she lifted her arm to wave I couldn't help but see a flash of bright color—the side of her bra. It was red, and lacy, such as Adam had just described to me."

"That could have meant nothing, of course. Millions of women might own such a garment . . . including Lady Duxter."

"But it was odd—a garment glaringly at odds with Jane's demure outward appearance, for one thing. And seeing her just then, it did make me start to wonder if I shouldn't err on the side of too much caution."

"For if Jane was having a rendezvous in those woods, it certainly wasn't with Colin. He wasn't even around."

"Precisely. Jane and Lord Duxter were almost certainly the couple little Tom saw in the woods. Also, once I realized Poppy's alibi for Jane was shaky . . . Poppy thought she left the library at a little after five o'clock and made a withdrawal from the bank at five twenty-five. But she dawdled on the way: it was actually five fifty-five, and the time disparity initially made us suspicious of her.

"I soon realized it could have been almost any time, though— she had her watch on upside down, so the digital display could not be trusted. I had a similar make of watch and more than once I put it on upside down after my shower, not realizing until the time showed as jarringly wrong. However, 5:05 and 5:25 and a few other times look identical when read right side up or upside down. It completely throws you off. I asked Poppy if she took the watch off to bathe. She looked at me like I was mad but she told me that although the watch was supposed to be water-resistant, she always took it off to bathe or shower. And besides, she didn't wear it all the time, except when she planned to do a lot of walking that day. So she wasn't completely used to wearing it, in other words.

"I realized that once Jane learned what had happened, Poppy would become very disposable, her alibi useless to Jane. In fact, it completely muddied the waters, just when Jane had been so careful to think of every contingency."

"The best-laid plans . . ."

"And then there was Carville, who also knew too much," Max continued. "He knew Colin was not Marina's lover. *He* was Marina's lover. Worse luck for Jane she didn't know that or she would have ditched the suicide pact idea. Instead she had to race around, covering up like mad. She attempted to kill Carville by setting fire to the studio while she thought he was inside as he should have been, sound asleep in the early morning hours. She also knew he kept a diary— because he told anyone who would listen he kept a diary. In pen and ink, but also on his laptop. What were the chances he wasn't telling his "Dear Diary" about his affair with Lady Duxter? The chances were zero. A writer like Carville never shuts up, anyway. That evidence had to be destroyed."

"He never heard of saving files to the cloud?"

"There was no wireless out there, remember."

"Ah. Another masterpiece lost to the world, then."

"When last seen, he was trying to rewrite everything from memory. I think he was as upset about the loss of his writing as about the attempt on his life."

Cotton sat back, and surveyed the polished tips of his shoes. "Come on, let's have it all now: When did you begin to suspect Jane?"

Max shrugged. "Not soon enough. Once I began to think Netta might have been murdered, it changed everything. But I never considered that possibility until the death of Colin and the attempt on Lady Duxter's life. Netta was so old any thought of her being killed for an inheritance made little sense. The murderer could almost be certain no one would realize she had been murdered."

"And no one did."

"No. Dr. Winship was called in, and he'd been treating her for years for all manner of ills. She'd had several heart attacks, and a mild stroke just last year. He assumed this attack was the one that finally carried her off, the last in a long string of events that had weakened her defenses. Any doctor in his position would have thought the same. What would be the point of an autopsy when every indication was of a natural death?

"Still, when Colin died, along with you I kept coming back to the possibility of murder, and I kept circling back to ask why anyone would kill an elderly woman who was already dying? There were three possible reasons."

"Apart from simple hatred, a murder committed in a spurt of sudden rage."

"Correct. But this murder was carefully organized to look like a natural death—sudden rage didn't enter into it. So one reason would be that you were in a hurry to inherit her money because of a looming debt. Or reason two: because you were unaware that she was in such poor health she was sure to die soon. Or reason three: because her death would trigger a funeral, and a funeral is the surest way to lure home a close relative.

"It would seem that this time, a funeral really *was* for the living."

Chapter 23

THE FLESH

The sun had long since set. Max made coffee, and got out the apple brandy and two snifters.

"Three options," he continued. "Now, the first option was a possibility, but Netta didn't have all that much money. Assuming Jane or even Poppy was the killer, surely waiting for Netta to die a natural death was the least risky way of inheriting, through Colin, what she did have.

"Then there was option two. But according to Dr. Winship, Jane and Poppy both knew Netta had a dicky heart. Just one look at her prescriptions, to which Jane had ready access, would make that clear. So again, it becomes a matter of just waiting out the natural course of things. Netta surely would die soon.

"Option three became the most interesting possibility, once Poppy told me Jane was running through pregnancy kits practically by the case. Why would any woman do that, I wondered? Because she was afraid of becoming pregnant? Or because she wanted to become pregnant and wanted—needed to have—the results as soon as possible?

"Lord Duxter goes into a panic when he hears her glad tidings: for him, there was no time to be lost in getting Colin home. So Jane, wanting to be helpful and perhaps 'prove' her love, killed Colin's grandmother."

"And Lord Duxter, seeing only that his wants were falling into place quite nicely, never realized that Netta's death was not just a helpful coincidence."

"Right," said Max. "It was something, in fact, that Jane may have had up her sleeve all along. To get Colin back—but not so people would assume he was the father of her child. She wanted Colin back so she could kill him, so she could be free to be with 'her' lord. Lady Duxter must die, also, to free up Lord Duxter."

"We are still asked to believe Lord Duxter had nothing to do with Colin's death? My super thinks he must have known or suspected."

"I don't believe he did. Psychologically, it won't mesh. Jane was seething that Lord Duxter wouldn't fall in line with her plans and own up to his responsibilities, but she pretended to go along and agreed she would make Colin think the baby was his. But what Jane had in mind was far more diabolical. She had to be rid of her husband and of David's wife, so she could become Lady Duxter. If you are able to follow her crazed logic, it of course made perfect sense. So by the time of Colin's return, she was ready to launch the second phase of her plan. The death of her husband and Marina."

"Three people had to die, not counting Carville."

Max shrugged. "Three people stood in the way to her happiness. I don't think she saw them as people."

"Lady Duxter in particular. Who had never done her a moment's harm."

"Jane was quite aware of Marina's tendencies—half of Monkslip had heard the stories of Lady Duxter's depressive episodes. Lord Duxter used to say it was like living with Virginia Woolf—he never knew when her spirits would plunge and she might do something to harm herself. She was on medication but too often the wrong prescription either makes no difference or makes matters worse. Or the patient starts to feel better and stops taking the needed medicine. So when she and her 'lover' Colin were found in a suicide pact, no one was that shocked. Jane put about the story of this tragic love affair between Colin and Marina, dropping hints of her suspicions that the affair was one of long standing. Tongues were already wagging at the Cavalier—*some*thing must be up with Lady Duxter.

"But where it all went wrong was that only one of her victims died, leaving the other behind to perhaps one day tell the tale of what really had happened, and even to say who the killer was. For Jane, the thought of Lady Duxter's surviving, waking up one night in hospital and starting to talk, was unthinkable. Jane started to go into a decline, herself. She was frantic with worry. When she heard—when I told her—that Lady Duxter was showing signs of recovery . . . well. That was all she needed to hear. She raced to the hospital to make sure Lady Duxter's recovery was stalled—permanently. I offered to escort her to make sure Jane wasn't left alone in the hospital unattended to do her dirty work."

"Of course I put the chief in the picture," said Cotton. "So long as Marina was in no danger—was in fact surrounded by policemen and policewomen dressed as doctors and orderlies—it seemed the best and only way to lure Jane out of her pretense of brave widowhood."

Max held his glass up to the fireplace, watching the play of the light through the amber liquid. He poured them both another drink.

"One odd thing . . . ," he began.

"It's all odd. What else?"

"I asked Awena to bring home a deck of tarot cards from her shop and of an evening I sat looking idly through them. Since we weren't by then playing with a full deck, as it were, with those two cards missing from Poppy's deck, I wanted to get the whole effect—see what was missing. And I saw that what was missing was the Star card. It depicts a naked woman. A naked woman kneeling by a pool of water."

"You think Jane got the idea for this seduction from the cards?"

Max shrugged: *Who knows?* "It can be a lucky card. A sign of renewal. But it also can mean a leaving behind, a following of a new path, and being guided by your own star and none other."

"How do you know all this? Awena, I suppose?"

"No, I looked it up on some website called Tabitha's Tarot. But I couldn't help but wonder if Jane had seen that depiction, looking through Poppy's deck of cards."

"And been inspired by it, somehow. Or maybe Colin or someone read her fortune, and she became convinced of her 'true destiny.' Well, we're agreed, she was the mastermind here."

"So it would appear. And a passable actress. That day she showed up at the vicarage, dripping with concern for Poppy: Every time she touched her handkerchief to her face, her eyes got redder and redder. I did wonder if there weren't some irritant on the handkerchief that was making her 'cry' more."

"Well, that's an old actor's trick," said Cotton. "My mother used it in her performances. God knows, natural ability was lacking so she had to resort to strategies like that."

Max nodded, his eyes absently roaming the shelves of the book-lined room with their dozens of versions of the Bible. "As with most women, we don't really hear from Bathsheba in the Bible. After this I have to wonder: Was she more a willing participant in the undoing of her husband—in sending him off to die in battle—than the old story leads us to believe? Now Lord Duxter claims Colin was brought home in part to protect Jane's virtue, just as David did in the Bible. And so a husband might be tricked into thinking the child was his. It didn't work out well for the biblical David and it didn't work out for this one, either."

Cotton said, "Be that as it may. Our David, Lord Duxter, wanted most of all not to be saddled with this woman who he was perhaps beginning to sense was crazy."

"And he didn't even realize she'd already murdered Netta."

"Ah," said Cotton. "So, whatever he felt at one time for Jane, he came to his senses and wanted out."

"King David had stooped to treachery and, effectively, to murder to get himself out of his own trap. But our David's first thought was to foist Jane back onto her husband, Colin, never dreaming that he couldn't just hand her back over, as if he were returning a lawn mower. She didn't want to go back. She'd tasted a bit of the high life, in her roamings about Wooton Priory, and she saw riches and prestige in her future. She wanted all that she'd 'worked' for to continue."

"She wasn't going without a fight."

"Not ever. Not Jane."

Destiny came for dinner the next night with Max and Awena, Cotton having settled back in at Monkslip-super-Mare with his own young family. Naturally, the table talk turned to the murder. But the two women had a slightly different take on the situation from that of Max and Cotton.

"It took me so long to see it," Max was saying, passing the homemade bread and offering wine.

"See what, Max?" Awena asked.

"That Jane was a cold-blooded manipulator. People tended to talk of her in clichés—if they talked of her at all—as the plain little librarian no one notices and everyone underestimates. With her hair in a low bun and her big wide eyes and her small stature, she always reminded me of a sort of Jane Eyre type—she even has the name. An intelligent young woman who has been told all her life that she was nothing special.

"What was it Brontë called her heroine? Obscure, plain, and little? Something like that. It summed up Jane Frost—but it summed up her outward appearance, merely."

Still, Max thought, this woman had at least one man in thrall to her. As with Wallis Simpson—no one could ever understand the king's fierce, nearly irrational attachment. History had repeated itself with Camilla and Prince Charles. Absurd rumors abounded of the ways Wallis kept the immature and strangely unworldly prince in thrall. But the fact was, Max thought, he trusted her. He simply grew to trust her. A man in his position, surrounded by sycophants and self-seekers, no doubt sank gratefully into her web with an enormous sigh of relief. To the devil with duty and with what the world thought.

"Shame on me that I couldn't see it," said Max. "What a complete conniver she was. She told me she'd seen Colin slip something from the archives into his knapsack, something he said was 'dynamite.' That was of course a red herring, a lie told to make me think Colin might be the target of outside forces."

"Funny," said Awena, with a glance at Destiny. "I don't think there was a woman in the village who couldn't see it. No one thought she'd stoop to murder or we'd have caught on sooner, of course. Well, Miss Pitchford thought she would—stoop to murder, I mean. But she thinks that of most people so no one pays her any mind."

Destiny took a sip of her wine, nodded her approval, and added,

"She always struck me as sly, Jane. Butter wouldn't melt in her mouth. You know the type: Whenever she saw me coming down the High, it was all, 'What time is Morning Prayer, then, Mother Chatsworth?' No one, absolutely no one, calls me Mother Chatsworth, at least not with a straight face. It makes me sound like someone on trial for witchcraft in *The Crucible*. Or it would be, 'Oh, I should love to donate something to the Fayre. I'll bring my special apple fritters then, shall I?' As if I'd care. But it was an act. I knew it was a performance of some kind, but I could not for a moment figure out why she would go out of her way to impress me with her piety. Let alone her fritters."

"Nor me," said Awena. "Perhaps she was collecting the character witnesses she knew she might need one day. Except, Max, I always rather thought it was a way of getting to you."

Max was astounded. "To *me*? Whatever for?"

The two women again exchanged glances, and they both sighed. One of Max's most winning traits was his obliviousness to how attractive he was to women; it was his blind spot. While it was a card he could easily have played all his life to get whatever he wanted out of almost anyone, he either didn't recognize it as an option or he chose not to use it. And that sense of fair play, as it were, of course only trebled his attractiveness.

"Never mind," said Awena and Destiny together.

"Why did you not say something before now?" Max asked, not unreasonably.

It was Destiny who replied. "We thought she was a conniver. A schemer. At worst a seductress. Not a murderess, I tell you. I never dreamed she *killed* anyone."

"Nor I," said Awena. "That was too big a leap to make. Now, try some of the wild mushrooms. They're growing like mad all over Prior's Wood now."

"Thank you," said Destiny. "And now, what about the stained glass, Max? Has Coombebridge decided to see reason? About the goat?"

Max had driven out to the artist's cottage again just the other day. He thought back to the conversation he'd had then with Coombebridge.

"About that goat," he'd begun.

"Oh," said Coombebridge—from his expression, much enjoying the thought of the hubbub he'd created. "You noticed."

"Of course I noticed. And I'm afraid I'll have to ask you to change it into something more orthodox. Like a lamb. And the Good Shepherd needs to be made to look, well, normal."

"You can't do that." Coombebridge was smug, sure of his footing. "The family commissioned the work, not you or the Church."

Oh, yes I can. "You'll have to change it," Max said again.

"What's in it for me if I do?"

"Reduced time in Purgatory," said Max. "Let's say I knock one hundred days off for you."

"Are you serious?"

"No. But I'll see to it that your payment for your work is withheld. Poppy will have the final say now, you know. And I think she'll enjoy exercising her authority in such a good cause. Once I've explained the situation to her."

"I don't care about money," said the artist. "I'm rich."

"Then I'll not permit the work to be installed. It will sit in a cupboard where no one will ever see it. Or, better yet, I'll tell the rubbish men to come and recycle it."

Max was bluffing on the latter threat, but it did the trick. Coombebridge's face fell. He was incorruptible when it came to money, but only because he didn't need money. It was his ego as an artist that was his Achilles' heel. Coombebridge was proud of the work he'd labored so long and hard to create, and he wanted the world to see it, not have it be hidden away on a shelf or destroyed.

In the end, grudgingly and with little grace, Coombebridge agreed to Max's terms. "But only if you promise to let me paint your portrait one day."

"When I have time," said Max easily, guessing that that had been Coombebridge's price from the very beginning. And knowing that the day when he had time hanging heavy on his hands would never come.

"And I'll take you up on the Purgatory deal, too."

"You'll have to talk with the Catholics about that. Although the last I heard they stopped selling indulgences at some point in the fifteen hundreds."

Now Max told Destiny, "He was fine with making a few changes. He actually said it was an easy fix.

"Really, he was just as gentle as a lamb. I think he's mellowing."

Chapter 24

AND EVERYWHERE, THE DEVIL

Lord Duxter also seemed to be a reformed man. Somehow, having learned he didn't know everything had had a humbling effect, as he confessed to Max.

He and Max had had many a conversation at both the priory and the hospital since Jane had been apprehended. The lord made daily visits to his wife. Even knowing she now was safe from Jane, he wanted to see for himself that all was well, and that Marina continued to thrive. He had not, he told Max, missed a visiting hour, and would not until she was returned safely home.

"Who would think any sane person would—?" Lord Duxter caught himself before he could finish the sentence. "*Is* she sane?"

"There is every chance she is not," said Max. "But under the legal standard of knowing right from wrong, she's as right as rain. She is quite aware she killed two people and wanted to kill four. And for no other reason than that she wanted what she wanted. I'm told by DCI Cotton her only regret is that she was caught. And for that she blames me. That is the usual psychology of the sociopath."

"Poor old Netta. They're sure?"

"Quite sure. Jane needed a good reason to lure Colin home. A person can't come and go on a whim from Saudi, and sometimes even a death in the family isn't enough. Add to that the fact that Colin, according to Poppy, had become reluctant even to be in the same country with Jane, only returning to England when absolutely necessary to see his daughter. It explains why Colin quickly jumped at the chance of a job in a foreign place that would keep him away for so much of the year."

"He was dying to get away from her."

"With dying being the operative word, as it turned out."

"I don't understand how Colin could have left his daughter with such a woman."

"Don't you? He badly needed the money, for her education, for his family. I'm sure Colin told himself that leaving Poppy with Jane was just a temporary but necessary expedient. Colin may have been weak but he was not an uncaring father, not at all. I just don't think for a moment he recognized the danger."

"He certainly wasn't alone in that."

Max nodded. "Anyway, Jane had to act quickly. Her pregnancy is what altered the dynamic."

Max shot a meaningful glance at Lord Duxter, who had the grace to look abashed.

"If all else failed—with you, I mean—she might still need to seduce Colin into believing the child was his. I admire her confidence, don't you? Somehow I am certain her confidence in her seductive powers is more than justified."

Lord Duxter looked as though he could say from sad experience that it was.

"All this, by the way, explains why Jane was suddenly all sweetness and light where Colin was concerned, as Poppy claimed—up to a point. Colin must not suspect he was walking into a trap. I suppose a case could be made that she did all this for you, to save your reputation—at least, for as long as it needed to be saved. There is no question her long-range plan was to get rid of Colin and live happily ever after as lady of the manor. Your manor, as it happens."

Lord Duxter seemed horrified at the thought. Say what anyone might about Lady Duxter, she had been born into the upper classes. The lord's innate snobbishness and need to social climb wouldn't have allowed him to consider Jane as being anything other than another temporary fling. Jane had refused to see that.

Max wondered: Had she similarly coaxed the malleable Colin into marriage—later trying the same trick on the lord? What worked once might work again.

"So Jane set up a scheme to do away with Colin and your wife."

"Using my wife's previous attempt on her own life to make it seem believable that she would try again. The cruelty takes my breath away. But she's a small woman. It is hard to picture how she had the strength to do it."

"She was strong and fit from running. And she made sure she had the time, or seemed to. Poppy and Awena both alibied her."

Max thought back to something Cotton had repeated to him, which showed the depths of Jane's callousness. "She was old anyway," Jane had said to the police, in making a full confession. "Her life was over. My life was just beginning." But Netta may have had many good years left to her, with proper care, and Max thought it a crime to steal so much as a minute from anyone. After all, a lot could change in a minute.

"I still don't know how she got them both in the car with her," Lord Duxter was saying. "What was the pretext?"

"That was easier than it seemed. But first, she waited for a day when you were in London, so you would have an alibi. She *was* protecting you, you see. And when she killed Netta, she made sure she had a cover story ready for herself."

"How so?"

"By trying to pin the blame for some doctored preserves on Poppy. She told Mme Cuthbert that she herself—Jane—had noticed they tasted off."

"Good heavens, man! All right. Go on."

"She had already invited Lady Duxter to come to the library earlier in the afternoon—say around four fifteen or four thirty—on the pretext of showing her some wonderful find in the archives about the Girl's Grave, knowing how interested she'd be. Once Marina was there, she offered her a drink—several drinks, doctored. Lady Duxter, already heavily medicated, would soon be unconscious, a dead weight. But Jane had made sure she sat in a chair with wheels. Once she was certain Marina was completely out, she wheeled her into a cupboard off the library. Then she telephoned Colin, who was in the grounds, and asked him to bring their car round to the library, as she now needed a ride. Once he arrived, she drugged him the same way she'd drugged Lady Duxter. Poppy came in briefly around five, before Colin was completely intoxicated. Poppy left for the ATM. Then, complaining that he was now too drunk to drive, Jane said she would drive them both home. But she made sure she walked him outside to the car before he could collapse on her. She couldn't handle a dead weight the size of Colin. She made him get in the backseat, where he fell completely into sleep, already approaching a state of overdose.

"She then pushed Marina out the French windows to the car, which was parked outside. She tipped the unconscious woman into the backseat beside Colin. That side of the priory is hidden from view, so Jane had no worries about being seen."

"Could she manage even Marina's light weight?" said Lord Duxter, doubtfully.

Max said, "Jane was nothing if not determined. She worked in a nursing home, remember, and was used to lifting people far heavier than she was. She knew how to do it without straining her back. The training came in handy with Netta but even handier in arranging a fake double suicide for Marina and Colin. She hoisted Marina out of the chair into a fireman's carry and shoved her onto the backseat alongside Colin, arranging them in a sort of lovers' embrace and planting the note and the poem alongside. And that Hanged Man card, for good measure, to point the finger, if all else failed, at some anonymous Saudi cartel or other."

"Diabolical."

"But, too—she was a romantic, remember. It has all the earmarks of a sort of overblown plot that spanned continents. Next, Jane drove the car into a secluded spot in Prior's Wood, where she attached the vacuum hose, which of course she'd readied in the boot of the car, to the exhaust. It so happened she chose the very spot in the woods where she met all that summer with you, Lord Duxter—chosen because she knew how secluded a spot it was. Naturally, she wore gloves the whole time. Probably the white gloves she used to handle old manuscripts in the library. She left the car running and left Colin and Marina to their fates. If the tank of the car had been full, no doubt Marina would have been finished as well as Colin. It was one of several mistakes she made. The car simply ran out of petrol."

"Another mistake was with the music," said Lord Duxter.

Max nodded. "The music added a ghoulish touch. But she got the music wrong."

"And Carville? She set the fire and tried to kill him, too. But, why?"

Because Carville never knew when to shut up, Max thought. "It must be an occupational hazard," he said aloud, "wanting to try to script and direct everything. And wanting to put everything that happened to him in a book, a thought that worried Jane greatly. She might have the threat of 'Tell-a-Tale Carville' hanging over her head indefinitely. Because, intending to spare her grief at thinking her husband unfaithful, Carville told Jane that *he*—not Colin—was Marina's lover. He furthermore confessed to her how he had been mightily confused by this chain of events. How he simply could not understand why Colin would be found in a suicide pact with Marina when he was not having an affair with Marina.

"Jane realizes that this unforeseen development—she had had no idea Marina and Carville were involved—means the authorities will never buy a suicide attempt and will start to investigate this as a murder. So Jane decides the only thing for her to do is to kill the writer that night by setting fire to his place, neatly getting rid of both him and any diary he was keeping.

"Her next mistake was in not realizing Carville wasn't in the St. George Studio that night. She'd advised him not to tell the authorities that he and Marina were lovers, in case the police started suspecting him, as a jealous lover or some such. As it happens, Carville finally did come clean about his affair with Marina, but Jane wasn't to know that. And luckily for him, as he was returning to Wooton Priory for the night, he was involved in a minor automobile accident that forced him to stop at a nearby inn while his car was taken in for repairs. That minor crash probably saved his life. He was lucky."

"I suppose you would say a higher power saved him."

"Undoubtedly I would," Max assured him. "So. Jane knows that *Carville* knows that the Colin-and-Marina setup is a sham. So she tries to kill him by burning the church down around him."

"And the police decided to let the arsonist, whoever it was, think they had succeeded."

"Right. That was an on-the-spot decision orchestrated by DCI Cotton. Carville's life appeared to be in real danger. The police seized the opportunity to keep him out of harm's way while they gained time to get to the bottom of things. If Jane thought she'd got away with murder yet again, she might start to think she was invincible—and that is when she might slip up. They do say 'pride goeth before a fall.'"

"Is that legal?"

Max shrugged. "More or less. The truth is that any case not cracked within the first forty-eight hours may never be solved. They were getting desperate for a solve, and flushing out the killer was much the best way. Once it was clear there was no actual victim of the fire, they staged the removal of a body from the scene. Jane, triumphant, thought Carville was dead, that she'd succeeded in killing him and destroying whatever he may have been writing—although she put on quite a show of distress at the scene. She felt she'd covered her tracks nicely. No Wi-Fi meant no record had been kept that could be retrieved by investigators. Carville had repeatedly said how wonderful it was to have to revert to pen and paper."

"Where did Carville stay all that time? Until he showed up at the hospital, when Jane was apprehended?"

"The police simply told him to stay put at the inn where he was already staying. Thoroughly shaken but glad to be alive, he did as he was told. But he insisted he wanted to be part of the sting arranged for Jane at the hospital. And DCI Cotton was willing to oblige, so long as he kept completely out of the way and at a safe distance." Cotton, thought Max, whether he would admit it or not, had inherited a flair for the dramatic from his parents. It went against procedure to have the writer there at all, even standing safely peering in through the small window in the hospital room door.

"The police, by the way, got the distinct impression Carville may have been coming from the home of one of his former paramours," Max continued. "You know the type of man he is: he thinks the sun doesn't shine when he's gone, and he assumes every old flame will be thrilled to hear from him again."

Lord Duxter grunted his agreement. By this time he was very worried his wife might want to continue her relationship with the famous author.

"Since that was not really our business," Max continued, "the policeman sent to talk with her didn't try to force her on that angle. Theirs was a relationship from some years ago and Carville claims it was pure coincidence she lived nearby. He found her on social media, as everyone seems to do these days. But their meeting was to all appearances what he says: a friendly get-together for old times' sake. Besides—the woman has remarried." Max noticed that Lord Duxter's anxiety seemed to increase with this news. Much better from his point of view that the woman be readily available to Carville. "Her husband was there for this reunion and apparently got on famously with the author. He had all of Carville's books on his bookshelves, and had Carville sign them. I gather the husband is a true fan and this little act of homage definitely won Carville over, probably for life."

"What a fathead," said Lord Duxter, showing more than a trace of residual jealousy.

"Hmm. Anyway, I think we can safely rule out the idea this old flame was covering for Carville for some unknown reason or was involved with him as an accomplice. I mean, what purpose would it serve? Beyond finding out for certain he was not at home, and that no one seems to have known he was away—that was the sum total of the police findings."

Max didn't mention to Lord Duxter that all Carville did, when he wasn't talking about his books that night, was talk about how much he cared for Marina. He claimed Marina was the love of his life. And he went on and on about how he knew for certain that suicide setup was just that—a setup. Marina was going to leave her husband for Carville, or so Carville claimed.

Max didn't feel Lord Duxter needed to hear that. Once Lady Duxter recovered completely, surely she would make up her own mind what to do.

Chapter 25

RESHUFFLE

With her great-grandmother, mother, and father all dead and her stepmother put away for a long time, Poppy Frost found herself quite alone at the age of sixteen. It was Lord and Lady Duxter who took her in, offering her a home until she could leave for Oxford and the start of her new young life.

She spent a long afternoon with Max one day as he babysat Owen, talking to the priest in ever-widening arcs and trying to come to terms with what had happened. Owen's contribution to the conversation was to punctuate any silences with gleeful babble. He was discovering the wonders of picture books, which apparently could be enjoyed upside down as much as right side up.

"Jane started making all the meals in that house," she told Max. "I would offer to help and she would shoo me out of the kitchen. She didn't used to do that—at one time she'd give me all the work to do if she could get away with it. Which generally, she could."

"Like Cinderella."

"Precisely! But then it changed. It got so if she caught me

watching her as she cooked—well, she'd practically jump out of her shoes. It would completely rattle her. Now, why was that? I wondered. One time she was mixing some herbs into the soup—but only into the one bowl, you know? The individual serving. That, I thought, was odd."

"Normally, you'd season the entire pot of soup."

"Yes, of course you would. It was that sort of thing, hard to put a finger on. It was more the guilty look on her face that made me afraid. Not a guilty look, actually, but a frightened look."

"Afraid of getting caught, she was," Max agreed. "You should have seen the state she got into when she thought you'd gone missing. You were out of her reach and beyond her control, and she suspected your disappearance could only mean you were getting wise to her. You were afraid of her. And rightly so."

Poppy nodded quickly, solemnly. "That's it exactly. And might she have given Grandmama a little something extra in her soup? To keep her docile, to make her sleep? I began to wonder. And then I wondered if Jane weren't up to something even more sinister."

"Old Mrs. Henslowe's death was viewed as being from natural causes. No one thought otherwise. Certainly, I didn't."

That earned him a look. That "how can adults be so dense" look that teenagers seemed to hold the patent on.

"Sorry," he said. "Of course doctors get it wrong, especially in dealing with the elderly."

"Don't misunderstand me," she said. "Dr. Winship is better than most. But in this case, he was thinking in clichés and he got it wrong. Anyway, it got so I was afraid to sit down to a meal with my stepmother. No way." She shook her head and the stylized copper feathers hanging from her ears danced, made to sparkle among the colorful strands of her hair. She'd had something done to it while she was in London, and now yellow stripes were added to the red.

"Besides, if she were planning a little accident for me—something unexpected, like, I dunno, an anvil falling on my head—I couldn't control for everything. I could avoid eating anything she might have messed with but I couldn't watch her day and night. I couldn't sleep—what if she tried to smother me in my sleep? It was exhausting, living like that. And I knew no one would take me seriously. I had nothing to go on, no evidence. Just a bad, bad feeling."

"And then your father, with Lady Duxter . . . No one knew what was going on. So you decided to run. I am very glad you came to me for help."

"I'd heard you used to be MI5. I never believed the stories, you know. Until now. Is it true you worked undercover at the Vatican as a Swiss Guard?"

"Stanley knew from the start, didn't he?"

She bit her lip and nodded. "I knew they might be suspicious of him if I upped and vanished. So first, I gave him my permission to tell—if it looked like they, the police, were getting ready to stitch him up for a bum rap or something. Then I decided it was better to tell you everything I *thought* was going on. Thank you for letting him come stay with me, by the way. It was ever so thrilling, being in a safe house. I'll write about that, one day."

A bum rap. What had the child been reading? Owen, having reached a particularly delightful passage in his book, let out a shriek of pleasure.

"You did well, Poppy."

"But . . . I am worried about my stepmother."

"Worried?" She couldn't be serious. Was this some form of survivor's guilt? "Surely, she has lost the right for you to worry about her."

"No, no. I mean . . . I guess what frightens me is that it took me so long to realize my stepmother was crazy. My father never saw it, either. Is this kind of denseness when it comes to people inherited? Will I go through life as some sort of gormless stooge?"

"First of all, you did start to realize something was off. And you realized it before a lot of professional investigators caught on to her."

"But my father?"

"Your father was solid as a rock and not given to paranoia and suspicion. I shouldn't worry, if I were you, but instead honor that solidity and be glad of his positive traits. Besides, you have such a spark of life to you. You are your own person." He didn't think it would be politic or necessary to mention that her rock-solid father had a reputation as being one of the dullest men in the history of the world. Poppy *was* different—perhaps the spark he referred to came from her mother, or it had skipped down a generation from her great-grandparents. He remembered Netta as being nothing if not lively, and Leo had been blade sharp. Poppy would be all right. She was already rebounding from what had been a shocking loss of nearly every blood relative she had had. And the stepmother who should have cared for her was of course no longer in the picture. Thank God.

"How are you getting on over at the Priory?"

"It's fine. S'okay. Everyone is looking forward to the arrival of the baby."

Jane had agreed to let Lord Duxter and his wife formally adopt her baby when it was born. Sadly, it would be born in prison, but that had not deterred Lord Duxter. Now that the truth was known he had, not without some trepidation, accepted responsibility for seeing that his child was not sent out to be raised by strangers. And Lady Duxter had shown what she was made of by agreeing to the adoption. Max was coming to appreciate the ties that bound that pair—marital ties much stronger than idle village gossip would have led anyone to believe.

Why had Jane Frost agreed to the adoption—apparently without much hesitation? According to DCI Cotton, she had reasoned it was one way of having a child of her blood attain a certain status in life—a status she herself had aimed for and failed so spectacularly to achieve.

"Lord Duxter seems to think I might have it in me to be a writer," Poppy was saying, "and he's doing what he can to help me. Arranging introductions to authors and agents. You know."

"And Lady Duxter? She is also encouraging?"

"Oh, yes! She's really rather sweet. I don't think people realize that about her. She's been most kind. She said to me more or less what you just said, when I talked to her. About things—you know."

"What was that?"

"She said Jane had everyone fooled. And that the devil has many disguises. It's how he gets away with murder so often. Normal people are trusting. Evil people know better."

Max looked at her, into those sad, sparkling eyes. The awful eyeliner was gone, he noticed. Today she had on only a pale makeup, nearly white, and she had painted her lips ruby red. He was reminded again how much Poppy had lost in her young life—too much, too young. Most would crumble under that strain, become bitter. They might even, in their grief, surrender to the worst of all temptations—the desire to see others suffer as they themselves had suffered. And still, through it all, Poppy had retained that grace. That heaven-sent spirit that Max believed would sustain her.

"Amen to that," said Max.